Francesca Pascal

Fredrik Nath

FINGERPRESS LTD
LONDON

Francesca Pascal

ISBN (pbk): 978-1-908824-11-0

Published by Fingerpress Ltd

Production Editor: Matt Stephens
Production Manager: Michelle Stephens
Copy Editor: Madeleine Horobin
Editorial Assistant: Artica Ham

www.fingerpress.co.uk

To

Alex, Stuart and Andy
My sons, my best readers, and my best friends

I would like to acknowledge the help and editing skill of 'Editor 182' from Scribendi who helped with this book from the outset.

About the Author

Fredrik Nath is a full-time neurosurgeon based in the northeast of England. In his time, he has run twenty consecutive Great North Run half-marathons, trekked to 6000m in Nepal, and crossed the highest mountain pass in the world.

He began writing, like John Buchan, "because he ran out of penny-novels to read and felt he should write his own." Fred loves a good story, which is why he writes.

Catch Fred online at:

www.frednath.com

Also by Fredrik Nath,

available from Fingerpress.co.uk

The Cyclist—*World War II Series, part I*

Farewell Bergerac—*World War II Series, part II*

Galdir: A Slave's Tale—*Barbarian Warlord Saga, volume I*

Francesca Pascal

Chapter 1

1

The two women found no relief from the torrid atmosphere, even when their taxi pulled up outside the station of the eighth arrondissement. The Paris summer of 1942 was as hot as a steel-mill, the kind of weather that prompted an exodus from the city. La Gare Saint Lazare buzzed with sweaty travellers swarming like locusts in the humid heat through the seven tall, stone archways leading to the platforms.

Perspiring despite her cotton blouse, Francesca Pascal tugged at the case in the open boot as the driver stood by and watched. She looked up at his bewhiskered face, hoping for help, but it seemed clear no assistance was forthcoming. He, too, was sweating beneath his beret in the scorching sun, but he smiled all the same as he opened the taxi door for Francesca's lithe young daughter, Marie. It was clear he did not intend to exert himself in the August swelter; he was a Paris taxi-driver after all.

'Maman, let me help you,' Marie said. 'You should not be doing that, it's too heavy.'

Her smile lit up her face; she showed no signs of urgency, despite the time. At eighteen she stood a little taller than her mother, but the resemblance between them was unmistakable. She wore her auburn hair in a bob, though the fringe was a little too long according to Francesca's critical eye. High cheekbones and wide green eyes gave Marie an instant eye-catching appeal. To Francesca, her daughter was the crowning achievement of her life.

The clock above them struck the half-hour and Francesca fretted because they were late. She hoped the train would be as tardy as they'd been made by the traffic on the Avenue de Gabriel, where she'd admonished the driver for taking a bad short cut through the park.

Together, mother and daughter extracted their luggage and carried it towards the platform. Marie smiled again as Francesca checked the tickets.

'Platform two I expect,' Francesca said.

'Yes, Maman, like last year. It's on the board, up there.'

'Perhaps he was German or something, that taxi-driver. Such an impolite man. He saw me struggle.'

'Maman, times are hard for men like him. If he just coughs in the wrong place the Germans will send him to a munitions factory. Poor fellow.'

The mother looked at her daughter, revelling in the young woman's youthful enthusiasm for everything in life. Marie was even-tempered and pleasant, such a contrast to most young people, in Francesca's experience.

'Is Papi meeting us?'

'I expect so, my child. The telephone was not working again and who can afford a telegram these days?'

'He might not be there?'

'I wrote to him but who knows? If he isn't there, we'll get another cab.'

'I love it when summer comes and we spend time with Papi and Mami. It's not like the old farm, of course, but Switzerland is super too. You remember that boy from the shop?'

'Yes, I remember. You encouraged him," she said. 'It was not his fault.'

'He was nice all the same.'

Francesca took in the high glazed ceiling of the old station, reflecting how it seemed much the same as in Monet's painting of it a hundred years before. She thought the old master had got it right, after all; the predominant colours, to her eyes, were greys and blues. The long, grey platform stretched away before them, filled with travellers and all of them waiting in endless queues, restless but powerless.

They shoved their way onto the platform, jostled by the crowd. There was a smell of humanity, body odours, scent and more. Francesca wrinkled her nose. Marie almost fell as a boy in his twenties pushed past, but he reached out strong, muscular arms towards her, grabbing her shoulders and keeping her upright.

'I apologise,' he said. 'I apologise but am enchanted to meet you.'

Francesca said, 'You can take your enchantment down the platform and take your hands off my daughter.'

He said, 'I apologise to her mother, also. To bump into two such beautiful women at once is both formidable and overwhelming.'

He smiled a smile of white teeth and radiant humour.

Francesca's frown saw him off. He shoved on through the milling crowd, pushing his way to the end of the platform. Marie stared after him. He glanced over his shoulder and the grin reappeared. The girl smiled back. Francesca could see it was a forceful, momentary connection.

She could not help watching too as he pressed on. He wore

a grey suit, tight enough to indicate it might not be his own and she thought his backside swaggered in masculine pride. He was young and attractive and she felt pleasure, because he was beautiful and because he was French. She sighed, catching herself in thoughts to which she was sure no woman of her age should have admitted, even to herself.

They now stood twenty yards from the young man and Francesca noticed how he turned towards Marie and grinned again. He raised his eyebrows, again with a smile. Even at twenty yards, its meaning was clear. It was an expression of appreciation and Francesca, despite herself, felt pride in the beauty of her daughter. As a mother, she also knew she must keep such men at bay. Enchanted indeed. Cheeky boy.

She stumbled forward and Marie gripped her mother's arm as four German soldiers dressed in green uniforms pushed past. One of them stood almost a head taller than the rest and his uniform bore flashes on the collar and badges of rank on the arms. He had a thin face and a grim expression in his pale, darting eyes. The features were strong and to Francesca, as an artist, they imprinted themselves in her memory.

The train was late. They always were these days. The occupation meant nothing functioned as it used to, even Francesca's finances, though she did still have means. Her thoughts wandered as they stood waiting in the heat and chatted, as only a mother and her daughter can do, about clothes, about details of the people around them, but they were careful what they said. Who could tell, Francesca thought, whether someone was eavesdropping? Truncating their conversations was almost a habit nowadays when everywhere seemed populated by informers and soldiers and false accusations and petty quarrels resulted in arrests.

Francesca heard the sound of raised voices. German voices.

The young man who had pushed past them only minutes before seemed to be in intense argument with the soldiers. He held up his papers. One of the Germans snatched them and then threw them onto the rails beneath the platform. He shoved the boy in the chest. To her horror, she saw the young man land a punch. The soldier collapsed. His colleagues turned as one. As if ordered to do so, they raised their Mauser rifles. The young man turned and ran up the platform towards the crowd.

A shot rang out. Only one shot. It echoed in the station building. Loud, like an instant of thunder, it seemed suspended in the air. The other soldiers took aim. The crowd ran or lay down all around on the cold, grey platform. Before Francesca could prevent it, Marie ran towards the now-crawling young man. Francesca could see a blood trail behind the boy and his face, once handsome, contorted by pain.

Then more shots.

Marie had almost reached the young man. The sound of the shots echoed as she fell. Francesca stood watching in silent disbelief. There was nothing else to do. Why was her daughter lying down? Incomprehension, then action.

She ran to Marie's side. She pulled at the limp, lifeless form. Turning her, Francesca realised it was pointless. The young man lay still; the very stillness of his corpse was reflected in her daughter's. Marie's forehead leaked blood, where the bullet had entered. It trickled down her face, her beautiful face, the face of Francesca's only life. She saw how Marie's eyes were open, pupils huge, and it needed no medical degree, no experience of death, to realise, to understand. Francesca absorbed the horror, but felt nothing for seconds. It was a numbness and an absence of pain which gripped her most in that instant.

She clutched her daughter to her breast. She rocked back and forth. Then she felt it: a pain worse than labour, worse than anything she had ever imagined. In her heart, it exploded like a grenade. Then she wept bitter tears. She wailed like a Bedouin. Her life was gone. Everything that ever mattered to her ceased to exist in that moment.

Death had come. Death, darkness and the everlasting cessation of hope.

2

A sparrow called to its mate in the autumn dawn, heralding the start of a new day. Francesca lay on her back, staring up at the yellowing, paint-peeling ceiling. Her eyes traced a crack in the plaster, meandering to the far left corner. As her gaze reached the wall, she broke the silence.

'Charles, when they shot her, I thought my life would end. The pain, it was so hard; I slept little. I roamed my apartment, drinking eau-de-vie for God's sake, and I almost folded then.'

'Hush, now, my sweet friend. We cannot, any of us, go back. She has gone to God.'

He stroked her cheek.

'No,' she said, pulling away and facing him. She stared into his eyes. A wild stare, insane almost. 'I did not cave in as I expected.'

'No, of course not.'

'Somewhere inside that world of pain, that sea of misery, stirred a thought. It was the smallest of things when it began, you know.'

'It was?'

'Yes, but it grew." She groped to explain. "It grew like a

green shoot in the spring sunshine. It took only a few days for me to comprehend that germination within me. It was rapid, complete," she went on. "It was the beginning of hatred, a hatred so deep and so enormous it now fills my every waking moment. It occupies my life as the Germans occupy our land. My sole reason for living now is to obtain revenge.'

'But revenge against whom? The entire German army? The SD?" He shook his head. "No, Francesca, that is not the right road; it will make you bitter. Resistance is the way. If enough people stand against the sauerkrauts, we will win through, but hatred makes for mistakes. There is no room for error.'

She leaned up on her elbow; the bed creaked.

'And what are you doing with your silly newspaper? Few people read it and you will be caught one day distributing it.'

'You have no contacts. You have never fired a gun. What do you expect to do?'

She stared at him again as her eyes filled with pain and moisture. She leaned in towards him and he stroked her hair, a gentle movement of his hand, a gesture of kindness as she pressed herself to him, sobbing. She knew he loved her. She was his closest friend and he, hers. Her pain was his but she knew he was right; there was no way to fight, only resistance, and the hope it would be enough.

Chapter 2

1

When she met Pierre for the first time in 1923, Francesca was twenty and it was raining. Irritated by the sloping drops, she took shelter in the entranceway opposite the Department of Art and Archaeology and waited, fidgeting. She needed to cross the square to her next lecture but the deluge kept her tucked tight into the lee of the building.

A boy walked past. He wore a raincoat and held an open umbrella. He looked at Francesca with clear blue eyes, his blond hair straggling over his ears. A warm feeling encompassed her when she looked at him, as if here were a refuge from the rain. When he smiled at her, and spoke, her heart leapt.

'Share an umbrella with a fellow student?'

This was too much. She wanted to hide this new feeling arising inside her. She had no time for boys.

'No. I'm fine, thank you,' she said.

'But of course. You are going nowhere, so it doesn't matter.'

'I'm going to a lecture.'

'Ah, a lecture. So the lecturer will wait for you? He would want a wet student?'

'Go. I'm in no mood for this.'

She smiled, despite herself.

'Cheri, come, I will shelter you from the storm. I ask nothing in return, only the favour of your smile.'

'Look, I've told you…'

'You'll be late.'

'Leave me alone.'

'Well, if you insist.'

He folded his umbrella. Raindrops pelted him. They pattered and bounced on his peaked beret-cap and the epaulettes of his long, black coat. He swung his folded, black protector in his hand and then….

He sang as he began to dance.

He moved his feet nimbly. He floated before her, light-footed and fast, dancing and singing as he stepped from sidewalk to road and back again, swinging his umbrella.

On impulse, she clapped her hands together and exploded in laughter; he was absurd.

Opening the umbrella, the boy, now drenched, offered his arm and she took it.

'I'm Pierre. I study Archaeology. You?'

'Art. I'm late now.'

'No point going. You'll only disturb everyone. Come with me instead.'

'I have to sign in.'

'Ah, they won't notice your absence. I will. It would break my heart.'

'You make me laugh; you're ridiculous. I must go.'

'Hot coffee is what you need. Rue de Pigalle. I know a nice little café with paper tablecloths on which poets write their work and artist draw sketches.'

'Artists?'

'Yes, it is where Rodin, Renoir, and Manet used to meet. You will experience more art there than from any Sorbonne lecture on perspective.'

'You seem to know a lot about art.'

'I flunked the course and they allowed me to convert to archaeology. I have been condemned to three years of boredom, but I'll come back and teach them that I am a great artist. I will have an exhibition at the Academie, you'll see.'

'You're crazy. I must go.'

He turned to her, their faces close.

'Please,' he said, sheltering them both beneath the black umbrella. He placed his arm around her waist and with his eyes closed, he aimed for her lips. Francesca pulled away.

'Crazy,' she said.

The rain pelted down around them and he improved his aim this time. She resisted at first, then yielding to the soft pressure, opened her mouth. As their tongues romanced, she embarked on a long, winding road to falling in love.

2

The dull, grey night was still, the curfew killing all movement outside. Dense drizzle obscured the view as she looked out of the window of her apartment. Francesca realised she longed for the sound of cars. She wondered why cars would be a welcome sound. Perhaps, she thought, they were a sign of happiness, signalling merrymakers travelling between destinations of enjoyment and gaiety. She wished with desperation that she could have time back, to hold Marie in her arms again and rock her as she once did in the night, or in the morning. Her little girl, her angel. All was dull, grey misery now. German soldiers, Nazi propaganda fooling no one, and hope lost forever. Head bowed, she crossed to the sofa.

Sitting on the gilded couch, she clutched a photograph and stared long and hard, emotions swirling within her. If only she had grabbed her arm. If only Marie had not felt that flutter of the heart for the boy, that feeling Francesca understood so well. If only...

She poured another glass of red wine and from long habit, sucked it, allowing the aromas to enter her nose. Swallowing, she reflected how life held nothing for her now. Her little girl had been everything to her in those years when there were just the two of them. She lit a Gauloise.

She smiled at Marie's face, engrossed in the photograph on her lap. Francesca gazed at the image, moisture welling in her eyes. A teardrop fell, round and still upon the grey paper. To Francesca, the droplet looked like a lake, so wide and impenetrable that nothing, not even God, could ferry her across it. She wiped it away and got up.

Stumbling, she reached the casement, and holding onto the thick velvet curtains, she stared out at the view below. Where once there had been traffic, milling people, now there was silence. Not a soul wandered the streets, and her view of the Tour Eiffel lit faintly from below made up for the absence of the people who would have thronged there in happier times.

What was the use? Her child was gone and all she had left was the paintings. Restore, paint, and covet. All her adult life she had cared. Cared for her daughter, cared for the great artworks on which she laboured so intently. Now the Germans had stolen so many of them away. The invaders hid them and then smuggled them back to Germany. It was not their art. It was not a German expression of beauty; it was French, unmistakeably French. The pictures she cared for were not only part of her life, but also part of the daily life of her nation. Art was

France and France was life for her.

How could she do it? Tablets? She had nothing like that. A gun? Even if she had access to one, she would not know how to load it. Even if she had known about firearms, she baulked at the idea of giving up her life to a bullet, as the Germans had forced on Marie.

Three floors. Was it enough? If she landed badly, she might not die. The prospect of paralysis and endless, crippled struggles held no attraction. Maybe gas. The oven in the kitchen drew her bleak thoughts. It could be easy. Turn on the gas and sleep. Sleep would surely come. It would be an easy exit. And what would God say?

"You have been very bad?"

"Go to Hell?"

Surely, God, with all his knowledge, omnipresent and forgiving, would understand. Yes. God. Yes, he would forgive her. There was nothing left for her apart from hatred and a revenge she was ill equipped to deliver.

Her feet felt heavy as she trudged toward the kitchen, across her treasured Chinese rug. She could recall the day she had bought it in Algeria. The man assured her how in a far-off country some child had laboured for weeks to produce this work of art. Looking down, she could not master her vertigo and clutched at the table, but she appreciated the dragon on the rug. It was a sign of peace and happiness, the man had said. No peace. No happiness. Perhaps a long sleep and an awakening at those pearly gates, St. Peter admonishing her for her weakness.

Turning on the gas, she opened the oven door. Kneeling, she thought how uncomfortable she would be unless it was quick. The sulphuric odour tickled her nostrils and she almost sneezed. She laid her head on her crossed arms and waited.

The hissing sound seemed a calm, soothing accompaniment to the act, like violins at a concert, and she closed her eyes.

A knock on the door.

Should she ignore it?

Perhaps they would go away if she kept quiet.

The knock persisted.

It became louder, violent, insistent.

'Francesca. Are you there? Let me in.'

She heard the muffled voice as if it were an angel summoning her back to life. It was a familiar voice. A voice of warmth and kindness. She closed her eyes.

'Francesca. Are you there?'

She heard banging, loud battering at the door. It did not stop. With her concentration disturbed—for suicide requires concentration, she thought—she stood, turning off the gas.

Stumbling towards the door, she gained the handle, and steadying herself, she called, 'Who is this?'

'It's me. Charles. I've brought you some wine.'

'Not now, Charles. I'm busy.'

'Too busy for an old friend?'

Hesitating, she stood at the door. Her quandary resolved, she un-bolted the door.

'I smell gas.'

'No, it's nothing. I forgot to turn off the oven. That's all.'

'The oven? What were you doing? You never cook these days. What were you cooking?'

'Please, Charles, I need to be alone.'

'Alone? In an apartment smelling of gas? I am homosexual, not stupid, my girl.'

'Charles, please. Leave me.'

Charles pushed past Francesca.

He checked in the kitchen first, then entered the living

13

room and opened the window. He sat down on the sofa.

'Francesca. You are the only honest friend I have. Do you think I would not care? If you died, where would that leave me? I love you.'

'Love? No, you love me only as a friend. It has always been so.'

He smiled up at her.

'Of course, you know the truth. No one else does. Our little secret. I love you, though.'

'Yes, I know you do. I love you, too. You are my father confessor, my only true refuge these days.'

'Then tell me what you were thinking. The gas, the smell. I understand. Sit here with me.'

She sat and he enveloped her in his long and angular arms. With her head resting upon his shoulder, she closed her eyes. It was like entering a soothing bath; warmth crept over her and her body relaxed.

'

Chapter 3

1

Francesca stood in a well-appointed apartment overlooking the Boulevard Saint-Germain, gazing out of the window at Leon's Café on the street corner opposite. An occasional car passed below and she could see uniformed soldiers sitting at one of the outdoor tables, their rifles carefully leaning against their legs, as if ready to spring into action despite the coffee and brioche in front of them. She swallowed her bitterness. They were everywhere.

This was an expensive place to live, more than she could afford herself, and heaven knew she was well off. This was her first day of returning to some semblance of normality, lured by Naomi Rosenthal's telephone call which intrigued her enough to put away her grief, if only briefly.

She turned to her friend.

'In all the time I've known you, you've never sounded so excited,' she said.

'Wait until you see it,' Naomi said.

She was a woman of middle years, small and dark, her thin wrinkled lips drawn into a smile, and her greying hair cut in a bob, swaying as she talked.

'Come,' she said and gestured at the adjoining well-lit room.

The floorboards creaked as she entered. There were contemporary paintings hung on the walls and a faint smell of lavender, though she could not detect its source. Francesca knew one of the paintings very well, having re-varnished it herself five years before. The furniture in the room was Louis Quinze and an open walnut chiffonier stood against the opposite wall in lieu of a desk. Even the silver inkwell on the opened front was antique.

The painting astounded her. It stood propped on a low mahogany table in the centre of the room. A Matisse. An early Matisse, but she knew it was genuine. It was something about the clarity of the blue sky and the signature she recognised so well.

'It's beautiful,' she said.

'Genuine?'

'Unmistakable. I've seen it before. I love this picture. It reminds me of happy times in the country with my parents and with my daughter.'

There was a catch in her throat as she spoke.

Hurrying to hide her feelings, she went on, 'That shade of blue can't be copied. The signature, too. The bigger size of the writing fits for Matisse in his earlier paintings. The use of colour too is classic Matisse. That alone gives emotional depth, can't you see?'

'You've seen this before?'

'When it was on display in the Louvre, on loan from a private collector called Fuld. It reminds me a little of "Les toits de Collioure", although that one is mainly in reds. Where will you hang it? It must have pride of place.'

'I'm not sure I dare hang it anywhere. These days, if the Germans know you have something of value, they send you away.'

'Not you, surely. I thought…'

'There is a limit to what money can buy. Henri may fool some of them, but every day it becomes harder to avoid arrest.'

'He bribes them?'

'Yes.'

'You have enough?'

'Oh, it's not that. It's the Nazi Party, exerting more and more pressure on the general. He said we would be safe but I don't know how long it will be before they take us.'

'Can't you get away?'

'Impossible, without help. General Herxheimer would never allow his golden goose to fly. He's had three million francs already and his greed seems limitless.'

'Perhaps you can hide?'

'No. At my age I don't think I could shut myself up for years in some cellar or attic. I'm tired of it all, to be honest.'

Francesca crossed the room and placed a gentle hand on the older woman's shoulder.

'Naomi, I wish I could do something to help.'

'There is nothing you can do. I should hide the painting from the Germans. It is important. They have stolen many works of art already. They tick us Jews off their list and then ship us away to Poland to work in factories. Of course, they confiscate everything we own, too. They get richer all the time.'

'Make sure you hide it well. This is an important picture and must never fall into their hands. It is, as you say, our heritage and a symbol of our nation. French art is French life.'

'If you ever need my help, come here and I will do what I can. Henri and I have powerful contacts, but whether we can save ourselves now, or not, is another matter.'

'Where will you hide the painting?'

'If I tell you, it won't be a secret,' Naomi said and smiled.

Francesca smiled back and they parted. As she walked home, she thought about the painting. This was the first time there had been something to occupy her thoughts, which did not involve Marie, and she knew it. The painting was important. The Matisse was a cultural relic for which it was even worth dying. It was not its financial value: it was the fact that it was a symbol of everything the Germans had taken from her country on the day they crushed the Maginot Line. Freedom, the right to be French and prosper.

She noticed her hands felt tremulous; there was perspiration where her neck touched her collar; her head throbbed. The walk home seemed to help, but as she mounted the stairs, a feeling of expectant fear overtook her, inexplicable but real.

Chapter 4

1

Francesca shuddered as she mounted the wide, spiralling stone staircase. Above the landing, she could hear booted feet stomping on the marble floors. She stood still and heard a banging from upstairs. A splintering sound of breaking wood replaced the thumping and she realised there was something wrong here. She hoped it was not her apartment. Some small fragment of prescience came to her however, so she turned to sit on the stairs. She sank her face into her hands and her arms and shoulders shook.

A scene appeared in her head.

Rue de Seine, the rising sun red and hard, throwing long shadows as she stood on the bridge. Behind her was a perambulator. She recalled how Marie must have been less than a year old. Francesca could hear her own voice, desperate, fraught.

'Pierre, dit moi la verité. Pierre, tell me the truth.'

Her beige raincoat, tightened hard with the belt at her waist, seemed almost to choke her as she grabbed at the man in front of her, frantic, desperate. 'Tell me the truth.'

She recalled the look on his face. It was one of irritation, not anger but some lesser cousin of that feeling reflected on his handsome features. His hat sat askew as she clutched his arm in the rain. A gust of wind took it and it flew away, bouncing and rolling across the bridge's empty roadway, though neither of the players in the little scene reacted.

Sitting on the stairs, she could almost feel the pain in her cold, white fingers, as he shrugged her off. He said nothing. He looked at her as if she were some machine, spouting words. Her mechanical sentences cried out for answers but he offered her none. She felt as if she had become an automaton, spewing words and questions, words unworthy of reply, answered only with silence.

She saw herself desist, her hands at her sides, glaring at him. He became an object of disgust.

'Pierre I want the truth. How long has this been going on?'

'I'm leaving.'

'With her? You bastard.'

'Look, leave me alone.'

'Leave you alone? That's the point, isn't it? I'm the one being left. I'm the one who is alone. You bastard.'

Francesca remembered how she had tried to grab him again and how he had pulled away and walked towards the Right Bank, never looking back. Not even a glance. She never saw him again. He left her, left her with anger and an infant child.

She stood there on the bridge for many minutes, staring, desolate.

Rue de Seine, six in the morning: the bridge where her tears merged with the raindrops, as they trickled down her cheeks.

2

Francesca did not count the time but the memories faded. She knew in a strange way, there was something to face in the apartment above. She had only fooled herself before, thinking it could be otherwise, and she knew it. Standing, she turned and mounted the stairs. Her apartment door was open. She caught sight of men passing by the open doorway. Black uniforms. Soldiers. They had no reason to arrest her; she was not a resister, though God knew the truth. If she had the ability, the strength, she would have shot or blown up the entire German army, but real life was different. She was weak and she knew it. If Jesus Christ himself had offered her a firearm and told her to use it, she would have been unable. It was not the mechanics, loading, firing, cleaning with oil, that made her feel hopeless, it was the thought that to take life, anyone's life, was wrong and against all she had ever learned in church or in her existence at large.

No, better to give in and capitulate. What had she to lose? Her life had ended with the death of her daughter. Marie had been everything to her and Francesca could no more shake that off than she could become a nun. As she neared the doorway, she wondered if prayer and turning to God were the answer, but she was a pragmatist at heart and knew it was not.

Francesca stood in the doorway. The lights were on and the door swung in a disconsolate arc before her.

A uniformed soldier came towards her.

'You are the owner?'

She said, 'Owner of what?'

'Come,' the soldier said. He reached for her arm and guided her into her violated home.

Men in grey-green uniforms wandered around, rifles on their shoulders, notebooks in hand and boots on their feet. She looked at them and wondered what they might be doing. They disturbed nothing; they simply milled through the apartment, making notes, as far as she could see.

'What are you doing in my home?'

No answer.

She raised her voice. She felt as if her words were faint and inaudible in the huge crowd that moved to and fro around her.

'What are you doing here?' she said, desperation adding volume.

Presently, a uniformed man in his forties, who had been staring out of the window, came forward. He clicked his heels and bowed.

'I am General Lammerding, Waffen-SS. I compliment you on your beautiful apartment.'

'Yes?'

'I am sorry, but I require it for the purposes of the Third Reich.'

Francesca understood at once. No anger arose in her. She found herself experiencing only relief that they were not seeking homosexuals or Partisans.

'But it is my home.'

'I'm sorry. It has been requisitioned by the Reich and you will have to leave.'

'What?'

'Leave.'

'But it's my home, I have nowhere to go.'

'Then you have much in common with many of your defeated people. This apartment is needed.'

'But I have nowhere to go,' Francesca said.

She experienced a feeling of hopelessness. It was as if the conversation had to go on. The longer it lasted for Francesca, the longer she could delay reality.

'Please,' she said.

'I will be fair,' the German said. 'I can give you until to-morrow morning at six. After that, anything you have not packed will belong to me... err... to the Reich.'

'But I cannot get ready by then.'

'It is as you wish. My men will be here tomorrow, and if you are still here, they will have to remove you. I'm sorry.'

'But you must find me another apartment.'

'I am sorry for you. The only accommodation we arrange is for Jewish people and you would not like that.' He looked her up and down. 'Of course you could always stay, we might become friends.'

A soldier behind the General laughed. Francesca knew the truth of it. This man, Lammerding, was taking away her home, a home she had worked to pay for, for fifteen years. The apartment was the place where she and Marie had once worked so hard to create a home. It was where Marie had her birthday parties, and where Francesca had lain in bed with Charles. The thought made her realise that Charles was more in her life now than any man she knew; she wished he had been there with her, to help her to cope.

Ridiculous thoughts. If they caught him, they would execute him for subversion.

'This is... unfair.'

A tear formed in her eye. She brushed it away with the back of her hand. It seemed to her the movement had become a spasm of habit since they shot Marie.

'As I said, I apologise. You will leave the paintings and the furniture. You may take your jewellery and any personal belongings but not more than one suitcase. I will leave a man outside to ensure you follow our protocol.'

She said nothing. She needed a drink but equally she knew there was much to do.

It would be a long night.

Chapter 5

1

A cool breeze greeted her as she descended her apartment stairs into the bright summer morning. Even an hour after dawn the air felt warm on her cheeks and she realised it would be another sweltering day in the city. Through the window, she could see that already people moved in the street below. A baker delivered bread, a child ran careless and smiling along the pavement, and a workman carried his lunchbox as he walked with determined steps away from her. This would be the last time she would witness the street where so much of her life had passed. The final page was turning, and it was time to close the chapter. Halfway down she stopped, shifting the suitcase to her left hand, then thought better of it and put it down. She looked up with bitter anger prodding her.

'My home,' she whispered. 'My home, Marie's. All gone. If there is a God in heaven how can this be?'

She wiped her eyes with the back of her hand and picked up the suitcase, then trudged down the stairs. It was as if every aspect of her life had become diseased, corrupted by the German occupation. When all the other Parisians fled, she had remained; secure in the belief the occupying forces had no quarrel with her or her daughter. She was an artist and had no political side. She never caused trouble for anyone. Besides, she kept to herself and did work of national importance for the Louvre. She never imagined her work would count for nothing in the scheme of things.

Now all she had, apart from money in a Swiss bank, was a suitcase, a case full of paintings, her memories. In her mind, an image rose of the picture of Marie doing her homework, the pencil-end in her mouth and the sun filtering through the sitting-room window. There was that charcoal sketch of Rodin's of the great poet Balzac, only a few lines that, put together, created shape and expression in a simple but unmistakable way. And the winter street scene Pierre once painted for her and which he left behind. Most of the pictures were of Marie in every stage of growing up and they meant more to her than to anyone else in the world, even a greedy German general. Besides, though the images were not valuable in themselves, they were her visual memories. Once, she had poured her feelings and emotions into creating them. They were all she had now, everything left of her old life.

The night before, Francesca had determined to take up Naomi Rosenthal on her offer of help. At the time of the offer, she had possessed no inkling she might need to take advantage of it. Perhaps Naomi did not imagine she would have, either. It made no difference. She needed somewhere to stay until she could get her life back together.

The taxi took more time to organise than she thought. In the end, she needed to go out personally and locate a driver, an old man who was willing to come, though he charged an exorbitant fee. The money meant nothing to her; it was the feeling the man was extorting it from her that rankled.

The driver refused to carry her case up, claiming he had a bad back, so she left it with him, hoping to get Henri to help her with it. She knew they would be home at this early hour.

Climbing the stairs, she found the front door ajar. She

called out to her friends. No reply came, but she only half-expected one. When she entered, she began to understand the meaning of Naomi's words. A smashed window, broken glass on the floor, a cold breeze lifting the white net curtain. Grey outlines on the wallpaper, the only evidence of all the paintings. She walked from room to room. There was not a single ornament, even the inkstand, remaining. It was as if some giant hand had swept through the place, removing everything of value. Naomi and Henri were gone, and that, to Francesca, was a much heavier blow.

She had nowhere now to run. She could no more stay here than she could return home. Then she thought about the contents of her suitcase. The taxi driver was an old man and she knew where he lived, so she had trusted him. Panic overtook her then. Suppose he drove away? Suppose he stole her suitcase. Everything she valued was in it, even if it was almost too heavy for her to carry.

Francesca turned and pelted down the stairs, made for the doorway, her heart beating like an express.

2

Her tiredness seemed overwhelming as she alighted from the taxi once more, close to Charles' apartment block. At six-thirty in the morning, the street was awakening and she stood for a moment on the kerb, watching the taxi depart into the shadows of another road. The sun probed the street now between the tall apartment buildings, casting long shadows across the roadway as the street began to come to life. Workers walked to their places of employment, café owners began to assemble their roadside empires and Francesca stood, a tightness in her throat and her precious suitcase beside her. It was heavy and she felt reluctant to begin lugging it into the four-storey apartment block. She should have known she could trust the old driver but nothing seemed to work out for her now and it was making her feel more insecure than ever before.

She buzzed up, pressing the button by the door. No one answered, but the door was unlocked and she let herself in. The hallway was dark but not dingy, with a high ceiling and a musty smell hanging in the still air. Rather than carry her case all the way to the second floor, she left it in the hallway, tucked away behind a dresser, which stood against the wall. It was out of sight and she reassured herself it was only for a few moments. Charles would carry it up for her, she was sure.

On the third flight of stairs, two things happened at once, two events that changed her life.

Above, she heard a door slam and footsteps ascending the stairs above. At almost the same time, she heard a loud diesel engine outside which someone switched off almost as soon as she heard it. Francesca pulled aside the net curtain and looked out of the tall casement window on the landing.

It was a German military truck, the swastikas clear and brutal on its sides. For a few seconds she stood there, wondering what to do. She had done nothing to warrant pursuit by armed soldiers but she was consumed by the feeling she did not want them to find her here.

A faint feeling of guilt came, too. The night before flashed through her mind. She could hear Lammerding commanding her to leave the pictures, but how could she have departed without her paintings? She had slaved over them when she painted them. They were an extension of her soul and personality. How could she have left the Rodin sketch? No, she had taken the time to remove all the good pictures, her own, Pierre's and those that were originals. It took her all night to replace the canvases with contemporary unknown works but in the end, as dawn bled into her apartment, she finished her work and felt the Germans would never notice, whether they made an inventory or not.

Frightened into action now, she leapt up the remaining stairs to Charles' apartment. The door stood open and she wondered whether it was he she had heard on the stairs above. Were they after him?

Below, she heard heavy-booted footsteps on the stairs. Francesca dared not enter. She removed her shoes and clutching them in her left hand, ran up the next flight. Leaning forward into the stairwell, she could see the open door. She still had the option to move upwards if the soldiers continued to climb. They could have been after another apartment, after all.

Seconds passed and then she saw them. Six uniformed men stood outside Charles' door. They waited. A full minute passed in which she could see they were listening. A seventh in a black uniform arrived. Then, clutching their rifles, they entered, one at a time, pointing their weapons. She heard some indistinct German conversation and one of the soldiers emerged. He began to climb the stairs towards Francesca.

In silent panic, she fled up the remaining stairs.

Chapter 6

1

Marie burst into peals of laughter as her mother almost over-balanced, clutching the punt-pole, trying to propel them to the island. It was a day worthy of laughter, a yellow day of sunshine and meadow-flowers. A heat haze hung on the slow-moving river and the water carried petals, leaves and water boatmen as the two of them floated along with their picnic.

Francesca wore a wide-brimmed straw hat and her cool, low-cut, floral dress merged with the summer background with its yellow, green and red colours. Marie, aged twelve, wore shorts and a short-sleeved blouse and together they complemented each other, mother and daughter, alike yet so different.

Marie pointed to a grassy bank.

'There. There, Maman.'

'I'll get the hang of this if it kills me,' Francesca said. She pulled hard at the pole and it came loose with her violent tugging. Again, she almost overbalanced, but she avoided a soaking by sitting down. It cost her extraordinary effort to direct the low boat to the spot where Marie was pointing. The boat struck the bank and the little girl jumped out, painter in hand, and began tying it to a willow sapling whose arching egg-yolk-coloured branches reached to the water's edge.

They unloaded their feast together. They had bread, paté,

cheese and blackcurrant juice. There was a bottle of white Bordeaux which Francesca's father had put in, warning her not to drink all of it, because in his opinion wine and boats were an unsafe mixture.

They spread the chequered cloth and weighted the corners with stones. They chatted. They ate, and Francesca became drowsy. The warm sun tempted her to sleep, but Marie would not allow it. She flicked water at her mother and they both laughed as they splashed each other.

The fracas ceased as fast as it began and they both lay on the bank, silent and smiling.

'Do you ever wonder about your father?' Francesca said.

'No.'

'But you must be curious?'

'No, Maman. I don't want to talk about it.'

'It is important for us to talk about him. He exists. Just because he and I could not make a life together, does not mean he is a bad man. Perhaps I should try to find him so you can judge for yourself.'

'I told you. I don't want to. He doesn't care about me. If he did, he would have stayed. He would have come to see me.'

'My little one, of course he cares. You are his daughter. Will you not let me?'

Marie stood, and with her arms by her sides, shouted loud enough to startle a duck nearby into flight. 'I hate my papa. He left us. I never want to see him.'

The two looked at each other for long minutes, neither of them speaking. Francesca opened her arms and Marie knelt next to her. They embraced.

'Maman, take it all away, all away.'

'Hush now, my angel. I was wrong to raise it. When you are older, perhaps you will understand.'

Francesca's voice was strong and even, but the tear forming in the corner of her eye told more truth than a thousand platitudes.

2

The staircase ended at a door. She tried the handle. It was unlocked, but would not budge. Francesca could hear slow, laborious footsteps below as the soldier trudged up towards her, two flights down. Panic made her sob and hammer on the door with closed fists. She no longer cared whether the soldier heard her. She had reached a stage now where if anything went right, it would have been a miracle worthy of Saint Jude.

Her strangled cry must have the alerted the soldier below. The pace of his ascent increased. She leaned against the door. With a speed taking her unawares, it swung open. Strong hands grabbed her and pulled her up to her feet and out into a windy place.

Charles said, 'In the name of all the saints, I knew somehow it was you. Your cry was unmistakable. A moment later and I would have been gone.'

He thrust a broken broomstick handle into the door catch.

'It will hold them for a while. Come.'

Charles gestured to Francesca, who stood confused and immobile.

'Where to? We are on the roof.'

'Yes, there is another one there. We must fly like those squirrels in the jungle.'

'Squirrels?'

'Never mind, come.'

Charles took a running jump, as far as she could see into

thin air. She walked towards where he leapt. There was another roof lower down, across a gap of three metres, and he stood, arms outstretched, indicating for her to follow.

Francesca hesitated. It looked too far for her to jump. A sound behind convinced her. The soldier fired a shot, then another. The sound echoed and two pigeons launched themselves into the sky by her left hand.

Without further delay, she stepped back. She ran the few steps towards the edge. She launched herself into the air. Her jump was short. Her feet missed the roof, finding only air. She struck the parapet of the roof like a body check. The impact took the breath from her lungs, as if a pile driver had struck her. Her outstretched hands scrabbled for a moment on the brickwork but the impact as her ribs hit the edge benumbed her. She slipped down and ended clutching vainly at the edge.

Charles again used his long arms to grab her. Struggling, she gained the roof and without time to recover her breath, felt him pull her up and they jumped to another building. The pitched roof there seemed an impossible obstacle to Francesca. Now she felt relief at being barefoot. One foot either side of the apex, she negotiated the ridge and down the slope to a skylight.

Charles pulled it up. It was as if he knew where to go. It seemed to Francesca, her friend must have rehearsed this stumbling flight, for he never faltered. When she fell behind, he slowed; when she wanted to rest out of breathlessness, he encouraged her. They flew down a staircase; they emerged into a quiet alleyway. They ran.

A wall at the end of the alley convinced her the race was finished. It looked unscalable. Without pause, Charles pulled a dustbin towards the wall and stood upon it. He pulled himself up and sat astride the mountain's summit. She looked up as the sun outlined him from behind. She could paint that.

It was a strange thought, which only an artist could have at a time like this, and she recognised the fact as she clambered onto the dustbin, grabbing his hand, and felt herself pulled to the crest of the brickwork.

He lowered her down on the opposite side and then holding the top of the wall, did the same for himself. They were off again. She could hear no sound of pursuit but knew they had to continue. The Germans were not stupid and would call for reinforcements soon enough. They would overrun the whole quarter in no time.

On they ran, until ten intersections away they came to a café with tables set out on the street. The owner was raising parasols as they approached. He was preparing for breakfast and looked askance at the couple, dishevelled and breathless, who occupied a table near the door.

'Not yet open,' he said.

'We need only a coffee and a brioche each. We have a train to catch.'

'Coffee? You joke?'

Charles smiled. 'I have grown so used to the chicory, I even call it coffee. You must think I'm stupid.'

'No. I understand. I just don't like to insult the coffee I used to serve by confusing the two. You are too early.'

'Is the place too busy?' Charles said.

'Please, we will leave quite soon,' Francesca said, her eyelids fluttering.

'It is no trouble,' the proprietor said. 'I will see if the water is hot.'

He went inside and Charles said, 'I preferred the yellow suit. This brown one is too tight on you.'

'Charles, how can you talk about clothes? The Germans

will come any minute.'

'If you wore looser clothing you could jump better,' he smiled to her as he spoke. He seemed calm. She wondered if he were trying to calm her down and if she looked as close to panic as she felt.

'Mad. The world has gone mad. We are in danger.'

'No. They don't know what I look like and they are surely not chasing you?'

A cold dread gripped her.

'I have to go back.'

'Where?'

'To your apartment.'

'Now who is mad? It will be crawling with soldiers. Impossible.'

'My suitcase. I left it in the hallway. A German general took over my home and I escaped with some paintings. I cannot leave them, whatever the danger.'

Charles leaned forward. He covered her hand with his.

'We will have to wait until tonight if we are going to do that.'

'What if they find it?'

'Then you will have to paint a new collection.'

'Why are they after you?' she said.

'The newspaper. Someone must have, as the Americans say, "squeaked". It means…'

'Squealed, you mean squealed.'

'Well, whatever they call it, someone has talked and the game is up. I will have to get out. I'm going home to Bergerac.'

'I must get my things.'

'Well, they aren't looking for you. Maybe you shouldn't have run.'

Francesca leaned forward. She lowered her voice.

'I have an original Rodin sketch. Balzac. It is my most valuable possession. The Germans told me to leave all the paintings, but it would have broken my heart.'

'Don't worry, Francesca, we will get your case tonight. We need somewhere to go first and we need tickets for the train. Not from a station in town, though. We will need to get out of Paris and then take the train. They may be checking the stations for me.'

'Just because of a newspaper?'

'Yes, they shot Henri Frenay a few weeks ago.'

'But they may be looking for me too.'

'They won't do that for a few pictures some officer wanted to steal. They might, to get me, though. I wrote an article about the death-camps in Poland. They would not like it.'

The café proprietor interrupted them and breakfast arrived. The only sign of pursuit was an open military vehicle with four soldiers passing by at a slow pace, staring around them. None of them showed interest in the well-dressed couple having breakfast at an open-air café.

Chapter 7

1

The straight yellow road wound around the corner of the pink-and-white-rendered building and a tiled roof, russet and black, sat upon it like a tiled hat, placed as if by a careless hand. The enclosed garden beyond the red brick wall held dark green trees and outside was verdant grass. A smooth, blue sea beyond, merged in a straight line with the grey-blue of an untroubled sky, yet the eye always returned to the building, the wall, the garden. It was a matter of balance; the lighter shades created to point and bring the eye to the building and the wall. The scene was true French art and Francesca squeezed Pierre's hand as they looked.

The newly married couple stood in the Louvre, staring with delight at the picture, on loan from a private collector.

'Eighteen-ninety eight,' Francesca said.

'What?' he said.

'Matisse painted it then. It is a masterpiece of simplicity and truly French. I love this painting.'

'*Le Mur Rose*, it's nice I suppose, but not my sort of thing. I like his half-nudes. They have a gentle eroticism which always makes me think of you.'

Pierre released her hand and placed his on her buttocks, kneading with gentle movements.

'Stop it, someone will see.'

'There's only us here. I sometimes wonder what it would be like to make love in an art gallery.'

'You think of nothing else. We stand here in front of one of France's great pictures and all you think about is sex. You have always been crazy.'

'That's why you love me.'

'Hah.'

She smiled.

'Perhaps we can go home in a while. I want to sit and look at this painting. It means a lot to me. It is symbolic. Matisse was such a great painter, even if they labelled him a "wild beast". Maybe he was a little like you when he was young.'

'You love my beast-like qualities. The sounds from your throat when we make love demonstrate this. Come, let's go. I want you.'

'But we may never see this painting again. It's in a private collection and goes back tomorrow.'

'One landscape looks much like another. Come on.'

Indignant now, Francesca stamped her foot. 'No wonder you failed the arts course. You are a Philistine.'

'Francesca, my love, I want to worship your body, not the great masters.'

She smiled a reluctant smile. He had a way of always making her anger dissipate. Turning, she held his hand as they left. An irresistible impulse took her. She glanced over her shoulder at the Matisse. It was her only way to say goodbye.

2

The faint redness as the sun sank behind the tenement roofs above her left long shadows on the pavement, as Francesca mounted the steps of Charles' apartment building. Charles waited in the shadow of a doorway further down, ready, she hoped, to come to her aid if necessary. They knew there was a risk in this, but Francesca insisted she would not go anywhere without her suitcase. Charles made her wait a full hour while they watched from the other side of the street. There was no movement, no one going in or out, and when it felt safe, he permitted her to go.

The tall, oak door stood ajar and she pushed it with tremulous hands, entering the hallway.

'Halt.'

The voice was German and she realised her mistake at once. Sweat glowed on her back and her mouth became dry as an Algerian summer.

'Hello?' she said.

'Stop there.'

She put up her hands and advanced one pace.

'I'm sorry. I came for my case.'

'Who are you?'

'I am Francesca Pascal. I am a conservator from the Louvre. I came earlier to appraise a painting but my bag was too heavy to take upstairs.'

'Papers?'

'In my bag. Here...'

'Keep your hands up.'

The man grabbed the bag she wore slung over her shoulder. He examined the wallet with her photograph and the stamped identity document.

'In Ordnung. What are you doing here?'

'I told you. My suitcase. I couldn't wander round Paris with it; it's too heavy.'

'In the suitcase is what?'

'My belongings.' Genuine tears formed in her eyes. 'One of your generals took my apartment and I had to leave. They took everything except what I carried away.'

The soldier, a man of perhaps fifty, lowered his rifle. His expression softened. He reached forward and patted her on the arm.

'It is a bad war. I'm sorry for you. I am just an ordinary soldier, I cannot help you. I will have to check the contents and I apologise for that.'

'There are some family pictures I painted before my daughter died and a few other belongings. Nothing which could obstruct the German war-machine.'

The soldier picked up the case.

'Heavy,' he said.

He opened it and glanced inside. His fingers probed for a few seconds, then he shrugged.

'You can go. Where will you stay? You have money?'

'I will be alright. Do you care?'

'Me? Not every one of my countrymen is heartless. You look a little like my wife. I often think how she would be if France had overrun Dortmund, in the Bundesland, where we live. There is no end to this. All I want is for it to finish so I can go home. I'm a Catholic, you see.'

'I see,' she said.

He carried the case to the door.

'I'm afraid I cannot carry it for you. I must stay here. I wish you good luck.'

Francesca smiled as she descended the stairs. The man confused her. He was not like any of the others she had seen and heard. Those men were brusque, sometimes courteous, but never humane. Her feelings of hatred blanched a little, then she thought of Marie and her determination returned. One day she would avenge her daughter's death, Catholic soldiers or not.

It made no difference, she decided, whether there were occasional good Germans. She wanted them all dead, for Marie, for France. Struggling with her case, she walked towards where Charles waited, and after she turned a corner, he took it from her. She was still sweating but this time from the effort of carrying her paintings. They walked on. Once again, it promised to be a long and exhausting night and she realised she had not slept for thirty-six hours.

Chapter 8

1

They stood on the platform, waiting. It was still hot and flies buzzed around Francesca's face as if she were now fair game, even for insects. Perhaps, she thought, they believed she was already dead. Losing everything in this stupid war meant she might as well be. She caught herself thinking this way and stopped short. It had to be the lack of sleep. Losing almost two nights' sleep in a row made her feel as if she could lie down on the platform right there and close her eyes for a week.

After walking out of the city they continued until, at six in the morning, they came to a small station at Massy where they bought tickets for Bergerac. They were not alone on the platform. Some road workers carrying their lunchboxes stood at the far end of the platform and laughter drifted down towards Francesca from time to time.

'Don't worry,' Charles said, 'you can sleep on the train. I will keep watch.'

'If we get a seat. There are only half the number of trains for civilians nowadays.'

'I know, but someone may stand up for you.'

'It's coming.'

'Yes, I hear it.'

A train appeared in the distance but it was heading towards

Paris, not away. Francesca sighed. It was not even a passenger train. It pulled cattle trucks.

The train stopped halfway along the platform and two soldiers stepped down. Francesca looked away, avoiding their gaze. She was shaking. Charles responded by putting his arm around her, his flat hand rubbing her back.

'Don't worry,' he whispered, 'they aren't looking for you.'

The two soldiers entered the station house and for a while, there was silence, apart from the steam issuing from the engine. She looked at the truck five or six yards away. There was a small grille close to ground level and she started when she saw a small hand emerge. It belonged to a child, chubby and pink. Francesca thought it would be a child aged maybe three or four. She shifted her gaze, peering closer to look into the darkness inside the carriage. She could make out a vague disturbance as of many shapes, moving, changing all the time.

Presently, a little face appeared. It belonged to the child with the hand still projecting from the cattle truck. The look on that face made her catch her breath. It reminded her, in her tired and emotional state, of Marie as a small child. It seemed to Francesca as if this picture had come to her to show what was happening in her France, the place where she had lived the formative part of her adult life and where once she had been happy. She made to go to the child.

Charles grabbed her arm.

'Are you suddenly crazy? What are you doing?' he said.

'But it's a child. A child in the train.'

'I know. There is nothing we can do.'

'But what is she doing there?'

'The whole fucking train is crammed with Jews and prisoners. They are going to concentration camps in Poland and Germany.'

'But it's inhuman.'

'You should have read the article I wrote. It is all we can do—tell people everywhere we can.'

'It's a small child.'

'Yes, yes. We can't interfere. They would arrest us. Leave it alone.'

She thought about her friends, the Rosenthals. Was this train going to stop for them? Were they going away like all these poor people?

Her mind travelled to the apartment above the Boulevard Saint-Germaine. She remembered the desolation she had found there, the missing pictures, the ornaments gone and the broken glass. It was as if the Germans had erased her friends' lives, everything making them individuals, human beings, rubbed out or stolen.

The two soldiers came out. They were laughing and swinging their rifles. They walked behind Francesca and Charles. One of them aimed a kick at the outstretched arm. It buckled and sagged with the impact before someone withdrew it. A child's scream came from behind the grille and Francesca jerked as she heard it. She wanted to go to the child, pick her up, comfort her, anything but endure this. Tears came. She leaned in towards Charles and he put his arms around her.

Francesca felt she was living in a black nightmare, as if she were descending into Hell and on her road all these horrible scenes were played out for her benefit, to hasten her journey. Why? It was the one question she asked herself almost every minute after that day. Why?

2

To Francesca's relief, their train, when it came, was not crowded and they both found seats in an almost empty single compartment. The train corridor was empty too, and Charles chose a seat next to it. Francesca assumed it was so he could look out for soldiers. He placed her case on the luggage rack and held her hand as they began their three-hour journey. It took moments only for her to rest her head on his shoulder; sleep came in seconds after she closed her weary eyes.

She awakened with a start and realised Charles was shaking her.

'Soldiers,' he whispered.

An elderly farmer sitting in the window seat looked up. She was not certain whether he heard or not. She smiled at the man.

'My papers are not in order. Please say nothing. Are we not French, all of us?'

The man smiled and nodded. It was all she could do. She had no time to look, as Charles guided her out of the compartment and into the corridor, clutching the suitcase. At the opposite end, a black-uniformed officer and two German soldiers stood opening the door of a compartment. Charles pulled at her arm.

'Come,' he said.

They moved along the corridor to the next carriage and kept walking, jerked from side to side by the movement of the train. They kept going. Three carriages on, there was a dead end. Reaching the end of the train, they had nowhere left to go.

'Look, they aren't after you. Go back. I'll take my chances. I can climb out of the window onto the roof. Go.'

'No, I'm not leaving you.'

'Go, will you? I will be all right. I've done this before.'

'Liar. Look. Here. Into the toilet.'

She opened the door to the tiny toilet.

'They will find us,' he said.

'Do it.'

He became meek and pliable to her command. It was as if she was changing her role and now took the upper hand. She knew it and so, it seemed to Francesca, did Charles.

Entering the tiny cubicle, she pushed him to the corner behind the door.

'Keep well back,' she said and pushed him again, but this time she encountered something hard at his waist.

'What's this?'

'Well you know it isn't arousal, Francesca.'

'What is it?'

He drew out a pistol out of his waistband, from under his woollen jumper. It was a Parabellum, the type used by the French police.

'You have a gun?'

'I told you; although you excite me, I'm not that kind of girl.'

She felt like slapping his face. She would have too, had it not been for a feeling of weakness. She felt nauseated and dizzy. She knew their lives were at even greater risk if the Germans found he had a pistol.

There was a loud knock on the door.

'Papers,' a man's voice said.

Another loud knock, more insistent this time.

'Papers, you hear?' The German accent was unmistakable.

With heart thumping, she said, 'One moment, please. I am ill.'

Francesca lifted the toilet seat. She poked her throat with her finger and began retching. Close to vomiting, she turned and opened the door. The black uniformed officer stood outside, regarding her.

It came then. It came full tilt. Projectile, disgusting. With superb timing, she thought, she leaned forward and instead of the vomit striking the uniform; it spewed onto the floor and splashed one of the man's black, shiny boots.

Francesca knelt. She clutched the doorjamb. She continued to retch. Wiping her mouth with the back of her hand, she said, 'I'm sorry.'

She turned. She leaned on the toilet and retched again, all the time pushing the door back, obscuring any view behind.

'Disgusting French whore,' the officer said. He retched a little himself and turned away to wipe his boot with a handkerchief. When he finished, he threw it at Francesca.

'Clean yourself up woman.'

Turning, he left. Francesca pushed the door shut with her foot and, standing, locked it. Vomit smeared, her lips broke into a smile. Charles smiled back.

He kissed her mouth.

Chapter 9

1

The hour they spent in the train toilet seemed to both of them a sweet relief compared to the tension of sitting waiting in a compartment for soldiers to check papers again as they travelled. Alighting on the platform, they both checked for Germans or French security police up and down, but all was clear.

'Do we have to walk now?'

'We are only one stop from Bergerac but to travel into the town would be an unnecessary risk. Don't worry, I'll carry your suitcase. With company like this, it will be like a picnic; I am going home, after all. I could carry you as well.'

'Charles, please be serious. How far is it?'

'Ten miles. We can go through woodland and maybe avoid any military patrols. With any luck, we will meet a group of partisans. My friends said there were some in the forests north of the town. If we miss them, then by evening we will be in the town and can dine on duck-breasts and foie gras.'

'Those things are not available even in the country. You know it.'

'It was a figure of speech. Let's go and find somewhere to eat and then we set off. I'm starving. I guess your stomach is empty, too.'

'When we get there, what do we do?'

'I'm hoping to find that group of partisans my friend told me about, in the forest, or maybe they'll find us. There is a risk we will miss them, in which case, we will have to go into town. I have a contact there, another journalist. We are like mushrooms; we spring up everywhere on German shit.'

He smiled at his joke but Francesca found no humour in it. They gained the stairs and, still looking around, descended on the far side of the platform to find no signs of troops. The station was as quiet as a Sunday, but they both realised it was because no one had money to travel, and even if they did, the constant delays made the trains unreliable. The war had ruined all the things in the daily life Francesca had once learned to rely upon. She was almost tempted to go to her parents but now she had no way of obtaining letters of transit. When she was a respected art conservator in Paris, getting passes for a holiday in the neutral countries had not been too difficult. But now? Things had tightened even more than before, in only a few months.

Besides, Francesca had felt she had reason to stay in Paris. She wanted some means of redressing the balance in her life. They had shot Marie. They had to pay. Now she hoped Bergerac might give her an opportunity to somehow help in the resistance against these monsters. Charles seemed to know all about how to do it. She wondered if she had underestimated her friend. He seemed calm, almost confident, as if he were not Charles the reporter, Charles the failed artist and writer. He had become Charles the resistance fighter, a soldier of freedom in her eyes. She loved him even more in that moment and found herself wishing their bond were more than friendship. A man like him...

They found a café serving hot sausages and bread and it was enough to fill their stomachs, though Francesca found pieces of bone as they ate. They drank Anjou rosé and water and she found the effects of the small carafe of wine more soporific than she could tolerate with her sleep deprivation.

'Can't we stay the night? I can't walk the rest of the day. There must be somewhere.'

'Stay the night? You are too soft to be a Maquis,' Charles whispered, but his smile showed his feelings.

'I need to sleep very badly,' she said.

'I will see what we can do. I don't have a lot of money.'

'I have plenty, both Francs and Deutschemarks.'

'You have?'

'Yes, I always kept plenty at home in case…'

'In case of what?'

'I don't know. Since they shot Marie I have been nervous and…'

'No matter. We will find a place to stay. I'll ask the waiter.'

When they left, they needed only to walk a short way to a small hotel down the cobbled street. Mid-afternoon there was no one in the tiny foyer apart from the proprietor and they obtained a key as man and wife under the name of Duboef. The stairs were dark and rickety and the room small and dingy, but it had a generous double bed and a rug beneath. Francesca felt the place was clean and would be comfortable enough.

She undressed, but for the first time in their friendship, she felt embarrassed. It was as if he had become someone else, not her Charles. Not the asexual person she had known and loved.

Charles for his part seemed to notice nothing. He removed his clothes, lay on the bed and patted the unoccupied half.

'What's wrong?'

'Nothing.'

'Why are you hesitating? I always look forward to cuddling

up to you. I love the feel of your body as we go to sleep. We need to sleep, you know.'

'Yes,' she said.

Francesca drew the curtains and although they did not black out the room, they provided enough darkness for her to feel comfortable. When her head hit the pillow, Charles nestled into her, his right arm around her shoulders and his left outside the covers, resting on her chest.

She knew she felt aroused. The feeling angered her. There was no passion in this love of theirs and she knew it. Closing her eyes, she realised she wanted passion; she wanted release. They loved each other but it was not enough for her. He was not the man she thought he was, and yet he was the familiar man she knew would never make love to her.

Turning towards him, she said, 'Charles, have you ever made love to a woman?'

'What? Silly talk, go to sleep.'

She propped herself up on one elbow.

'Charles, you don't see me as a woman at all.'

'Oh, for the love of Christ, will you sleep?'

'Please, I want to know.'

'All right. Here it is. I appreciate beauty. You are beautiful. But as for the other thing, I have no interest. It just does not happen that way for me. I love you but not in that way. It is not because you are not a wonderful, sexual woman, because you are. It is because of who I am. Look, you like the same things in men as I do. I cannot escape it.'

'Why then do we lie naked next to each other?'

'It's... It's friendship, is it not?'

'Yes, Charles, I suppose it is. Sometimes , I cannot help it, I sometimes wish it were different.'

'My dear sweet friend. How can it ever be? Yes, I love you

51

but not that way, you know this. Would you rather I slept in the chair?'

'No, hold me,' she said.

He wrapped his arms around her and stroked her hair.

Francesca closed her eyes and sank into a deep and dream-less sleep.

2

Purchasing a length of rope from the village chandler, Charles created a kind of rucksack out of the suitcase and slung it onto his shoulders They had far to go, most of it through the autumn woodlands. Francesca, in her new low-heeled shoes, realised there would be blisters soon. She wondered how it would be if Marie were with them. Her feet always blistered in new shoes, her little girl. The catch in her throat was a warn-ing. She needed to keep her focus, and she knew that thinking about the greatest source of grief in her life was not going to help her. As they walked in the russets, browns and greens of the woods, memories came, fast and painful. It became unen-durable in the end and since neither of them conversed much as they walked, she demanded they rest so she could talk instead of think.

Sitting on an ancient, moss-covered, fallen elm, they shared water from Charles's bottle and Francesca listened to pigeons cooing above them. It was a still, quiet place, verdant grass and tall pines across the meadow calming her, giving some semblance of peace in her war-torn world.

Presently, she said, 'I wonder so often how it would have been if only I had grabbed her arm. You see…'

'I keep telling you. Part of grief is guilt. You know this.

Stop torturing yourself.'

'No, not torture. Torture is when pain comes and you are alone. The Germans, I think, know all about that from what I've read. Anyway, I'm not alone, am I? I have you and it warms my heart.'

He smiled and took her hand.

'Come, Francesca, we must go on. We've hardly started and it will be another two hours yet.'

They stood up. A sound to their left made him stop and listen. Francesca stiffened. It was the sound of a snapping twig but there seemed to be no one visible. Soldiers? No, she thought, soldiers would rush in, not observe.

'Who's there?' Charles called.

No answer.

Her mouth dry, she whispered, 'Who can it be? Where are they?'

Charles stepped forward; he pushed her back with his left hand and with his right, drew his pistol. They stood like that for minutes. Another sound, this time off to the right, then a voice.

'Who are you?'

Charles said, 'We are from Paris. Going to Bergerac. Who are you?'

'Put down the gun and step away from it. There are four rifles pointed at your chest.'

Francesca saw him hesitate.

'Do as they say, Charles, for the love of God.'

'You could be anyone. How can I trust you?'

'We are Maquis. If you are here to spy on us, you're both dead. Put down your weapon.'

Charles put down the gun on the fallen tree and they both stepped back.

'Put your hands on your heads and kneel.'

'We are on your side,' Charles said.

'Now.'

They obeyed the voice. Two men and two women came out of the woods. Francesca studied them. All of them wore berets or caps. One of the women wore a long, dark raincoat and carried a rifle. She had blond hair and a beautiful face with high cheekbones. She stood out as competent and determined. The other was brown-haired and remained in the background. One of them caught her eye. He was tall, wearing a soft, peaked cap and fair-haired, judging by his eyebrows. His big-boned face was handsome and a smile adorned it, as if life here were a joke to be savoured and enjoyed. His grey eyes sought Francesca's and she experienced an unfamiliar feeling within her, warm but unfamiliar. His smiled broadened.

The brown-haired woman said, 'Seppo, check their papers.'

'Josephine, I wouldn't know if they are real or not. You check them.'

With a look of irritation, she stepped forward.

'Papers,' she said.

Both Charles and Francesca produced their papers and the woman examined them.

'So, who are you?'

Charles said, 'This is Francesca Pascal, an artist and conservator who worked at the Louvre. I am Charles Delacroix, the editor of *Le Franc-Tireur*. You may have heard of my paper?'

'*Franc-Tireur*? Yes, I've heard of it. We don't get copies of it down here but I've heard the name. You have contacts? Passwords?'

'A friend in Paris suggested I ask you about your holiday in

Gibraltar.'

'All right, I believe you. What are you really doing here?'

'Who are you? You want me to tell you everything but you give me nothing. Should I trust anyone who has a rifle? I don't know you. You could be Milice spies, for all we know.'

Josephine considered his words.

'Yes, you are right.'

Francesca noticed a softening of the woman's expression. A wave of relief came over her. She realised her hands had been clenched hard and she relaxed them.

She said, 'The Germans are not after me. They killed my daughter last year. I want to help and I could be useful.'

Josephine said, 'Just now, all hell has broken loose. A few months ago, we attacked a convoy taking prisoners to Lyon. The whole of Aquitaine will be swarming with German soldiers and Milice, even travelling here is dangerous. You would be wise to wait in the forest with us. We are well hidden. Just don't expect us to trust you.'

The second woman, the blonde one, said, 'The Germans are not looking for you?'

'No,' Francesca said, 'they threw me out of my apartment and when Charles had to flee, I came with him.'

'You came with him? Why?'

'I… I had nothing to keep me in Paris and took things with me the Germans forbade me to.'

'Things?'

'You are not French.'

'No. I'm English. I'm surprised you noticed.'

'I have a good ear.'

'Shirley Doone.'

The woman stepped forward and offered her hand. Francesca took it. It was warm and dry. The two looked each other in the eye and Francesca realised this woman was someone she could trust. There seemed to be no guile in her.

Josephine turned and signalled with her hand. 'Come,' she said.

Charles and Francesca followed. A little rain began to fall as they wound their way through the autumnal forest; the trees, increasing in density, protected them from the drizzle.

Stumbling on occasional tree-roots, Francesca wondered where all this was leading. Yes, she was a sympathiser, but joining a group of fighting Maquis was never the kind of revenge she had planned. She entertained only doubt about the outcome. She knew she was not a woman who could live this life in the forest, wielding weapons, killing Germans. Her role had to be more subtle than this if she were to achieve anything at all.

Chapter 10

1

The autumn sky grew overcast and the sun, peeping through now and then, did little to lift Francesca's spirits as they trudged through the forest. Once, she stumbled and fell and Josephine, the dark-haired woman, poked her with the rifle barrel.

'Get up,' she said.

Nothing else, a simple command, without a smile, no platitudes. Charles, for his part caught up with the blond man, Seppo, and she could hear them talking in low tones, but Francesca could not follow the conversation. She heard them laugh and once Seppo slapped Charles on the back. She began to feel isolated. Hot, sweating, and unused to walking so far, she wanted to rest but there was no sign of anyone else letting up with the pace.

The blonde girl, Shirley, caught up with her. She smiled, inclining her head towards Francesca.

'You're tired?'

'Yes. Can we rest a little?'

'Josephine is in a hurry. We're meeting the others at camp in another hour. Do you think you could carry on that long?'

'If I must, then I must.'

'Game of you. Charles is your man?'

'No.'

'Just friends then?'

'Yes, but we are close.'

'You are going to Bergerac for a reason?'

'I stole some pictures. They were mine but the Germans took my home and ordered me to leave them. I couldn't.'

'Ah.'

'Look,' Francesca said, 'I'm not strong. I don't even know how to load or shoot a gun but I want to help in any way I can. I want France to be free.'

'We all want that, even us Rosbifs.'

'Will you help me to do what I need to do?'

Shirley looked her up and down.

'Well, a city girl like you won't like the forest much, I guess.'

'No. I suppose not. I was going to set up a gallery in the town. I could perhaps carry messages or something.'

'It depends on whether you can persuade Josephine to trust you. Her man, Jules, is in charge but she pulls his strings. She is very strong, but a bit too serious.'

'And you? What do you do?'

'I'm with SOE. British Intelligence.'

'An oxymoron?'

Shirley laughed. 'I think you are very rude and ungrateful.'

'Sorry, it was a joke.'

'I'm going home, actually. There is a very tight net around Bergerac just now. We can't get out but the Germans will have trouble finding us, since we shift camp all the time. That's why we have to hurry. Our friends may be gone if we are late.'

Presently, they came to a small clearing in the lee of a tall rocky outcropping surrounded by pine trees and protected at ground level by gorse and blackberry bushes. Seppo at the front of the little column whistled and Francesca saw a young man dressed like the others emerge from behind a pine-bole.

'Hah, little Amos. How are you?'

'Not so little, Seppo, you great Swedish meatball.'

Seppo laughed as if he had not a care in the world. He turned and waved a hand towards Francesca.

He said, 'This, my little friend, is the beautiful Madame Pascal or is it Mademoiselle?'

'Madame,' Francesca said.

Amos murmured something under his breath. Seppo stood next to her and whispered, 'And where is Monsieur Pascal? He is not here?'

'No. I am divorced.'

'This gets better and better,' Seppo said, 'a beautiful divorcee. Perhaps my luck is turning, after all.'

Seppo, a big man with a loud voice, became silent and smiled to Francesca, indicating the camp. This camp consisted of three real tents and several tarpaulins on sticks. There were two upturned baskets and a packing case around a fire. Francesca wondered how they could exist here. Seated at the fire were a man and a girl. She was skinny as a vine cane, no more than late teens, and she did not look up as they entered. The man stood.

Francesca assessed him as maybe fifty years of age; he wore a beret on a balding head and he looked rough, unshaven and grubby. She could think of no other word for him but grubby. In his mouth was a battered pipe and his face had a weather-worn look.

'François Dufy, at your service,' the man said, bowing slightly in old-fashioned politeness. He spoke with a cultured accent. Francesca had difficulty reconciling his appearance with his voice and manners. He offered her a place on the packing case beside him and she noticed he walked with a limp. He had an odour of ponds and tobacco.

'The appearance is my disguise,' he said, 'or at least it was. Now I can't even get a change of clothes to become myself again.'

'Uncle,' said the girl, 'I could wash all your clothes. Shirley would be pleased.'

There was a smile in her words but none on her face. She looked bruised and malnourished. Francesca wanted to ask if she were all right but thought better of it. It was none of her business if these Partisans beat each other up. Charles talking in a low voice to Seppo again at the far side of the clearing. Francesca noticed a look in his eyes she had not seen before. They glistened and followed Seppo, as if glued to him. That, too, was none of her business.

Dufy said, 'Shirley tells me you are an artist.'

'Conservator and critic, too.'

'I was a school teacher in St Cyprien. You know it?'

'I've never been there. I don't know Aquitaine well.'

'You will like Bergerac, once the Germans leave. It is a nice place.'

'I'm not here to enjoy myself. I came to help in the war. My daughter…'

'You have a daughter in Paris?'

'No… She… She's dead. Germans killed her.'

'I'm sorry. We all have baggage to carry,' he indicated his forehead with an index finger, 'in here. I understand you now. It's good. And the man? Your lover?'

'No. He's a close friend.'

'Perhaps Seppo will take you both to the right road. If we keep in touch, you might be useful to us. Our eyes and ears in the town have disappeared.'

'Disappeared?'

'Yes. We raided a convoy of prisoners a few months ago and things are difficult now. We plan to go north. I have a cousin in Dun-Les-Places.'

'Then who will there be here?'

'Jules and Josephine are staying. Seppo, too. They will need contacts in the town. You have a job there to go to?'

'No. I can rent somewhere. I have money and the sauer-krauts are not looking for me here, I think.'

Josephine approached. Looking down at Francesca, she said, 'I need to talk to you.'

'About?'

'About whether to keep you alive or not. I need to know if you are genuine. The Germans use spies. Milice spies. If you lie to me, I will know. Believe me.'

François said, 'Josephine, there is no need...'

'Need? Need? You take risks with your life, Dufy. You aren't taking risks with mine.'

Francesca could feel the tension between them.

'I have no objections to your questions,' she said. 'I have nothing to hide.'

The two women walked to the other side of the camp and began talking, Josephine, expressionless, Francesca gesticulating with her hands. The interrogation continued until Josephine was satisfied and both of them smiled. Francesca realised she had found some measure of understanding with this hard young woman.

When they had eaten some cold rabbit, cheese and dry bread, Seppo picked up Francesca's case and indicated the tiny path out of the camp.

'But what about Charles?'

She could see him cleaning his pistol by the remains of the

smokeless fire.

'He's staying. He didn't tell you?'

'No. I will be alone in the town? I won't even know where to sleep.'

Seppo said, 'Josephine is coming too. Her aunt will let you stay there and then you can rent somewhere. Hotels are not safe, according to Jules.'

Francesca's parting from Charles was brief. She gained the impression something was preoccupying him, but what it was, she could only guess. He kissed her on each cheek and then was gone. Confused, she watched as he turned his back and she began to feel alone again as she had when Lammerding took her apartment, when the whole awful business began.

She felt as if her "father confessor" no longer wanted her beside him, as if he were now home and she had become some baggage to be discarded. The realisation caused not anger, but disappointment. She was now alone with strangers; there was no one here she could lean upon. In her mind, she reasoned that whether Charles remained with her or not, she needed to do something to right the imbalance in her life. She needed to fight back. Marie, dead in her arms in that station, called out to her for revenge, and it was a vengeance which only helping the Maquis in any way they demanded of her could satisfy. Doubt left her and despite her feeling of tiredness, she wanted to follow Josephine.

2

Josephine led the way and Francesca began to feel she was embarking on another exhausting forest trek. She felt worn to a ravelling and her legs ached. Scratches on her legs stung and her feet hurt. It took only an hour before she began to wonder what she was doing here in Aquitaine, alone with two strangers who carried guns as if such things were a normal part of everyday life. Who was she becoming? Where was her old life? Life with Marie, with Charles and with the Louvre?

The forest path emerged at a field and beyond that was a road running towards the old, ruined Chateau Beynac. They walked across the field and along the road. A farm on their right lay on the lower side of the road and she could see smoke emitted from a chimney. Two cows stood outside, all brown hide and grey horns. She saw no one but assumed there was no reason for anyone to come out. They descended the twisting, cobbled path through the Chateau to the village far below.

'Is that Bergerac?' Francesca said, pointing to the village down the steep hill, on the slopes below the chateau.

Seppo laughed his raucous laugh. He slapped her on the shoulder. It felt like being hit by a falling tree but Francesca said nothing. She looked up at him. He had a rugged, handsome, stubbly face with grey eyes and curly blond hair.

'No, my beautiful divorcee. That is Beynac. We are twenty miles from Bergerac. Bergerac is much bigger. We are here because Josephine's aunt lives here.'

'But how will I get to Bergerac?'

'You can ride a bicycle?' Seppo said.

'Yes, of course.'

'Then you are less than an hour away.'

'My aunt lives a little further down the road leading to St Cyprien in Saint-Vincent-de-Cosse. We have a few miles to go yet.'

Francesca's face must have betrayed her disappointment. Seppo put an arm around her.

'Josephine,' he said, 'can't we stop in the village? I would love a beer.'

'You're mad. If we are seen and recognised…'

'No one knows us. We killed all the Germans in the convoy but one, and he never had a chance to see faces. We can hide the rifles. Come, how long has it been?'

Josephine relented. Perhaps, Francesca mused, she too was tired, though it did not show in her face or movements. They entered a small café opposite the little Mairie. It was dark inside but the proprietor lit some candles on the tables and they sat, enjoying the rest. Seppo and Josephine placed their rifles under the table, leaning them up between their legs, invisible but available beneath the chequered tablecloth.

They ordered beer and Francesca had a local rosé with water. She had never liked beer. As she sipped the wine, she realised how much she missed Charles and she wondered what he might be doing.

'Santé or kippis, as we say at home,' Seppo said and began drinking his beer as if it were saving his life.

'You're Dutch?' Francesca said.

Josephine smiled. 'He is about as Dutch as Hitler's moustache. He's a Finn. Like a Russian but with blond hair.'

'I don't know Finland,' Francesca said.

Seppo said, 'Finland is a wonderful country. It has mountains, sea, and is cold in the winter but hot in the summer. People there are friendly and hospitable. They make a schnapps that puts Russian vodka to shame.'

'I'm sorry, I didn't recognise your accent.'

'Not many people here have. They think I am Swedish, most of them.'

'Seppo,' Josephine said, sitting bold upright and picking up her drink as if she could hide behind it.

Francesca looked in the direction she indicated. Framed in the door was a soldier. A German soldier, rifle slung on his shoulder and a map in his hand. He was asking the proprietor directions. The three of them tensed and Francesca noticed Seppo's right hand reach down between his legs.

Presently, three more Germans entered and the four men sat at a table near the doorway. One of them glanced in their direction as the café owner served them with a bottle of wine. The man smiled and raised his glass to Josephine. The reciprocal smile on her face seemed to Francesca to be as forced as if she were greeting a poisoner who offered her a cup of coffee.

None of the three dared to move. They could not now get up with their rifles nor could they leave them behind and Francesca understood the predicament well. They sat in silence, hoping the soldiers would not order a second bottle. But they did. Francesca felt cold fingers of sweat tickling her back beneath her blouse.

Chapter 11

1

1932 birthed a hot summer. Alighting from the train, Francesca felt an eagerness she had not experienced since she was a young girl. The tiny station with its long, grey platform and the tubs of red and yellow flowers was a welcome sight and brought back many memories of other journeys ending here in Brittany as she grew up. The thought of her mother's apple almond tarte, the sound of the cows in the byre and the birdsong in the mornings filled her with nostalgia. She grasped both the suitcase and her seven-year-old daughter's hand as she descended from the train, searching for her father. There were few people on the platform and she soon saw him. His beard tickled her neck when they embraced and Marie, delighted, almost jumped into Jean's embrace. He took the case and swept Marie into his arms almost at once. He was silent for the most part during the journey but Francesca knew he was not a man to chat idly. Some might have called him stern but his affection for his daughter was never in doubt.

The small Breton farm seemed parched to Francesca as they drove the long, dirt road to the farmhouse. Francesca turned to her father. His grey beard and his balding head, and his smile as he talked, sank deep into her mind and seemed framed there like a picture, suspended on a canvas, one of infinite worth to her.

66

'We have bought a house already and we have a buyer for the farm. We will make enough on the sale to live comfortably, though not as rich people. It is exciting, is it not?'

'I... I don't know,' she said.

'But you must be happy for your Maman and me?'

'Well yes, but without you, I don't know what Marie and I will do.'

'But you won't be without us. We will be a little further away, that's all. A simple train journey.'

'We only see you twice a year as it is, Papa.'

'It will mean we have to make more effort, that's all.'

'Papi,' eight-year-old Marie said, 'is Switzerland a long way from Paris?'

'No, like I said, it is not a long way by train.'

'Will you take the piglets? I love the piglets.'

'No, my darling. Piglets become big pigs in the end and we will not be able to look after them in our new house.'

'Are the people there German?'

'Hush now, Marie,' Francesca said.

'German?' Jean Pascal, Francesca's father said. 'Why do you ask?'

'Uncle Charles said all the Germans are pigs, but I think he meant they keep pigs, like you do.'

'You are still friends with that man?' Jean said.

'Yes. He's been very good to me and Marie.'

'*Il est pede*. He has nothing for you.'

The car stopped outside the farmhouse. Francesca put her hand on her father's arm.

'Papa. He loves me as a friend. He has been very kind.'

'I don't care; he is an infamy.'

'How can you be so old-fashioned? This is the twentieth century. Such things are tolerated in Paris. No one remarks upon it.'

'Paris is Paris. I live in Brittany. It is against God's law.'

'Papa. Please, not in front of Marie. You are very old-fashioned and behind the times.'

'If I am as you say, then I'm old-fashioned. I want to be. I don't like people like that. We never saw any of them fighting alongside us in the last war. They were in Paris as you say, flaunting themselves. It's a bad thing. I never liked him.'

In exasperation, Francesca opened the car door and grabbed at the suitcase in the open boot of the car. Her father tore the case from her and stomped up the veranda steps and the front door slammed.

'Is Papi angry?' Marie said.

'Only a little. He is not angry with you, my flower. Come.'

She stretched out her hand and Marie took it. Francesca led her to the house and as she entered, she called her mother. There was a strange feeling in her heart. This would be the last time she would be here, the last holiday in Brittany, her home, and a place of memories. She bit her lip.

2

They drank more. The Germans ordered more wine. Seppo became jittery and Francesca realised he was planning something. He kept reaching down between his legs, either reassuring himself or, she thought, readying himself to fight. She began to feel as anxious as she felt on the train. It seemed to Francesca, everywhere she turned in her war-torn land, there was fighting and anger. Yet in her heart, she understood it. These men, these German soldiers, had no right to be here; they were the real infamy that her father had accused Charles of being. She hated them. The memory of the kind soldier in Charles' apartment house came to mind but it did nothing to soften her thoughts. If killing a man like that could help, she would have no hesitation.

She felt frustration for she knew she had no talent for such things. She had no experience in her life to equip her for a fight. All she could offer was subtlety and panache. What good such qualities could be in the situation in which she found herself today, seemed elusive—almost fruitless. She stood up. She leaned towards Seppo and whispered, 'Get out through the back. I'll keep them busy.'

Seppo pulled at her coat, attempting to seat her again.

'You're mad.'

'No,' she said.

Josephine shifted with discomfort in her chair. She looked at Francesca and her eyes narrowed.

She said in a whisper, 'These are not nice men. They are soldiers. Sit down.'

Francesca wondered if it were the wine. She felt strength as never before. If she had to distract the Germans, she would do it. In the back of her mind, she wondered if she were truly capable of sex acts with four soldiers of the army she hated, but she wanted above all to allow her newfound allies to escape. To do so, she would have to put on a superlative show, hold the soldiers' attention, and then what? She did not think of the aftermath; she shrugged it off. It was automatic. It was like the train, like when they shot Marie.

The picture of that moment on the platform when the Germans approached, insinuated itself. They kicked the body of the young man. They apologised to her for the death of her daughter and the face of the man who spoke remained burned into her memory, into her soul.

Yet none of these men was responsible. They were part of the vehicle causing Marie's death; they were not the drivers. Could she prostitute herself for the two Partisans? Could she allow such people to defile her body, men whom she hated? She concluded she could. It was life or death for her companions. What use was her body now, anyway? Marie, her only reason for living, was gone. Who cared about what went on now? Not Francesca.

'Get out the back. They won't notice. I promise.'

Seppo sat with his mouth open and watched as Francesca walked up to the Germans, glass in hand, seeming somewhat the worse for the two carafes of wine. Neither Josephine nor he seemed capable of moving. They sat watching a performance they afterwards could only call a masterpiece.

Francesca tapped the nearest soldier on the shoulder.

'Pardon. You have more wine?'

'Fraulein, we will be delighted. Will your friend join us too?'

'No. She is menstruating.'

The soldiers roared with laughter and one of them raised a glass towards Josephine.

Out of the corner of her eye, Francesca saw her companions sitting at the table, frozen in time, as if they were now creatures of marble. She cursed mentally. 'Not me, though.'

The nearest of the soldiers grabbed at her and tried to pull her onto his knee. The reality of the moment came home then. The truth of what she might have to endure for the two Partisans who remained immobile at the other table came home to Francesca and she realised. That realisation was as sudden as if a freight train had struck her. She could no more endure this than she could have killed herself. The hatred within her made her feel flushed. She noticed a feeling of blood rushing to her head, throbbing, pounding.

I hate them, she thought. Damn it, I hate them.

She knew she would rather die than have one of them touch her and although afterwards she attributed it to the wine, she became angry. She picked up the bottle from the table. Raising it above her shoulder, she swung it at the forehead of the soldier who seemed so intent to have her sit upon his knee. Red wine sprayed across the table. The bottle connected. It struck him with a force Francesca never realised she possessed. The blow surprised her almost as much as it did the other soldiers. Her victim, however, crumpled. She backed away.

The Germans reached for their rifles, stacked in an upright pyramid near the doorway, but seconds away from their hands. Shots rang out. The noise made Francesca startle and raise her hands. A sound of tables splintering, bodies falling, surrounded her. She protected her head as she fell away, backwards, against the bar-counter. She closed her eyes. She curled up and heard shot after shot, then silence. Then a hand on her shoulder, shaking, rousing.

'Francesca. Francesca? Are you all right?'

She opened her eyes.

Seppo said, 'It's alright. They're all dead.'

'Who?'

'The Germans. Whatever possessed you?'

'What?'

'To start a fight.'

Josephine knelt before her.

'Crazy woman. Now look at the mess. We have to clear up. Get your wits together and help.'

In a daze, Francesca helped the other two drag the bodies to the rear of the café.

The proprietor seemed to be panicking; he waved his hands, sweating, and remonstrated. Seppo calmed him and then tied him up in case he might seem implicated. The tidying process took a short time and they all three knew they had to flee. But where to?

Chapter 12

1

The cobbles jarred on her new shoes as they ran down the hill and then off to the right, trying to escape the scene of the bloodbath. Francesca had no idea where she was, no concept of where they were going, and she realised she was in trouble.

'Stupid,' Josephine said as they jogged along the riverside.

Francesca said nothing. She stumbled but stayed on her feet. Seppo put his arm around her waist to steady her and they paused to catch their breath further down a narrow road beside the Dordogne.

Josephine said, 'What were you doing? You could have got us all killed. You were supposed to distract them.'

'He touched me.'

'What did you expect? Flattering words and humour?'

'You don't understand. I was going to distract them in any way they wanted but you sat still. What did you expect? You didn't leave.'

'How could we? We had a meter and a half of metal between our legs. You think you can just get up and shoulder a rifle like that? Stupid.'

'When the soldier touched me. I realised I could not do it. They shot and killed my daughter. All I could see was a group of murderers.'

Josephine was silent then.

Seppo said, 'Don't be too hard on her. If you were like her, you would not have tolerated their hands on you, either.'

'What do you know about it? You're a man.'

'They killed two of my brothers. You think I don't know?'

Francesca said, 'Please. I'm sorry. I realise I risked your lives. It won't happen again.'

Josephine's expression softened. In the ensuing silence, Francesca shifted from one foot to another.

Josephine said, 'I'm sorry to shout. Everything has gone wrong now. We can maybe still make it to my aunt's place in Saint-Vincent-de-Cosse, but what we do then, I have no idea. We need to get off this damned road. Here. We cut off to the right.'

They walked and ran until they found a path to the right and followed a road, heading always north and west. A farmer with a horse-drawn cart full of hay passed in the opposite direction. He ignored them. Francesca thought it was because he saw the rifles. He acted as if he hoped by ignoring them, he could avoid involvement.

'Josephine. You are too hard on Francesca. It worked out well,' Seppo said.

'Well? Well? Four ordinary German soldiers dead and for what? Nothing.'

'Four dead Germans are better than four live ones, that's all.'

She turned to Francesca and said, 'Every German we kill results in reprisals. They kill two for every one we shoot. It has always been strategic before. Officers, generals, anyone who is important. These four men achieved nothing for us but put us in danger.'

Seppo said, 'You have never lost anyone. They killed my brothers. I hate them all, whether they are rankers or officers.

It gave me great pleasure to despatch them. Francesca, you did nothing wrong. I think you are one of the bravest women I have had the pleasure to meet.'

'Shut up, you stupid Finn,' Josephine said.

'Please don't fight over me. I'm sorry. I allowed my hatred to get the better of me. It will never happen again. Maybe I should learn to shoot a gun.'

The sun peeped out from behind a grey cloud as if to indicate she was right, but they ran on, oblivious. It could have been snowing, for all Francesca cared. She wanted respite. She wanted rest and a place away from danger. She felt she had been running forever as they made their way along the road, and the raw blisters on her heels smarted and burned with every step.

Josephine said, 'We have to hide the rifles. We are too obvious on this road.'

They stopped by a low wall and did as she suggested. They marked where they had left their two Mausers and walked on, trying to look casual to any passersby but jogging in between. Francesca found the running hard. The nearest she had experienced to exercise in the last few years was walking up the stairs to her apartment in Paris and she soon felt she could not go on. She stopped again by a low dry-stone wall.

'Please, I can't run any further.'

Seppo said, 'Your life may depend on it.'

'I don't care. If they shoot me, I will die in peace if only I am allowed to breathe a little.'

Josephine laughed.

'Come on. Not far now. Ten minutes maybe.'

Seppo grabbed her arm. His grip was strong and she looked at his face. He was still smiling. Francesca wondered whether anything could dampen his humour. Killing four

German soldiers was not enough; she could see that.

On their left, they came to a farmhouse. A barn stood next to it and an animal shed stood across the road. Josephine knocked on the door. There was no answer at first, but she continued to knock and Francesca could hear a faint voice behind the door.

'Who are you?'

'It is Josephine. I need your help.'

'Josephine?'

The door swung open. An elderly woman, her back distorted and bent, emerged from the doorway.

'Is it really you?'

The old lady proffered her arms and Josephine bent forward, leaning down to hug her aunt.

Francesca, witnessing the scene, wondered whether she had misjudged Josephine. There was tenderness and love in the embrace and she wondered whether there were depths to this Partisan she had not suspected. The aunt, whose name was Madeleine Duval, showed them in. Sitting in the kitchen, Francesca realised this place was her France, the way she recalled it. It was not part of Germany. It was her home. Nothing could persuade her otherwise.

2

Seppo peered through the lace curtains at the road outside. A military truck passed by and he drew away, standing against the wall next to the casement. Francesca could hear the truck pull up. She waited, drumming her fingers on the table, and she noticed a faint glow of perspiration beneath her collar.

'Are they coming?'

'No, they've gone across the square.'

'We aren't safe here,' Josephine said.

'Poor little one, what is happening?' Madeleine said.

'Auntie, we had some trouble with the soldiers in Beynac. They may be looking for us. We had better go. You could be in danger.'

'But my poor little one, at my age, I don't care what they do to me. You can hide in the hayloft and I will shoo them away.'

'They might search there too.'

'Then you can get out on the other side.'

Josephine stood; she leaned forward and kissed the old lady on the cheek. They ran through the kitchen into a small yard, cobbled and grey, moss between the stones, an uncared-for place. A barn stood behind the house, a remnant from the days when it had been a real farm. It had a brick base, but the upper part was wood with several windows, barred and shut-tered.

'Come,' Josephine said.

They pulled open the door and the three of them crossed the high-ceilinged barn to the opposite side where there was another smaller door. Seppo put his weight against it but it would not budge.

He said, 'If they come now, we are trapped.'

The wood must have swollen and try as he might, it re-mained shut.

Francesca could hear a door slam in the farmhouse.

'Hurry,' she said.

They heard voices from the yard.

Seppo found an edge and slipped his fingers round it. Bracing himself, he placed a foot on the rotting doorjamb; he heaved, using all his considerable strength. With a creak, enough of a gap appeared and he grabbed Francesca by the arm, almost ejecting her through the space. Josephine was next and the two women stood outside. Francesca realised she was shaking. She wished she had a cigarette, a drink, anything to calm her nerves. Ten yards away, a thick forest stretched up a hill and on as far as Francesca could see. She tugged at Josephine's gabardine coat, indicating the wood. She did not move. Still they waited. Her heart leapt to her throat.

Thirty seconds passed.

Francesca swallowed hard. Her palms were damp, her breathing fast.

Then a minute flew by.

'Go. Go.'

It was Seppo, climbing out.

'What were you doing?' Josephine said.

'A little surprise if they force the door, that's all.'

'The grenade?' Josephine said.

A sound of hammering came from the now-empty barn.

Seppo smiled, donning Francesca's suitcase in its rope sling, and with his arm around her shoulders, the three of them fled again. Francesca knew they were in deeper trouble than she had ever experienced in her life and she was no closer to making her fresh start in Bergerac. She felt like a character in a Kafkaesque story, always seeking a goal and never reaching it because of constant, invisible obstacles in her path.

The tree line loomed in front and the density of the trees forced them to push their way through, in single file, past grey and brown branches scratching and sticking, impeding their progress. They stopped for a breather after ten minutes; it was heavy going and her suitcase on Seppo's back, she felt, must be an impossible impediment.

Josephine said, 'Leave it. You're slowing us down.'

'No, it's all right,' Seppo said.

'No. You can't leave it. It's my life on your back. If you leave it, you leave me, too,' Francesca said. There was a hint of horror in her voice.

Seppo said, 'Don't you worry. For you, I would carry it all the way to hell.'

'You may have to,' Josephine said. 'We can't afford to be sluggish. Maybe I'll go on ahead and leave you both.'

'Now, now,' Seppo said, 'I know you're not so heartless. I saw you with the old lady.'

They walked on and found a path. It climbed in a steep meander up the hill. Then they heard it. There was a distant explosion. They turned but saw nothing through the trees.

'I think they found my surprise,' Seppo said, smirking.

'You can be quite childish sometimes,' Josephine said.

Francesca stopped. She looked at them and said, 'That wasn't your real aunt was it?'

'No, she was my great-aunt's best friend. The two of them brought me up when my parents died. She is all I have since my great-aunt died. She gave much to bring me up. She even paid for my tuition at university.'

'University?'

'Yes. Just because I sleep in a forest and kill Germans, doesn't mean I am an uneducated woman.'

'I'm sorry, I didn't mean to imply...' Francesca said. 'What were you studying?'

'Law.'

'Ah,' Francesca said.

'I, on the other hand,' Seppo said, 'am thoroughly uneducated. I am a carpenter by trade but I've picked up a few other skills on the way. I can do electrical work, like wire a bomb. I can exterminate vermin like the sauerkrauts. I can even cook.'

Francesca smiled. She said, 'But not sauerkraut, I hope.'

He laughed and pressed on. Presently, they came to a road bisecting the forest and Josephine led them west.

Francesca began to wonder where it would all end. She felt the gnawing pangs of exhaustion. Wondering whether it might have been the wine in the middle of the day, she said, 'I need to rest.'

As they sat by the roadside, they fell silent. It was as if now that they had space to converse, none of them had more to say. There was awkwardness between them, as if each of them regretted giving away any part of themselves to the others. Francesca wondered whether they were camping in the forest or finding somewhere to sleep under a roof, but she dared not ask. She felt as if the simple act of asking would make her look dependent and weak. She thought her companions were the strong ones, the ones who did not complain, and the ones who knew what to do.

Reflecting how she was useless, she said nothing; she sat, trying with desperation to regain some kind of control over her life and limbs.

She was becoming passive, almost as if she were giving up the person she used to be. No longer the famous, wealthy art expert; now she was an impoverished woman ready for others to tell her where to go and what to do. She would never have imagined she could have become such a person. In Paris, she had been competent, strong. How else could one bring up a child in the aftermath of the Great War? Yet now, others were leading her, directing her, as though she had no strength to resist, and she knew deep inside they were the experts here. They understood the dangers. They knew the way and what did she have to offer such people? An art appraisal? It was ridiculous and she began to question what she was doing in

Aquitaine at all. She should have stayed in Paris or fled to her parents in Switzerland.

No, she would learn the competencies these people possessed. She wanted to contribute to the resistance against the occupying force and to its ultimate destruction, the freeing of her beloved France, even if it killed her.

Chapter 13

1

When Pierre left her, Francesca became strong. She realised early that there was no one else to care for Marie. It was true she often sat alone at night, wishing the doorbell would ring and his smiling face would be there to come home to her and make it all better. In her more realistic moments, she hated him. She felt abandoned but she was not a woman to either accept it, or to fold. She became motivated. She worked harder. She wrote articles, papers. She presented her theories in conferences, she taught at the University, and in the end, she became a national expert in her field. Pierre could not take away the person deep inside, whatever he did to her confidence with men. When men paid her compliments she shunned them. When they asked her out she refused. She did not want another man to let her down. And sex? She did without. She was a sexual woman by nature but without it she developed other priorities in her life. Marie became her reason for living.

It was then she met Charles. She knew him from her time at the Sorbonne. They qualified together but were never social as undergraduates. They became friends by accident.

The sun baked the grass in the Jardin de Tuileries where Francesca sat on a bench, admiring the fountain spouting cool water twenty feet into the air, Marie in her perambulator next to her. The walkway around the fountain was busy with pedestrian visitors, French and foreign. She had a good view from her seat. The statue of Theseus slaying the Minotaur, the Avenue de General Lémoniére behind it and the oblong facade of the Louvre itself, gave her a feeling of contentment, as if her world were unshakeable and would last forever.

Marie began to cry. Francesca leaned forward and lifted out her baby.

'See, my little one,' she said in quiet tones, jiggling her up and down on her knee, 'there is the home of our heritage. Where the greatest pictures in the whole world are hung.'

She settled Marie on her lap and pointed. She meant the words. She felt them deep inside; it was as if her heritage were her greatest source of pride. Something to cling to in a changing world, where people could let you down, disappoint and desert you.

Marie, for her part, at the age of eighteen months, wriggled and seemed less interested in her heritage than Francesca had expected. Like anyone with children, she knew her child would be a prodigy. Had Marie not begun to walk early? Had she not made sounds like words? Did she not show signs of interest in drawing with crayons? At the age of one-and-a-half this could only be the signs of a developing artist.

A man interrupted her thoughts. He approached and stood, shading the infant girl, and Francesca looked up with surprise.

'Monsieur?'

'Francesca?'

'You are?'

'Charles. You must remember me. I drew that sketch of you and Joseph in the life-drawing class.'

She stood up, Marie clutched to her hip.

'Of course. Sorry, it was the sunlight; I could not see your face. Naturally, I remember you. You drew that picture which caused all the embarrassment.'

'Hah. The teachers in the Sorbonne are prudes. Everyone knows about men being together but no one wants it seen. It was a biblical picture and they made me destroy it.'

'It was a wonderful drawing. You have real talent. I was sad when you had to take it down.'

'They are Philistines. But, even Rodin had to put up with such things. He was on the outside looking in for a long time. You know he was unrecognised until he was almost forty?'

'Yes, I know. You are still painting?'

'No. I'm a journalist now and a writer. I'm working on a book about Degas. Not that they will ever publish it. And who is this young man?

'Girl.'

'Sorry. I'm not good with babies. She is beautiful. Don't tell me, her name is… Let me see…Camille?'

'No. Marie. My husband's mother was called Marie and now I have to saddle my child with her name.'

'She at least must be pleased. Where is your husband?'

Her face clouded over. There was a moment of silence and she said, 'He left us.'

'Left you with little Marie? He was a fool.'

'Another woman. She got her claws into him and there was no going back.'

'You see him still?'

'No. He shows no interest in us. I think he has moved away. I never hear from him.'

'Look, I have to go. I am meeting a friend. Can we meet again?'

'No. I think not. I don't need another man in our lives.'

'I don't mean in that way. We may become friends, only friends. I have other people in my life for that kind of thing. I always liked you because you were one of the few people who understood my work.'

Charles extracted a broken pencil and a scrap of paper from his trouser pocket.

'Your address?'

He scribbled and turned away.

Over his shoulder he said, 'I will perhaps contact you sometime. We could walk in the park or something.'

He pushed his way through the tourists.

'That would be nice,' Francesca lied.

In her head, she thought she would never see him again. She had always thought he must have been a homosexual and she felt safe with that. She did not think he would contact her anyway and she remained puzzled why she had given him her address. She bit her lip. What if he wanted her?

Another man to keep at arm's length.

No. No more men.

Men cannot be trusted.

2

They spent three days hiding in the forest. By that time, Francesca felt impatient, angry and dirty. She had never slept rough in her life and the added discomfort of sleeping on damp leaves in her overcoat made her feel she wanted to give up. They had water and a little bread and cheese from Josephine's backpack. The rifles, hidden on the way, were now inaccessible. They must have looked dishevelled, she thought. Surely, any passing soldiers would know who they were.

They trekked across fields, through woods and forest and avoided farms and towns. It was on the outskirts of Bergerac Josephine decided to find a contact she knew she could trust. They hid in a disused railway yard during the afternoon. It was a place of weed-strewn ground, rat-holes and wreckage. The brown, rusty rails piled in one corner and the rotting sleepers next to them, adding to the feeling of despondency pervading Francesca's heart.

At dusk, they made their way along muddy tracks in drizzle and puddles, until they came to a two-storey house at the end of a narrow street. Francesca looked up as they stood and waited for someone to answer the bell. The house had two upper rooms with open shutters, underscored by green-painted window boxes, from which last year's dead flowers peeped down at the street below. It had an air of past glory, as if this were once a happy place, but time and circumstance changed it, as the seasons changed the now dead, disconsolate plants in the boxes.

A man in a grey shirt, braces and a frown answered the door. He leaned out looking up and down the street and pulled Josephine in by the arm. The others followed and he shut the door, standing with his back towards it. Francesca found herself in a narrow hallway, with stairs leading up to small landing and a passageway through to the kitchen. On her right were two doors to other rooms but the man showed them into the kitchen. His name was Roland Duboef and after the introductions, he offered Francesca a bowl of hot water and a grubby-looking towel, which she took out to the washhouse behind the building. Even a strip-wash was a pleasure and she felt almost human by the time she crossed the cracking, grey concrete of the yard and re-entered the kitchen.

Panic took her when she did. Roland wore a Vichy-police

uniform and was strapping on a firearm as she entered. She backed away but Josephine called her back.

Josephine said, 'No. it's fine, he is one of us.'

'He's police.'

'I am a policeman but I am one of you as well. I was persuaded to join. Ask François Dufy if you must know. My chief, Assistant-chief Ran, killed a German SD officer and ran away because he could not stand what was happening in our country. He was a good man and like me, he learned to hate the Germans. My presence in the Prefecture is often useful. They have listening devices all over the place and I can pass wrong information to the sauerkrauts when Josephine's group needs me to. Don't fear me.'

'Is it safe here?' Seppo said.

'Roland said, 'Safe? Of course. It is probably the last place they would look for you, but if you put a foot outside, looking as you do, I'm afraid...'

Seppo nodded and took the towel from Francesca's trembling fingers. Noticing her hands shaking, he squeezed them and said, 'Relax yourself now. The journey is almost over.'

He patted her hand and left to clean up. Josephine, however, seemed to Francesca to be in no hurry and she wondered how Josephine could have become so hardened to the discomfort of living in the rough circumstances they had experienced in the last few days.

'Roland,' Josephine said, 'how about some food?'

'I made a cassoulet. It's on the stove. There's some bread in the bin on the table. I'm afraid there was no meat, so I put fish in it. You can finish it if you like. I found it disgusting.'

Josephine grinned.

'After what we have had in the forest, it will be a feast.'

Roland shrugged and said, 'I must go. I'm on nights. Keep

all the lights out. Everyone here knows when I'm on nights. If they see a light of any kind the game's up. Open the curtains. The moon shines through the back windows. Sorry.'

He left them, slamming the door behind him. They could hear him whistling a tune as he mounted his bicycle outside. They stood there in the dark and wondered how they could find plates and forks, but Francesca knew how; where there is a will, filling one's stomach presented few problems.

As they sat in the faint light of the moon, eating the bean-stew, they fell silent. Eating took priority.

Presently, pushing her plate away, Francesca said, 'Josephine, what happens now? I need to find a place of my own to rent where I can both paint and sell pictures.'

'You have money?'

'Yes. I brought quite a lot with me in Deutschemarks and francs. I also have money in a Swiss bank but not huge wealth. I can rent somewhere.'

Seppo said, 'If you have money in Switzerland, why are you here? You could have gone there and been safe.'

They could not see Francesca's face with any clarity but there was no mistaking the determination in her voice.

'The Nazis came to our country and began stealing and killing in 1940, almost four years ago. Since then they have killed my only child, taken my home and all my possessions, apart from a few paintings, and you ask why I'm here? I want what you want. I want to learn to do what you do. I'm not equipped for the revenge I seek, but I can learn.'

Neither of her companions replied. It was as if they wanted more, so she gave it to them.

'You look at me as if I am some pampered lady of the city who cannot endure what you do. Maybe you are right and my place will not be to shoot people, to throw bombs and grenades. But I will do my part. Never doubt that.'

Seppo said, 'Francesca, I never doubted you. Maybe you can't aim a gun, but you swing a bottle better than anyone I've ever seen.'

This was the first time they had laughed together. The bonding was slow to come but this was a start and Francesca could feel it. Even the reticent Josephine laughed. She reached forward and placed a hand on Francesca's shoulder.

'We will make you a Maquis before you know it. First, you must become a spy for us like Shirley, the Rosbif you met. You will become our eyes and ears in Bergerac. I already have the ideal place in mind for you.'

'You have?'

'Last year a sniper killed a German called Meyer on the steps of the Mairie, where the SD have their headquarters. The owner of the shoe-shop was called Camille. She ran away when the killing took place and later, the Germans shot her. Her nephew told them how the killer must have broken in. They accepted his explanation and apologised for her death, the pigs. The nephew owns the building now, though it stands empty. The place is ideal.'

Seppo said, 'The Germans won't let anyone rent it, surely?'

'It's worth a try.'

Francesca said, 'Before I do that, I need somewhere safe to stay.'

'François had a place on the south bank. It's not very comfortable but it will do for a few nights. We can take you there tomorrow morning. A woman on her own with genuine papers won't be questioned. They aren't looking for you for any real crimes.'

'I took paintings with me. The man who stole my home told me to leave them.'

'He won't be pursuing you all the way here. Doubt if anyone will know about such a small thing in a big war. They are more bothered about the Russians now than anything you may have done.'

'I suppose not. Tomorrow then?'

'Yes, tonight we sleep here and before Roland even returns, we will be gone.'

That night, to Francesca, even the sofa in the front room was a luxury when she closed her eyes. She felt as if she stood on a precipice, eager to fly, but reluctant in case she was inadequate to do it. As sleep took her, she thought of Marie and what her daughter might have done. She had always been a staunch believer in her country and Francesca was determined not to forsake her memory by running away.

Chapter 14

1

The house of François Dufy stood close up to the tree line of a dense forest south of the Dordogne River. The tiled roof sported moss and the guttering hung in places as if torn away years before. The bright front door with its peeling red paint added no hint of cheerfulness as Francesca followed Josephine into the place through the backdoor. Her heart sinking, she looked out of the window of the single-storey house at the bleak, cobbled roadway and lonely street-lamp twenty yards down the lane. Looking around inside, she felt even worse. There was a pervading smell of damp and the tattered rug beneath her feet looked as if it belonged in an outhouse. Seppo stood next to her. Josephine, efficient as ever, was busy searching the back to be certain it was safe.

'Will you be all right?' Seppo said.

'I… I don't know. I don't know what to do. This place is terrible. There is no inside toilet or wash-room and the bed looks disgusting. François lived here?'

She recalled the odour of the man and shuddered.

'Yes, he was pretending to be an alcoholic wastrel. He succeeded in that until we rescued Rachelle.'

'His niece?'

'Niece?'

'She called him uncle.'

'No they are not related. She's Jewish, but I think he loves her. He risked much to save her when the SD captured her.'

'But she is a child next to him. It's an infamy.'

'No. Not like that. I think he really cares for her as a friend. He would no more touch her like that, than I would. He rescued her from the Germans and hid her for many months.'

'Ah,' Francesca said.

Seppo put an arm around her waist. It felt strange for her. She had never allowed any man to touch her since Pierre. It was true, she and Charles sometimes slept together, but it was never sexual. It had been as if they were children, seeking warmth in each other's bodies and nothing more. They had a kind of closeness through friendship and she knew it never aroused him, either. This contact was different. In her mind, she wanted to push him away. There was something, however, staying her hand. A positive feeling came over her. To her own amazement, she enjoyed his closeness, his large, firm hand on her body.

Catching herself in these thoughts, she pushed him away.

'Don't,' she said.

Defences up.

'Sorry. I won't do it again,' he said.

'No. I didn't mean that. It's just…'

'Just?'

'I don't want that kind of thing with anyone just now. I've been away from men for so…'

'Look. I admire you. You are a beautiful woman. How can you not understand? I've watched you all the time since Beynac. Your green eyes, your hair…'

A sound behind them interrupted them.

'Your green eyes? Is this what you say to your women in

92

Finland?'

It was Josephine. She wore a broad smile, lighting up her long face.

Seppo pulled away and, scowling, said, 'Stop it. You make fun of me. I just meant…'

Francesca reached up and stroked his square, bristly face. 'No one could make fun of a man like you. I think you are brave and kind and…not bad looking,' she smiled.

She glanced at Josephine. The look on her face showed defiance. She said gently, 'I am here alone and looking for a way to help in the fight for my country. It is just not the time for such gestures, Seppo. That is all.'

A silence followed. It contained an awkwardness they all felt. Presently, Seppo said, 'Maybe we should be going. We can't afford to be seen here.'

'But what will I do?' Francesca said.

'Do?' Josephine said, 'Do nothing. One of us will return and let you know about the shoe shop. If that draws a blank, we will find somewhere else. You stay here. In the morning, walk into town and buy some food. You will need to be here a few days until our contacts find out about the place. We will send someone when we know.'

'But I need to choose. I can't just work anywhere.'

'Nor can we.'

Seppo and Josephine made their way to the back of the house where the forest encroached. The look in Seppo's eyes told her what he was thinking. She could not fathom Josephine's thoughts. The two Partisans left as quietly as they had arrived and she stood watching as they melted into the forest.

Francesca was now alone.

2

She missed Charles. She wished, as she cycled into Bergerac, he could have been there with her. He had brought her here and then left her. It puzzled her. What could be so important for him in the Partisan camp to stop him coming with her? It began to irritate her in the end and she put him out of mind.

It was a Friday, the day before the market but she guessed markets were not the affairs they used to be before the war. The most she expected was half-empty shops with barren shelves. Today there would be even less to buy than on a market day, but she had to have food of some kind. After the deprivation of the previous days, she admitted to herself she would have eaten almost anything.

She cycled across the bridge and glanced at the brown, cold swirling waters below her. She did not know the Dordogne River and she knew its towns and people even less well.

There was a German military vehicle stopped at an angle across the roadway at the far end and she began to wonder if they might stop her and arrest her. Tempted to turn around, she realised how suspicious it would look and she knew she had either to take her chance with her papers or be seen running. She reassured herself she had not committed any crime. Her papers were after all genuine identification papers, but she had no relocation permit.

She stopped, hesitating.

'Good morning,' said a deep female voice behind her.

She ignored it at first. She had no desire to speak to these country folk. Her heart was beating fast and she noticed her mouth was dry at the prospect of showing her documents, even though she was sure the Germans were not after her, either as an art thief, or as an associate of the Partisans.

A plump old woman on a bicycle pulled level with her. She wore a brown raincoat and a wide-brimmed straw hat. She turned her lined and serious face towards Francesca.

'I said, good morning. You did not hear me?'

'I'm sorry, I was thinking. Good morning to you.'

The older woman held out a hand. As Francesca took it, the older woman said, 'Marquite Arnaud. Pleased to meet you. You are?'

'Francesca Pascal.'

'From Paris?'

'My accent?'

'Yes, it is unmistakable. Particularly here, where the chance of meeting a cultured person is miniscule.'

'Please forgive me,' Francesca said, 'I'm next.'

The soldier by the vehicle called her to him.

'Papers,' he said.

He looked at them with more care than Francesca felt was warranted and he turned to his colleague, muttering low in German.

'Wait here,' he said.

The soldier picked up the earphones of a radio and spoke fast into the microphone. A moment later, he indicated Francesca to the side. Her heart leapt. She felt faint and sweaty. She moved as if in a dream to the side of the bridge. What could be wrong? Were they after her?

She noticed how the older woman, Madame Arnaud, accompanied her. She looked at the old face. Madame Arnaud had her mouth in a tight smile. She patted Francesca's hand where it rested on the handlebars of her bicycle.

'I will stay with you. I don't take bullying from these pigs.'

Francesca smiled at the woman. She felt that even the company of an unexpected stranger felt welcome.

Within minutes, a junior officer arrived in a black Mercedes. He approached with a bored expression. He clicked his heels and bowed a little towards the two women, then turned to the soldier.

'It had better be good. This is twice in one morning.'

Francesca heard the soldier say in German, 'This woman is from Paris. She has no relocation documents, Scharführer.'

The officer turned to Francesca.

'You are from Paris?'

'Yes.'

'Did you apply for papers to come here? All travellers need permits.'

Madame Arnaud interrupted. 'This my niece, Francesca. She has come all this way to visit me because I have been ill. There was no time for papers or German obstruction. I needed her by my side. I am dying of cancer.'

'You look alright to me,' the officer said.

'You are a doctor, you silly boy? I need a certificate to say I'm dying before I'm allowed my family to be with me? You think I should die alone?'

'But you are riding a bicycle. You say you are dying. I'm sorry but…'

'I can't walk so I ride a bicycle. I am the cousin of Judge Dubois. Perhaps you should telephone him to enquire over my health?'

'I… I…'

'Enough of this,' Madame Arnaud said. 'Come, Francesca, we are going. Perhaps these men are brave enough to shoot a dying woman in the back. Let us test them.'

The old woman remounted her bicycle and, teetering, began cycling.

Francesca followed. She shrugged and grinned to the officer as if to say she could do nothing; her aunt was her aunt.

Chapter 15

1

Francesca and Madame Arnaud shared a lunch of rustic paté and homemade bread at the wide kitchen table in "Maison Anglais", the house in which the old woman lived. The house, an old and comfortable place, stood on the west side of town south of the river. They talked at first about the war and the changes it had brought to both their daily lives. There seemed to Francesca to be some kind of affinity between them, though she did not understand why.

Madame Arnaud said, 'I'm glad you came to stay.'

'Did I have a choice?'

The old lady smiled. She stood up and walked across her kitchen. The tiled floor echoed her clacking heels as she reached into the ancient, wooden wine-rack.

'My husband always offered wine to new guests. Shall I do the same?'

'It would be a pleasure.'

'Is this any good?' She proffered a bottle from the rack. 'To be honest, it all tastes good to me. I don't know what top quality is, but I think my husband only had good wine.'

'You miss him. I can hear that.'

'Yes. He was a fool but I loved him as much as he loved France.'

'But he loved you too?'

'Yes; he was foolish sometimes, but he loved me.'

'Foolish?'

'He misbehaved with young girls, but he never wanted to leave me. It was a difficulty between us. I was patient with him and I ignored it. In the end it killed him.'

'Killed him?'

'Yes. We had a maid and he could not keep his hands off her.'

'Yet you say you loved him?'

'We were married for forty-five years. From before the time of the first war. He should have realised a young girl like that would not have been involved with an old man like him. I was tolerant. Perhaps it was a mistake.'

'You said it killed him.'

Francesca had visions of the old man in bed, dying of a heart attack.

'He talked to her. She worked for the SD. When she had enough information, she told them everything he said in his boasting, his stupidity. Is this wine good?'

'Chateau de Fieuzal? Fantastic. You have the '29, too. Your husband may have been foolish but he had good taste in wine.'

'They arrested him and beat him to death.'

'My God, I'm so sorry,' she said.

'My cousin the pathologist told me. André was covered in burns and bruises. Eugene signed the death certificate as a heart attack, but he told me the truth.'

She opened the bottle with the rusty old cork-pull on the wall.

'I'm sorry... I thought your cousin was a judge.'

'His brother. My husband died a hero. He told them nothing, I'm certain. He was as obstinate as a goat, believe me. I lived with him all those years. They say everyone talks under torture, but I know he would not. Maybe that's why he died. His obstinacy. Here.'

Madame Arnaud poured two glasses of wine and passed one to Francesca, who sniffed, then swirled it around her mouth.

'Magnificent,' she said.

She noticed tears forming in her hostess' eyes. Now, it seemed to Francesca, the old woman had passed beyond her barriers. Madame Arnaud, sitting on her stool at the rough wooden table, put her hands to her face. She leaned forward in silence. There were no sobs, no histrionics. It was a silent grief. A way of letting out something Francesca understood. It hung in the air between them.

The old lady wiped her eyes with the back of a hand and said, 'I don't understand what you are doing here.'

'I wonder myself sometimes. I have parents in Switzerland; maybe I should have gone there.'

'It would have been better than coming here. The place is crawling with Germans, SD, SS and even the French traitors, the Milice. They've taken away all the Jews to a camp at Drancy and a lot of innocent people, too. The ones whose enemies have informed on them for personal revenge. This war is destroying our culture and our fraternity.'

'I had friends in Paris, dear friends. They took them away and stole all their possessions. When they took my home, I thought they might search for me because I took a few paintings. I'm an artist so I didn't want to part with them.'

'If you took nothing valuable, why would they be after you?'

'I couldn't shake off the idea. The man I came with was wanted and we were together.'

'Your lover?'

'No… Only a friend. I think I needed a change and some way to get even with the Germans.'

'We must all resist. It is our duty to do so in any way we can for as long as it takes.'

'Yes. I hate them.'

'No more than I do. What made you feel this way?'

'They shot my daughter on a platform at Sainte Lazare. They said they were sorry, as if that could make any difference. They were killing a young man and Marie was shot by mistake. I don't know how to fight back.'

'There are resistance groups here. Perhaps they can find a use for you.'

'Perhaps.'

'Where are you staying?'

'In a little house on the outskirts. I met a man, François Dufy, who allowed me to stay there.'

'Sergeant Dufy? You know this man?'

'I only met him once.'

'He was in the first war with my husband. André said Dufy was one of the best killers of Germans he ever had serving under him. My husband trusted him, but he has run away. He was a dirty, disgusting fellow, though. The Germans think he killed one of the SD in a restaurant a few months back. You must tell no one you have seen him. You hear?'

'I didn't realise. I told you because I trusted you.'

'Trust no one. You don't know me. I could be an informer, for all you know.'

'I could be one, too.'

'I have told you nothing secret, not that I know anything, but all the same you are right. Maybe I need to keep a closer eye on you. You can stay here until you find a studio.'

'I couldn't impose.'

'Of course you can. I need the company. Since André was murdered, I find this house too big for just me. It will be better for you than living in that pigsty where Dufy used to stay. I used to cycle there to fetch game and fish. Disgusting way to live. Now, no more nonsense. Go and get your things when the wine is gone. I shall still be here. There is nowhere for me to go, you see.'

2

Francesca made her way in the drizzling dusk, wondering whether her motives were becoming confused. She knew nothing about this Arnaud woman, apart from an instinctual feeling they both needed each other. How she could fit this into her plans of becoming part of a resistance movement whose extent and effectiveness were unknown to her, she still could not fathom. She knew she did not belong with the Partisans in the forests, yet she wanted somehow to fight back against the killers who had taken Marie from her.

As she cycled and raindrops trickled down her nose-tip, she wondered whether the Partisans would have discouraged her from an alliance with Marquite Arnaud, if that were what it was. Francesca reasoned that if the woman's husband had been a resister, it must be safe to trust her, but she also knew there were many pressures the SD could put on ordinary folk to make them inform. For all she knew, their meeting was no accident; some German spymaster could have planned it, to lure her into a false sense of security. Perhaps, she wondered, this old lady could even be on the wrong side, but she discard-ed the thought when she recalled the look on Madame Arnaud's face as she spoke about her husband. Women know these things, she thought.

Arriving at the single-storey house, she dismounted and fumbled the key into the latch in the half-light. It was dark inside and as she closed the door, she experienced an uncomfortable feeling as if someone were in the room with her.

She startled when a light came on in front of her. She was not one to scream, but she felt shivers down her spine and jumped back towards the door.

'It's only me.'

'Seppo? What are you doing here?'

'François sent me to make sure you were all right.'

'You scared me. I didn't know who you were.'

'Sorry. I didn't mean…'

'I'm moving out. I met a lady called Arnaud, a widow. She said I can stay with her until I find a studio.'

'I know that name, but I can't remember in connection with what. I will ask François when I get back. I brought you some food.'

'I went into town and bought some today.'

'You went into town?'

'Well?'

He was silent then and they stood facing each other across the small candle in Seppo's hand. He said, 'When do you go?'

'Now. I mean, when you have gone. Where is Charles?'

'Charles? He is in the camp. He follows me around all the time. I like him but I don't want his company every moment. It's as if he needs friendship.'

'Ah.'

'Ah? What does that mean?'

'Nothing.'

'Nothing? What does "Ah" mean?'

'Look, I have to gather my things. I'll take the bicycle with me if it's all right.'

'I can help you?'

'No, it's all right. You go. Will you come back?'

Seppo said, 'Where is this woman's house?'

'West of the bridge. It's an odd, red-brick building. Looks almost English.'

'I'll ask the others about this woman. Try not to tell her anything about us. Who can be trusted?'

Seppo reached forward and squeezed her hand, then left through the back door, leaving the candle burning on the table. Francesca surprised herself then. She wished, somewhere inside, he could have stayed. She felt less safe, less competent without him. The feeling did not go away while she packed and lifted her case onto the parcel-rack at the back of her bicycle. Unable to ride with the heavy suitcase, she walked, holding onto the case and the handlebar. It was slow progress, but as she made her way to the English House, she recognised it was with a sense of relief. There was something about the home of François Dufy that gave her the creeps.

Chapter 16

1

The passing months brought colder weather, and as Francesca stood with her back to the market square and inserted her key, she reflected how her life seemed to have altered, almost as the seasons change. She was not expecting spring, only winter. The grey, scratched door with its glass pane and the shop-front where she hoped to display her paintings both needed painting, and she knew she had much to do to her rented gallery. Her pictures too, were becoming wintry and cold. The only one she had painted since coming to Bergerac was a view of a window from inside a darkened room, tattered lace curtains blowing in the breeze, framing a view of a bright landscape of grass and distant hills. One customer, who showed interest, asked if she felt imprisoned.

She said nothing in reply, and the man left without buying the painting.

Shutting the door, the bell clinked as she flicked on the light and crossed the stone floor to the rear of the three-storey house she rented from Madame Arnaud. A faint smell of damp greeted her nostrils as she pushed aside the curtain separating the front room from the back.

The house possessed a back room with stairs leading up to two floors of empty rooms. The shop front held her one lonely painting; she had not been able to frame any others.

Hardwood was in short supply and her framing skills were limited. She knew she could not make mitred frames on her own and there seemed to be no one to help. Available tradesmen were scarce in these days of deportation and arrest. At times she wondered if it was because she was now situated a few doors down from the Prefecture on the main market square. No one went near there in these troubled times, as far as she could see. Without customers and art lovers, her gallery was destined to failure, even if she populated it with the entire contents of her precious suitcase. Over the last month, she had thought it did not matter as long as she could do something useful, but the Partisans sent her no word and she was languishing.

It was a Sunday, the day after the market, when things seemed to change for her. She had done no more than put on a pan of water to make some diluted chicory, the usual poor substitute for coffee, when she heard the doorbell ring.

Pushing aside the curtain, she re-entered the shop area, her "gallery-of-one", as she called it. A man of medium height stood looking at the only picture on display. To Francesca he looked like an orange on sticks. He was round and protuberant but his legs seemed small and thin, despite his generous, grey flannel trousers flapping as he approached. He wore gold-rimmed spectacles and his balding head displayed a wide, high, freckled forehead.

'Pardon me,' he said, 'I came only to see if you had any pictures of merit. My home is a little sparse these days.'

'Sparse?'

'Yes, I apologise.'

The man put his heels together and proffered his hand.

'Eugene Dubois, at your service.'

He bowed his head a little and Francesca took his hand. It

felt dry and cold but his handshake was firm. She always remembered her father saying one could judge a man by his handshake and a man with a loose or sweaty handshake should never be trusted.

'You are a doctor?'

'No. I am like a kind of voyeur. Surgeons do everything and know nothing; physicians know everything and do nothing, but we poor pathologists? Well, we know everything and do everything, but too late.'

He smiled at his joke and Francesca warmed to him immediately.

She said, 'In this case you are too early. No one here is dead and I have only painted one picture in a whole month. I do have other pictures but they are not framed yet.'

'I am desolate to hear that. I had hoped for something to adorn my fireplace, something bright and colourful. In these days of gathering winter, a beautiful painting would be so welcome.'

'You could commission one perhaps?'

'I am afraid I have insufficient funds for that. I had hoped…'

'The one I have finished is perhaps not a cheerful scene.'

'It is beautifully painted. A window on what?'

Doctor Dubois looked at the solitary picture, hanging so lonely on the gallery wall. Francesca reflected it must have seemed strange, even to a pathologist—only one picture and a huge floor-space.

'I would hate to cause offence, Madame,' he said, 'but this one seems to capture only the mood of our occupation. I want something to reflect happier times.'

'But it is a picture of hope.'

'Hope?'

'Yes, the open curtain is an allegory of our eyes as we look out from a dark place, into a future which is lush and green. Well, that is what I wanted it to say.'

'It is superbly crafted, but I cannot fall in love with a painting which, when the war is over and the Germans gone, will only remind me of the dark place they made our country.'

'I'm sorry my picture does not please you.'

'Ah, Madame, now I offend you. It is like insulting someone's child; the parent, the creator, becomes full of rage. Honoré de Balzac says something like that in one of his poems I don't recall which it was exactly but…'

'Monsieur Le Docteur, you do not offend me at all. Perhaps you are right. It is hard to paint with optimism in this time without being absurdist.'

'You are clearly an intellectual. I cannot discuss such things without showing myself up. When will you have more pictures to sell?'

'I need someone to make frames and then I can populate my little shop.'

'Then I will return. I have optimism and so it breeds patience.'

They shook hands again and the man left. Francesca remembered with a jolt how Marquite had said her cousin was a pathologist. She wondered whether she were making a mistake and should call him back.

It was too late. The door clanged shut and the bell rang its cheerful chime as it closed.

She felt no inclination to chase after the man. It would have looked as if she were touting for a sale and such behaviour was beneath her. They wanted to buy, or they did not. She had money, anyway, so it was of little interest whether the clients bought her paintings or criticised them.

108

2

There was only bread to eat in the gallery. Francesca did not mind what she ate; her figure was perfect for a woman of forty and she knew it. Her long, brown skirt complimented the polka-dot blouse with its puffed sleeves, a birthday gift from Marie one Christmas. When she had donned it, in the dark of the morning at Maison Anglais, it awakened memories and she wore it with love. Memories were always painful now but anything palpable reminding her of Marie was welcome.

Francesca lit a Gauloise and went outside into the back yard. The overcast sky reflected her feelings as she thought about Charles. Her gaze moved from the high, grey brick wall and the green-painted gate to the rain-barrel standing in the corner. She reflected how some pots with flowers would brighten it up in the spring, at least, if she were still here then. She intended to stay on at any rate.

She blew the smoke straight up in a grey plume and decided she did not want the cigarette, so she squatted and extinguished it on the concrete. A noise attracted her attention and, startling her, a figure appeared on the wall. It was a big man. She almost jumped upright, ready to flee into the back-kitchen. Then she recognised him.

'Seppo? What are you doing? You never come here and when you do, you make me jump.'

He placed his index finger to his lips, indicating for her to be silent, and pushed past her, entering the house. Francesca followed him. They went through into the gallery-of-one.

'What's going on?' she said.

He stood with his back to the door, the light outlining his big frame. She thought he looked huge, almost bear-like, in the early morning gloom of her sanctuary.

'I'm sorry you have been on your own, without any contact.'

'Never mind that. What's happening?'

'We need to have a place to stay in the town. We may need to hide some people at times.'

'People?'

'Yes, it's best you don't know too much at this time. Shirley wants to set up an escape route to Switzerland.'

'What kind of people? Is it dangerous?'

'Of course. I can't tell you details now but I will come back in a few days and let you know.'

'I thought Shirley was leaving to go to England.'

'She is, but she has instructions to set up a route for escapees first.'

'What do you want me to do?' she said.

Seppo approached her and took her hand.

'You are very brave.'

Francesca drew her hand from his.

'What do you need me to do?'

'Nothing yet. I'll come back in a day or so and have more to tell you. Meantime, you need to prepare the rooms upstairs so you can look after visitors for a few days at a time. I will miss…'

There was a sound of approaching footsteps at the window. Seppo moved fast for such a big man, withdrawing to the back room. The curtain swirled as he disappeared and the bell rang its merry chime. The sound was beginning to irritate Francesca now. It was too cheerful for the world in which she existed. She realised with a pang of irritation that she had wanted Seppo to stay.

The door opened and a German soldier dressed in a green-grey uniform entered, rifle in hand. He nodded and smiled.

He said, in a guttural German accent, 'Please forgive.'

The man studied every corner of the room, then walked to the back room.

'That's empty,' Francesca said.

'Please.'

'It's true, there is nothing to see there. Why do you search?'

The soldier pushed aside the curtain. Her heart leapt. A man of Seppo's size could never hide there. Her eyes searched the room for some kind of weapon. There were no wine bottles here. She followed the man as he opened the back door through the kitchen. Seppo was not there either. Floods of relief took her and she held onto the table by her side. Her pulse slowed.

The soldier returned.

'Good. Good.'

His French was rudimentary, it was clear. He pushed past her. She heard the doorbell ring and the sound of others entering. She went back into the gallery.

The sight hit her as hard as if the soldier had shot her. Ossified, she stood rooted. Dizziness swept over her and a feeling of nausea, too. The German SD officer who entered was familiar. Too familiar. His face had burned itself into her memory long before and it was not one she could ever have forgotten. He was the one. The man on the platform. How could he be here? He was stepping out of her nightmares. He was here in Bergerac, where she imagined she had escaped from all the tragic events forcing her to leave Paris. It was as if he were pursuing her. Of all the men in the German army,

111

how could he be walking into her gallery?

He had commanded the men who shot Marie. He was the one who had given the apology. It was this man who had turned his back on her and ignored her grief, as if the life they had taken away from her was cheap. As if it were a necessary price to pay. As if Marie did not matter.

But Marie did matter. Marie was everything, and though Francesca swore revenge, she knew even then, she was powerless in reality. Now a slow change came over her. Her eyes narrowed and she recovered faster than she would ever have imagined she could.

The man approached. He was tall and fair-haired. There were bags under his grey eyes and his expression was drawn, as if too much wine and too many late nights clouded his face, but the pale eyes moved fast like an animal's, never still, probing, absorbing. He wore a black uniform like that of a Waffen-SS officer, but she had no way of knowing what rank he might be. If she had held a gun, she would have shot him without compunction. All she did have was her hatred and her intelligence, and they had to be enough.

The man stopped in front of her. He clicked his heels and bowed, then looked down at Francesca with cod-cold eyes, his thin smile like a knife-cut.

'Madame. I am Hauptsturmfürer Egger. At your service. I came only to enquire.'

'Enquire?' Francesca said, her voice tremulous but controlled.

'Yes. You have opened a gallery. There are no paintings? It is like a shoe shop with no shoes. Is it not so?'

He spoke almost perfect French, cultured and clear. He still smiled.

'I have only just started the gallery. I have other paintings and I am painting some myself, too. I have no frames.'

'If frames are all that are required, I'm sure we can help. We have men who can make them.'

'Very kind of you. There is a shortage of hardwood. I can find a wood-turner but I have no wood. I may put up my canvases without frames if nothing turns up.'

'It would be a shame, would it not? A picture is always best displayed in a frame.'

'You seem to know a lot about it.'

'Yes, I am a collector of paintings. I even dabbled a bit myself before the war. You know, watercolours, that sort of thing.'

Francesca felt like grabbing his throat. She wanted to tear at his face with her nails. She said nothing. The feeling of faintness was returning. She staggered to her left and held onto the counter.

'You are unwell?' the German said and reached for her arm. He held her upright. The touch of his hand was like the fiery finger of Satan himself and she shrugged it away.

'No, not unwell. I had no time for breakfast, that's all.'

'But we are going to breakfast. You must join us. I and the boys here would be delighted.'

'No, really, I cannot leave the gallery.'

His smile broadened. 'Are you afraid someone will steal your only picture? You can lock up for half-an-hour, I'm sure. I insist.'

'I…'

'Please. I did not learn your name.'

'Madame Pascal.'

'No, your first name. If we are to be friends and I am to be your customer too, we should put away the formalities; I am Kurt.'

'Francesca.'

'At your service. You are Italian? Why, your people are noble allies of the Third Reich. They have formed an enduring friendship with the German state. It will be a privilege to have you.'

'No. My mother was Italian. My father was French and we lived on a farm in Brittany. I am French.'

The words came as if she were an automaton. It was as if her voice were mechanical and she felt as if she stood outside herself, witnessing a conversation between her dissociated body and a monster looming large and grotesque before her. In the back of her mind, she wanted to tell the figure who talked to this murderer, to kill, to fly at the man, to spend the rage welling up inside.

'Ah, even better. A mixture of two noble allies in the struggle. You have a coat?'

'Yes, it's…'

'You there,' he said, pointing at the soldier who had entered first. 'Get the lady's coat. Come,' he said, gesturing to Francesca.

She found herself entering the square, with its tall elm trees shedding their leaves in the autumn wind. She was walking into that square with a German officer who was part of the murder of her daughter. The irony overwhelmed her.

She was breakfasting with the Devil.

Chapter 17

1

Francesca still experienced a feeling of unreality as she walked next to the tall SD Officer. He put an arm around her. Considering her options, she understood there was nothing she could do about it. She knew she could be passive if circumstances required, but her brain was teeming with hatred. The anger seemed obstructive yet she could not shrug it off. It was her reality, as tangible as her physical presence there on the pavement as she passed the empty bakery, as she entered the café facing onto the market square, on that Sunday morning.

As she walked, she glanced at the man beside her. He smiled often; he offered her his arm, guiding her to a seat under the red and white awning and summoning the waiter.

'You would like?' Egger said.

'Just coffee.'

'But you need to eat. A brioche, perhaps? Yes.'

He turned to the waiter. 'I will have coffee and a croissant. Madame will have a brioche. My men will enjoy the same.'

'Yes, Monsieur,' the waiter replied, writing fast on his pad.

'You are not cold?' Egger said. He seemed attentive.

'No.'

'You are not from Bergerac, is it not so?'

'No. Paris.'

'Ah, Paris. A beautiful city. I was there for six months, then

115

this opportunity came my way. Colonel Barbie in Lyon is a close friend. He suggested me for this post and here I am. The man here knows that when I order coffee, I mean coffee, not this chicory rubbish.'

'Do they have coffee?'

'Yes. I supplied them with some a few weeks ago. Cigarette?'

Egger took out a gold cigarette case and offered her one.

'No, thank you,' she said.

Francesca took a crumpled pack of Gauloise from her pocket, 'I like these.'

She felt a gush of pride in saying it. It was as if she wanted to say, 'I am French, I like French cigarettes, and I hate you, too.'

'How elegant,' he said. 'Where were you in Paris?'

'You mean?'

'Where did you live, Francesca?'

'I had an apartment near the Pont Neuf. It was acquired by one of your generals, so I left to come here.'

'Who? You know his name?'

'Lammerding.'

'Yes, I know him. He has been sent south. A great man. Perhaps he has finished with your apartment. I will try to find out.'

'No, please don't bother. Paris was becoming tedious, anyway.'

'Tedious?'

'I had personal reasons. I like it here.'

'This is more rural, but pleasant enough. The local wine must be an acquired taste, I think, but fortunately, I don't have to drink that. I have my own supplies. You must come to my place sometime and try some. I have good taste in such things. I love your country.'

'You do?'

Egger reached forward and took her hand across the table. He brought it to his lips. 'The women here are so feminine, so beautiful.'

The touch of the man was enough to make her cringe. When he kissed her hand, she wanted to vomit. It was the way he puckered his lips. They showed a kind of lasciviousness and self-indulgence, revolting her. Yet she did not react. It took as much courage as hitting the German soldier in the tavern. Her inaction was as much an expression of self-control as a physical action might have been. Somewhere inside her, she realised she could do anything to survive and if she could bring about the downfall of this particular man in doing so, she would do it. She decided to play her part with more vivacity.

Francesca broke the brioche with her fingers and drank the coffee. All the time, Egger talked. He began extolling the virtues of French art and sculpture. He talked of the great painters. Francesca realised he possessed some knowledge of such things, but she could think of nothing but how to hurt this man whom she saw as responsible for Marie's death.

The meal finished, she lit another cigarette. She was smoking too much and she knew it.

'I will send a carpenter to you. You may have to pay him. These French tradesmen do nothing without robbing you.'

'That is very kind of you. Now I must go and open my gallery. I try to paint for an hour each day. Thank you for the coffee.'

She stood and Egger stood up, too. He bowed in that formal German way, clicked his heels and smiled again. She was sick of his face, let alone the smile, which she knew held no meaning or sincerity. She thought he wanted either sex or intelligence and she was offering neither.

As she walked the twenty yards to the gallery, she wondered what Seppo had done. Was he hiding in the gallery upstairs or had he disappeared over the wall in the same way in which he had arrived? In a few moments, she would know.

2

The autumn evening brought a cold forceful wind, and when Francesca shut up the gallery she was glad of her thick woollen coat. She walked along the pavement, the tall elms to her left shedding leaves and offering no semblance of a windbreak. The days were drawing in and it was almost dark by the time she reached her bicycle, fixed into the stand at the southwest corner of the market square. She unlocked it and shivered as she mounted, knowing she would warm up as she cycled.

It was then she saw a figure obscured in part by a tree. The man wore a beret and a long coat. He stood watching but there was insufficient light for her to make out his face. She stared in his direction but in the fading light, as she blinked, he seemed to disappear behind the elm tree, or perhaps he moved away; she was unsure.

The bicycle wobbled a little in the wind as she set off. Francesca turned left at the end of the square and headed south towards the bridge to cycle to the home of Madame Arnaud. Behind her, she heard a motorised cycle. Glancing over her shoulder, she wondered where the engine sound came from but she saw nothing. The English House was fifteen minutes away and she pedalled fast, driven by the uncomfortable feeling that someone was following her.

After five minutes, she stopped, a straight leg propping her and her bicycle up at the side of the road, and she glanced again over her shoulder. The motor sound changed to an idle but still she could not ascertain where it came from. It disconcerted her. Her Partisan friends would not follow her in this way and she wondered if it meant she was under suspicion by the Germans.

The motor sound pursued her all the way home and when she dismounted outside the Arnaud house and wheeled her cycle around to the back, she noticed the sounds of pursuit had ceased. They were following her, though she wondered whom "they" might be. SD? Soldiers? Milice? It could be anyone, but why would they be after her? It made no sense.

3

Marquite was in the kitchen when she entered. The old woman smiled at once and began opening a bottle of wine. Francesca imagined she had treated her husband in the same way when he came home from the Gendarmerie. A cooked meal and a glass of wine, a smile, and a welcome. She wondered if she had become a surrogate partner in some way, a reason for ordinary life to go on in pantomime or even a caricature of Marquite's past life. She reflected perhaps it was always so for people whose long-term partners were gone; they became unable to lead new or different lives.

'Come, sit my dear. You look tired.'

Again, Francesca could imagine the same words greeting the old colonel after a long day.

Removing her coat and hanging it up, Francesca said over her shoulder, 'That is very kind of you. I had a bit of a shock today.'

She explained about Egger. She described what transpired at the café.

'Filth. What does he want with you? Keep away from him. Whatever he says, you can trust nothing coming from him. These people are demons, sent from Hell. If I could shoot a gun like François Dufy, I would kill them all.'

Francesca smiled at the thought of the old woman armed with a rifle, decimating the German occupying army.

'A time may still come for us to do something I suppose. By the way, a doctor came into the shop, a pathologist.'

'Eugene? There is only one pathologist in Bergerac. Did you tell him you are staying here?'

'No, I didn't realise he was your cousin until after he left.'

'My uncle named him after a great archaeologist who discovered some sort of ancient monkey-like ancestor of ours. We always laughed; we said it was because Eugene looked like an archaeologist's find.'

The older woman grinned and Francesca, despite herself, smiled back.

'I think I was followed here. I heard a Puch* behind me but never saw anyone.'

'You are sure?'

'Yes.'

'We have nothing to hide. Everyone in Bergerac knows me. Even the Germans do not molest me since they murdered André. My cousin, the judge, put in a protest to the German authorities but they simply apologised. Since they had no real proof of his guilt, they cannot arrest me without serious protest.'

'I don't think they care what protests are made. Maybe you should be more careful, Marquite. If they think I am a Partisan spy, it would implicate you. Perhaps I should leave.'

'No. I won't hear of it. You will be safe here. I will make some enquiries about this Egger man.'

'No. Please don't. I…'

'Why? I have friends. You might call them gossips but they know everything that goes on in the town.'

'Please, say nothing to anyone. Egger is my problem.'

'Ah, I understand,' Marquite said.

She raised her glass and smiled before drinking.

'Understand?'

'You are frightened. It is understandable. You can rely on me. Now, more cassoulet? I know the meat is a little scarce but the beans are beautiful.'

They continued the meal in silence for a few minutes. Francesca began to flag. Her day had been emotionally draining and all she wanted was a few more glasses of wine and a long sleep. It was not to be, however. Marquite had prepared an almond apple tarte just as her own mother used to, and despite her protests, Francesca found second helpings welcome on her plate.

Their meal finished, the two women regarded each other.

'You know, Francesca,' Marquite said, 'I am glad you came here.'

'I am glad I met you on the bridge.'

'André and I never had children. Although I have family nearby, I have no one I can talk to. I can talk to you, can't I?'

'Naturally.'

'Men are poor company when you get to my age. They are so grumpy, if you know what I mean. Maybe you don't; you are perhaps a little young to know that.'

'I have no man in my life. When Pierre, my husband, left, he took away all my desire, my passion, for such things.'

As she spoke, for no reason she could understand, the smiling face of the big Finn came into her mind, as if to belie her words as soon as she had voiced them.

'What will you do about Egger?'

'Egger? I don't know. One thing is certain. If I ever have an opportunity to damage him, I will take it. Even if I accepted that they did not intend to kill her, they should not have been in our country, on that platform with their guns and their hatred. You know, Egger didn't care what his men did to my girl, but I care. My God, I care. I hate them all.'

'To hear a young woman like you talk about hate fills my heart with gloom. You should be with a man, happy and far from here.'

Francesca took her leave of the older woman. As she lay in bed, she questioned why, in all their talk of war and revenge, the only mental picture recurring in her head was Seppo's face, and try as she might, she could not erase it.

Chapter 18

1

'Maman, what's the Maginot Line?'

Francesca stood at the apartment window, looking out at the square below. In the distance, she could see outlined against the spring clouds the Tour Eiffel and the Seine flowing by, as if nothing were happening in the world. She knew, however, things were about to change in her life and in the life of her daughter.

'The Maginot Line is the line of defence our country has maintained against the Germans.'

'Uncle Charles says it has fallen.'

'What? When did he say that?'

'This morning at breakfast. He said it was a terrible thing and we should prepare.'

'There is nothing we can do, my dear one. He said nothing to me.'

'Here. It is in *Le Figaro*. It says the Germans are in Holland and Belgium and they have taken the Maginot Line. What does it mean?'

'I... I don't know. They will never get to Paris. Our army will stop them, I suppose.'

'If they don't? Will the Germans kill everyone?'

'No, my darling. I don't think they will come so far into France.'

'That isn't what Bernadette at school said. Her father is a soldier. He has gone to fight, but they haven't heard from him in weeks. Her mother said he might not come back ever. She was very upset and it was very sad. The teacher sent her home.'

'Come here, my dear one,' Francesca said.

She took her teenage daughter in her arms, knowing how holding her like that hid her own face, to conceal her concerns, her confusion.

'Maman, many are leaving. The teacher said there may be no school next week.'

'Hush now, my angel,' Francesca said, fingertips stroking a soft, gentle caress on her daughter's back.

'Will we leave Paris?'

'No. We stay. The Germans want a political victory, that is all. They will go away if France surrenders. I hope we will fight, though. There is much here to protect.'

'What do you mean?'

'Here in Paris we have everything that makes up our heritage. We are proud of that. I am sure our brave soldiers will defend Paris. We will be safe. Anyway, it is cowardly to run away.'

'Will you fight?'

'Don't be silly. Maman is an artist. Artists cannot fight. All we can do is show what is happening. Enough of this, now. Tomorrow is a school day. You have homework to do and I must finish my painting.'

'What is it?'

'I am painting an angel sitting at a desk. That angel, unlike you, is doing her homework. Now if you don't do your homework, how can I finish the picture?'

'Charles said your oil on canvas is messy.'

124

'He is a journalist, not an artist anymore. What does he know? Messy, indeed.'

'If we have to run away, where would we go?'

'We will never run away but if we need to go, we will go to Papi and Mami in Switzerland.'

'I don't mind that, but I would miss everyone at school.'

'Yes. Homework now.'

Francesca picked up her palette and began to paint. The strokes were hard and coarse. In her mind, she was elsewhere. She was thinking about Pierre. She wondered what he was doing. Was he in Paris? Had he run away from the Germans? She knew he was not the type to join the army, nor was he the type to stay and await the outcome of the conflict. Francesca knew she was made of a harder fibre than he ever was.

Beyond her personal wish to stay, she recognised it involved risk if the Germans were at their doorstep and she questioned how she could run a risk of anything happening to Marie. Had she become so complacent and self-serving that her daughter would be at risk because of her own stubbornness? No, they had to stay together and Francesca would not run. She shrugged and began focussing on her painting. God would provide. She would never run.

2

It was a Monday when the carpenter arrived. He held an armful of hardwood slats and a tool-bag slung over his shoulder. His thick coat of grey wool kept out the wind and above his up-turned collar, beneath his peaked cap, a bearded face looked down at Francesca with an expression of irritation.

'Hauptsturmfürer Egger sent me. He ordered me to make

125

frames.'

'Oh, I see. I will pay you, of course.'

'Egger has paid me already.'

'You are?'

'Bassereau. Where can I work?'

'Over here,' she indicated a space by the counter. 'You have done this before?'

'It's no different to an architrave. I do good work.'

'I will get the paintings. All of them either are on canvas, or have card mounts already. You will need to nail the canvases to wooden frames first.'

The man grunted an acknowledgement and pushed past her. She wondered at his brusqueness. Perhaps, she thought, he resented working for the Germans, or he misunderstood why Egger had paid him for the work. She had no wish for anyone to think of her as a collaborator.

'I don't sleep with Germans,' she said.

'Didn't say that, did I?'

'No, I just thought…'

The man grunted and began extracting his tools from his bag. He ignored her.

She looked out at the wind-swept square. The brown leaves, whipped up by the autumn wind, flew and danced like a coffee-coloured smoke to her eyes. They were the eyes of an artist and she saw a picture she could paint. Francesca recognised it was the first time her imagination had stirred in that way since she came to Bergerac. Shutting the door, she glanced at Bassereau, who seemed to be staring at her. He looked away as soon as she did so, but she wondered what went on in his head. She went upstairs to fetch her paintings.

It was a long day, both for Francesca and for Bassereau. There was no doubting his skill but she had to show him how to tack the canvases and stretch them. He spoke little, and although polite, she detected no friendliness, even when she offered him soup and bread at midday. It was like being hostess to some grumpy child and she found his ill-humour impenetrable.

By the end of the day, he had made fourteen frames and outer frames of a simple fluted design and had mounted the pictures. Francesca hung them and was pleased with the effect. It made her little gallery look real for the first time.

When the man left, she noticed he rode a motorised bicycle and the sound seemed familiar.

Still no word from Seppo.

Chapter 19

1

Francesca stood at her easel. She wore an apron over her green, flower-print dress and she was concentrating hard. Mixing a light blue on her palette, she applied it to her canvas. She stood back to examine whether it created the right effect and she sucked the wooden end of her brush, contemplating the scene. It was the market square outside but not in autumn as she had planned when she started. She made it a summer scene with a bustling crowd, stalls laden with goods and children playing with a ball in the foreground. She felt sure no one would blame her for putting Marie's face onto one of the children, even though six of the pictures on display were also of her daughter. She was prepared to sell the ones in the gallery but she kept her favourites to herself. The one she called "Angel" was her best. Marie sat at a desk in their apartment doing her homework, the tip of her pencil touching her mouth.

Unsettled now, Francesca covered the picture, even though it required only minutes to complete. She half-decided to change part of the foreground because she felt the perspective was not precise enough, but painting required the right mood and thoughts of Seppo kept intruding. She wondered where he was. She pondered the fact he was not in touch, since it had now been three days since her trial-by-breakfast with

Egger.

The doorbell rang. She wondered who it could be in the afternoon. Her mood plummeted when she saw Egger enter, flanked by two soldiers.

'Ah, there you are Francesca,' he said.

He wore a black SS uniform again, smart and crisp. He held his stiff, black, peaked cap in his left hand and his right rested on the polished bible-black pistol holster at his waist. He waved to his men, who, like the previous time, pushed past Francesca and searched the back of the gallery. She heard them go upstairs and their booted footsteps thudded on the floor above.

This time, Francesca felt no surprise. She had acclimatised. She knew how she would deal with this swine and she already knew what game to play. It was almost as if in the three days since she had realised he was in Bergerac, her mind had adjusted and become determined to somehow get revenge.

Egger clacked his heels together and bowed at the hips. He advanced towards her and, placing a hand on each shoulder, kissed her on both cheeks. She hid her revulsion. Francesca Pascal was no fool. Determination grew in her as her hatred once grew. The germination of it was the thought that if she played along with this monster, she would one day find a way to bring him down.

The Sturmfürer began looking around the gallery. He paused, hands behind his back, and leaned forward towards one of the pictures. There was a look of faint recognition as he raised his eyebrows.

'This face is familiar.'

He was looking at a portrait of Marie. It was a river scene and Francesca had placed her daughter in a punt, reviving memories of the picnic she and Marie had once shared in a hot summer so long ago. There was another similar and better-painted canvas upstairs, which was why she did not mind this one being on display.

'Really?'

'Yes. I seem to recall…'

'It is a picture of my neighbour's daughter. I always found her a good sitter. As you can see, there are a number of portraits of her.'

'Her name?'

'Sara Rosenthal.'

'I know no one of that name. Jewish?'

'I don't know. I never asked.'

'But you must have guessed?'

'I never thought about it, to be honest. She was just a child.'

'Honest? Honesty is a rare quality these days. I did not think you would be one to mix with Jews.'

'I didn't mix with her. She sat for me.'

'Doesn't look Jewish to me, but there you are. Himmler seems to think you can tell; I'm not so sure myself. You aren't Jewish, are you?'

There was contempt in his voice but his grey eyes seemed unmoved.

'Jewish? No, but I am not a subscriber to your Nazi views.'

'Well said. I'm not sure I am, either. I am a politician at heart, not one of these party purists. Look, I'll take this one. How much do you want for it?'

'You may have it as a gift,' she said.

'A gift? Surely not? I am willing to pay you.'

'You have already paid the frame-maker. It is only fair you should have something in exchange.'

'Very well. Charming. I will be pleased to accept.'

It was the first time she saw a genuine smile of pleasure on the Sturmfürer's face. The thought of slapping him to remove it seemed attractive. She turned away and approached the counter.

'Where are you going?'

'To wrap your present, of course.'

'No, no. There is no need.' He turned to one of the two soldiers. 'Günter. Take this out and put it in the car will you?'

'Fraulein, I wonder if ...'

'I'm French. Not German.'

'Ah, yes, Francesca. Mademoiselle, I wonder if I could trouble you for a favour.'

'Favour?'

'Yes. I have a painting. I bought it very cheap when I was in Paris. A landscape of sorts. I am told it may be an original but I need it to be appraised and valued.'

'How did you know I could do this?'

'I have a wealth of information at my fingertips. You were a well-known art expert in Paris, were you not?'

'Well, yes.'

'I spoke to General Lammerding. He is quite cross with you, it seems.'

Francesca began to feel faint. She grabbed at the counter in front of her. If he had spoken to Lammerding, the game was up.

'Who?'

'The general who borrowed you apartment. It is now occupied by a German couple until he returns but he was upset that you took some pictures with you when you left. Oh, don't worry. I told the old thief they were not valuable and only of sentimental value and he accepted that. He enjoyed the view from your apartment so much he would never have noticed the pictures anyway, or so he said.'

'So I'm not in any trouble?'

'No. Not as far as I'm concerned. I need that favour from you, of course.'

'The painting?'

'Yes, can you come in a few weeks? I am away in Lyon next week and then I have to go to Berlin.'

'Yes, if you wish.'

'Good. I will send a car. I bid you guten tag.'

Egger leaned across the counter and kissed her on the lips. She noticed his left hand on her breast. It was almost an imagined caress, it was so brief. Francesca began to wonder what she had embarked upon. This German whom she hated seemed interested in her. Before, she had thought she was safe, because such men had access to much younger women, women who would gladly satisfy them, yet he was pursuing her. Now, she felt powerless to escape. She could run and shelter with the Partisans in the forest or she could stay and face the consequences of her own stupidity.

As Egger left, she thought about where she was in the scheme of things. She was becoming closer to the man who had killed her daughter, or at least had been instrumental in her death. She knew also how, even if she were alone with the man, she would hesitate to take his life. In one short moment, she had entrapped herself. Worse still, no one was looking for her. No one wanted to arrest her and she was the one who had caused her own downfall. It was a fall engendered by her own foolishness.

As the doorbell chimed its friendly tune, she stared at the blotter on the desk. Thinking about it, she felt there was no choice but to follow the road ahead, wherever it might take her. She knew also that she did not care very much about the outcome. The oppressive thought of her own child dying before she did made death seem overdue and almost attractive. Francesca held no fear of the consequences of anything bringing her closer to vengeance. She was not a Partisan, a Maquis, or even a killer, but she was a mother, experiencing a bitter need for some kind of end to the emptiness filling her heart. Marie, my angel, she thought, how could the world take you away from me?

2

Francesca often thought about Charles. She missed his company. For years their friendship had been a source of support, and without him to hand she wondered what she would do. She sat alone in the gallery, drinking brewed chicory and smoking her Gauloise. She fiddled with the sky-blue packet, half-empty in her hand. It was French and she wondered whether the main reason she smoked these cigarettes was some kind of patriotism, a wish to remain French. She inhaled deeply and blew the aromatic, blue-grey smoke across the hazy gallery. No one had entered since Egger had left and she was alone with her thoughts. They were blue-grey thoughts, like the Gauloise smoke. Recollections of times with her daughter and with Charles often played in her mind, but uninvited and always insinuating themselves these days, were also pictures in her head of Seppo, as if he were some kind of support too, though she did not even know him.

Dusk came and she wondered whether the mysterious follower would be there today again or not. She locked the door from the inside and pocketed the key. Crossing to the back door, she locked that, too. She left the back gate slightly ajar, a thought in the back of her mind reminding her of how Seppo had needed to climb the wall last time he came. Where was he?

Francesca walked behind the shops lying to either side of her gallery and turned left into a narrow, cobbled alleyway. She stumbled once on the rounded granite stones in the half-light. Reaching the square, she looked out. At first, she saw nothing. Then a figure seemed to materialise as her eyes became accustomed to the poor illumination.

She waited. Immobile and hidden at the corner, she watched as the man paced between the now leafless elms. He turned to walk back towards her and she realised who it was. A shiver ran down her spine. It was Bassereau. The bearded face seemed in no better humour than the last time she saw him. He hid behind a tree. He was waiting. She knew he waited for her.

Francesca realised how, if she went straight to her bicycle, he would know she was leaving the building by a different route, so she went back to the gallery. She reversed her leaving process, exiting through the front as she usually did.

She cycled home fast, testing the speed of the following moped. It kept up as far as the hill below her destination and she realised the rider was more than likely having to pedal to keep up. Arriving at Marquite's house, she took her bicycle through the narrow passageway between the houses and then around the back to the opposite gap. Standing between the houses, she watched as Bassereau stopped fifty yards away. He took out a notebook and wrote in it, licking the lead of his pencil often. He turned and began to descend the hill. She let him get down to the main road and noted how he turned left. At a lightning pace, faster than she was accustomed to, she followed. The hunter had become the hunted, she reflected.

134

Chapter 20

1

Francesca needed to pedal as fast as she could, to follow Bassereau. She was breathing hard when she saw him cross the bridge and turn left. Still out of breath, but determined, she followed as soon as he was across. It was dark now and she had no difficulty disguising her presence. Bassereau stopped and switched on his dynamo. Francesca smiled; he would never get away from her as long as she had the stamina to follow. She knew she was invisible to her prey.

The carpenter turned right after a few yards and ascended a cobbled hill, then turned right again. Unfamiliar with the streets, Francesca wondered whether he was heading home or whether he was going somewhere else. He stopped after another ten minutes, to Francesca's breathless relief. She found herself in a narrow street with several shops set into the ground floors of taller buildings than those on the west side of town, three storeys, she thought. Leaning her bicycle up against a shop-front, she kept close to the walls and glass panes of the shops and doorways. Bassereau, she could see, dismounted and looked up and down the street, as if uncomfortable. He entered a glass-fronted building. Francesca sneaked along until she was diagonally opposite, hiding in a doorway. There was a faint smell of urine and the wind blew her scarf in a colourful spiral across her chest.

The ground floor of the building where Bassereau entered housed a café. The external appearance was like a shop with a large glazed window and a glass door. Across the frontage pane was a blue line, a picture of a red parrot and a sign painted on, reading "Le Perroquet Rouge". Bassereau sat down at a table near the window and spoke to a waiter. Francesca cursed to herself. She was watching the man have his dinner while her own stomach rumbled in sympathy. She was wasting her time.

Turning to go back to where she had left her bicycle, she stopped. A car approached from the north end of the street. In the dark, she could not make out the type of vehicle but she pulled back into the doorway and waited. She felt uncomfortable about anyone seeing her, though she knew there was no reason why anyone could interpret her presence there as suspicious. She might, she thought, have been there to eat.

The car parked outside the café and she realised there were red-and-black flags, one either side of the bonnet. Swastikas. A moment later, two soldiers, one from the front, and one from the back, emerged and entered the café. Francesca watched as one of them came back to the car after what seemed an interminable time and opened the door.

There he was. It was Egger. She realised now who was having her followed. Perhaps he was not after her, but examining whether she had links with anyone suspicious. If Bassereau saw her with Charles, Seppo, or any of the Partisans, she knew her arrest would be certain and swift. She waited until she could see Bassereau, notebook in hand, standing to greet Egger, and she left. This time she clicked her dynamo onto the front wheel and cycled home without haste.

She knew now Egger was suspicious of her presence here and she knew she could do little for the Partisans in town if Bassereau continued to follow her.

When she arrived at Marquite's house, the old woman fussed. Francesca knew she looked dishevelled since it had begun to rain on her way home.

'Where have you been? It is much later than usual. The fish is ruined.'

'I'm sorry, I had some things to tidy at the gallery. Egger came. He took away a picture.'

'Took away?'

'I gave it to him in return for the help with the framing.'

'Why does he show an interest in you like this?'

'I don't know.'

'For that matter why do you bother with him? You must be careful to stay away from such filth. It can contaminate you.'

'Marquite, after what I told you, you surely don't think I have any feelings but hatred for such a man?'

'Well, all the same, stay away from him. I've heard things in town.'

'You promised not to enquire. Besides, I have no choice over who enters the gallery and he knows where to find me now.'

'Well it was just the usual gossip. We had a particularly evil SD officer called Brunner here last year. He was the one who tortured my husband. Happily, a policeman shot him as he deserved but he has been replaced by a new group of SD officers and the word in the town is that they are more security-conscious than their predecessors.'

'So?'

Marquite looked her in the eyes.

'You think I'm a foolish old woman don't you? You think I can't put two and two together? You are quite wrong there. I can guess why you are still here. I can even understand your motives and wish I could do something to help. But I will say this: you cannot act against a man like Egger alone. You need help from the Partisans.'

'You are quite wrong. I am only here to get away from Paris since they stole my home.'

'Why don't you trust me? You know my history. You know we share the same feelings of revulsion for the Germans and the collaborators. Trust me, girl. I will help you any way I can. I may be able to find the Partisans if you want me to.'

'You know where they are?'

'No, not exactly. I do know that my cousin helped Sergeant Dufy once. The man had been shot and although Eugene is only a pathologist, he was in the First War and treated many wounded soldiers. He may know how to contact them.'

'I don't think so. When I met Dufy, it was by chance in the forest north of here and they moved camp every day. No one can find them if they don't want to be found.'

'Will you not let me try?'

'No, Marquite. A wrong move now would cause serious risk for us both.'

'You've already been in touch with them, haven't you?'

'No.'

'Ah, I understand now. You don't want to tell the old crone in case she talks. Well, nothing would make me talk. Nothing. If André could keep silent, then so can I. Just remember, you can trust me. You never know, you may one day need even me. If that day comes, you will see how strong we women can be. Now let's eat before the wine gets oxidised, is that the right word?'

They ate, almost silent; each was engrossed in her own thoughts. Francesca questioned why she seemed unable to commit herself to trust Marquite. That lack of faith was not borne of a belief the old woman might betray her; it was more the thought she herself might let slip information about the Partisans by mistake. She wished she had someone to confide in. Seppo and Charles seemed a world away to her and still she had no more news.

2

The wind blew leaves into the gallery whenever anyone opened the door. The chime of the doorbell, incongruous as ever, announced the arrival of every visitor and every brown elm-leaf arriving in accompaniment. Francesca began to wonder if her Partisan friends were abandoning her, as she swept up the leaves. She had sold a canvas. It was not the one she expected would sell first. It was the picture of the window. A young woman with a small daughter in tow considered the painting for a few minutes and then bought it, saying it was a perfect accompaniment to the curtains in her daughter's room.

Surprised but pleased, Francesca wrapped it in brown paper and issued the receipt. She swept up again when they left. She felt uncomfortable about the painting for the first time; she had been experiencing a darkness in her soul when she painted it and worried it might affect the child. She shrugged off the thought and set about finishing her market scene.

She heard the sound of the back gate shutting and she anticipated Seppo. Covering the painting, she walked through to the back room. There he was. Tall, fair and vital. She watched the way he moved, his limbs relaxed and strong, and she wondered how she could portray them on canvas.

'You said a few days, Seppo. It's been five already. I was worried.'

'I'm sorry, Francesca. There was much to do. Shirley and François have left to go to the north. They took Amos and Bernard with them. Josephine and Jules and a few others remain. They are recruiting.'

He approached and took her hand. 'I've been worried about you.'

Francesca could see the look in his eyes. It signalled concern and the touch of his hands felt warming.

She said, 'Not worried enough to send word.'

'Send word? How? I have no means of communicating with you. I wish I had. Cheer up, Charles is here, too.'

'Charles?'

'Yes, he's outside making sure we weren't followed. You're pleased?'

'Of course. You are looking after him, aren't you?'

'He doesn't need much looking after, that one. It's as if he was born to be a Partisan.'

She heard the gate again. The back door opened and she ran to it. When Charles appeared, she threw her arms around his neck. He responded with a warm and affectionate hug.

'My little Francesca. It's been too long. And now, you are a saleswoman of pictures. Can I look around your gallery?'

'Look all you want. It contains only pictures you have seen before. I've missed you.' She looked at his face. 'How are you? No. I mean, how are you really?'

'I am fine. Seppo looks after me. He keeps me right. We are close friends now.'

There was a look in his eyes when he said those words and Francesca wondered at it. It was as if he were bursting to tell her something, but the words did not match his meaning.

140

Charles looked at Seppo and she could see how his eyes lit up when he did so and the realisation came to her there was more here than she wished to acknowledge.

Seppo said, 'Have you any food? We are starving.'

'No,' Francesca said, 'only a little bread. We can eat that together but I have things to tell you.'

'Oh?'

'Yes, an SD officer came here three days ago.'

'Here?' Seppo said.

'Yes, I know him.'

Charles said, 'You know him? Since when…'

'He was there when Marie was shot. He was responsible.'

'Who is Marie?' Seppo said.

Francesca explained. She told them about Egger and about her cycling detective work.

Seppo said, 'So this Bassereau works for the SD? If he sees us, everything will be gone. Kaput!'

Charles said, 'You think this SD officer suspects you?'

'No,' Francesca said, sitting down at the kitchen table. 'I think he likes me. It's almost as bad. He is maybe having me followed to make sure I am who I say I am. He already knows I live with Madame Arnaud, and she has been a suspect since her husband was accused.'

'Either way, this place is becoming too hot. Maybe we can't use you,' Charles said.

'Charles,' Seppo said, sitting down next to Francesca and placing his big hands over hers, 'this place is ideal. Francesca is one of us and she, like us, wants the Germans to suffer. Who could blame her? No, if it isn't safe, then we have to make it safe. Where is this café?'

'What have you in mind?' Charles said.

'Egger poses a risk and so does Bassereau. If they are together, we can eliminate them both.'

Francesca said, 'But how?'

'We can teach them to fly.'

'Talk sense,' she said.

Seppo smiled and glanced at Charles, who grinned back. He said, 'Next time they exchange information, we give them each a grenade. I need to know what Egger looks like and to know they are both in the same place and pouf! They are gone.'

'I will identify them for you,' Francesca said.

Charles said, 'It would be better if we could keep you out of this.'

'Maybe, but I'm the only one who can identify them both. Give me a chance.'

Seppo said, 'Come on, Charles. Francesca is one of us and we can protect her. We just need to lay some plans.'

Reluctance showed itself in Charles' face but he said, 'If that's what you want, Seppo. You know I would do anything for you.'

Francesca looked at her friend's face and she understood his thought. She could not fail to see the affection Charles held for Seppo. She understood also what Charles must be feeling every time Seppo held her hands. She withdrew them from Seppo's grasp and smiled at Charles. She had no wish to stand in his way. If Seppo and Charles were together, they were so with her blessing. She looked at Seppo. His strong features still attracted her and she could see that face on canvas, painted in oil. She wondered if she possessed the talent to depict the look on his face. It was one of boldness mixed with humour and she acknowledged the challenge. It was her nature to take on things she found difficult and to triumph in doing so. She decided then, he would be her next painting.

'Do you think they meet every night?' Seppo said.

'I don't know. Someone will have to follow Bassereau and find out. I don't think I can do that alone again. If I am seen…' Francesca said.

Charles said, 'Following people is what the Maquis are good at. We need to get back to Josephine and make some plans. If she agrees, we will come back.'

'You're not staying?'

'No, with Shirley gone, the idea of an escape route is weakened. We will still work on it but the Rosbifs only want their flyers back so they can fight again. We would be taking huge risks and for what? A few fly-boys?'

'When will you be back?'

Seppo said, 'Tomorrow or the next day.'

'Egger wants me to appraise a painting. He said a few weeks, so it could be anytime.'

'Don't worry,' Charles said. 'With any luck, he'll be dead in a couple of days.'

'He lied to me.'

'What about.'

'He said he was going to Berlin and would be away for weeks, but I saw him with Bassereau in the café. Maybe he suspects me.'

Seppo said, 'Doubt it. If he really did suspect you, he would ask you his questions in the Mairie, don't you think?'

'Perhaps,' Francesca said.

The two Partisans left then. They went without the ceremony of lingering farewells or hugs. Her information seemed to change everything and Francesca wondered what would be the next step. It seemed to her, every time Seppo came, he left her with more questions than answers.

When the back gate closed, she sat at the counter of the

little gallery and thought about Seppo. Were he and Charles now together? She wondered about that since Seppo never expressed any affection for Charles, though she could see how Charles hung on every word Seppo uttered and she knew him well enough to anticipate how he felt. Surely, Seppo was not a pede? There was no indication of that in the way he behaved, nor in fact, in the way he treated her, either. She shrugged and began to feel it made no difference to her. She was not, after all, looking for a romantic liaison with the Finn any more than with any man.

Then she thought about Egger. She knew Egger had not pulled the trigger when Marie died. True, he did not order her death, but he remained in her eyes, culpable. There was also the way the German had shrugged off her daughter's death. The curt apology, the turned back. The summary glance and the denial. She knew she hated him. He represented everything she hated about the occupying Germans troops. They carried out atrocities; they killed her people and then shrugged it off as if Frenchmen were nothing, as if their lives were not worth a thought. No. She would be pleased to see the man dead and she would piss on his grave. Marie had deserved to live. Marie, her child, should have lived. Marie would be avenged and now Francesca felt she had that chance to restore some dignity to her own life and bring justice to bear upon Egger, the killer of her little angel.

Chapter 21

1

Jules and Josephine picked her up. The evening had been one of constant worry for Francesca, not least because she found telling Marquite the truth difficult. As Seppo always instructed her, she never opened up, not until today, and now she had swallowed the jagged pill, telling the old woman everything.

She felt like a woman in the confessional who had not attended for months and now confronted by the priest, felt relief in unburdening herself, despite the forthcoming penance. Sitting at the old, oak-topped kitchen table, with a glass of Bordeaux in her hand, she found it less of a struggle than she had imagined it would be. Nonetheless, she recognised how her earlier lack of trust could be a cause of contention between them.

'I knew it all along, you know,' Marquite said.

'You did?'

'Yes. I am old, but age does not always bring stupidity, my girl.'

'You are angry. I understand that, but they told me not to tell you. The less people know of my links to the Maquis, the better, surely?'

'I understand. I do not blame you. We are relative strangers, after all. For my part, I have always trusted you. As one gets older, time teaches one whom to trust. It is a skill.

My poor husband never had it; in fact, he was clumsy in his clandestine activities. It came as no surprise to me he was caught in the end.'

'Marquite, I hope you can forgive me for not telling you.'

'Huh, it is nothing. When will they come?'

'Soon. I don't know who will pick me up. They only want me to sit in the car and tell them when Egger arrives. I will be back in no time.'

'Won't they just recognise his car?'

'Any of the SD could be in the car. They need me to point him out.'

Madame Arnaud reached across the table; her bony, liver-spotted hand took Francesca's and gripped it hard. The old lady looked into her eyes. Francesca realised her mistake in not trusting this woman.

Marquite said, 'I wish you luck. No. I wish you more than that. I wish you the revenge I could never achieve. Perhaps it is because I am old, I don't know, but I envy you the ability to fight back. I was never able to avenge André's murder by these savages. If I had been your age, who knows? Help the Maquis. Resist. It is all we can do. If I can ever help and do my part, I will. I don't care about myself anymore. Losing my life means nothing at my age, remember that.'

'I have always known that. I worried you might tell something by accident, you know what I mean?'

'Yes. You must understand that we women do not have the same vulnerabilities as our men. I am not André, I don't have his weaknesses, and in my head I have not aged enough to lose my common sense.'

'No. I understand that now.'

'I hear something.'

'Yes, it will be them.'

Marquite stood up and as Francesca made to leave, the old lady embraced her. Before Francesca left, they stood and each regarded each other. The older woman, grave-faced; Francesca trying to make the best of the situation. They both knew there was blood-work to come this night. That fact stood between them like a spectre, though neither of them shunned it.

Her face grim, Francesca opened the door and walked to the waiting car. Glancing over her shoulder, she could see Marquite peering around the curtain of the front room and she knew she had found someone upon whom she could rely, the ally she had sought ever since coming to Bergerac. Here was someone who cared about her.

2

The night was dark and starless as she crossed the road to the waiting car. Heavy rain came down, soaking her shoulders and hair, as Francesca ducked into the back of the black Citroen. Jules drove and Josephine sat next to him. Their faces showed strain and Francesca realised she too felt the tension. Her heart raced and her mouth was dry.

She swallowed and said, 'Are Seppo and Charles coming too?'

'They have their part to play. I won't say too much; you'll find out soon enough,' Josephine said.

Francesca noticed the sharp tone in the woman's voice but put it down to the tension of the moment and realised she was not the only one worrying about the night's outcome.

Jules looked straight ahead and Josephine looked at her watch. Francesca lit a cigarette. The aromatic smoke hit the back of her throat and it jolted her back to the present as the car set off. They went north first, then doubled back on a parallel road. Francesca realised it was in case they were followed, but she could not see any lights or other signs of pursuit through the rain-painted rear windscreen.

Presently, Jules said, 'We are going to park near the café, close enough for you to see who comes and goes. When both of them are in, you need to tell us. We will signal to the others. When they have done their job, we will check to see if we have been successful. You will need to come with us to identify the bodies.'

'Identify…'

Josephine said, 'Of course. We have to know whom we have killed.'

'But you said all I had to do was point out when they arrived.'

Jules said, 'Getting scared?'

'No.' Francesca said. 'It is only I thought I was not going to get involved, in case I am seen.'

'Change of plan then,' Josephine said. 'You'll have to be versatile, you know, if you want to become one of us.'

Francesca said nothing. It was as if the two in the front did not care about her. She felt like a chess piece on a board, pushed hither and thither at the player's whim. It added to the feeling of danger. She tried hard to swallow between lungfuls of smoke but her mouth was dry.

The car crossed the bridge. The street was quiet and the only other vehicle she saw was a motorcycle zipping past them halfway across. They followed the route Francesca described and parked at the end of the street in which the café stood.

Chapter 22

1

Francesca recognised the motorised bicycle. Bassereau must have been a trusting soul, she reflected, judging by the way he left his Puch propped against a lamppost, twenty yards from the café. To her eyes, it stood there looking as if its owner had not a care in the world but she questioned how an object could convey a mood. Deep inside, she knew it could if the beholder possessed the talent to express those feelings in an image. In her abstraction, she viewed the scene as something on canvas, something she could one day create, if only time would pass and let her have some kind of peace.

Again, it was dark, the cobbles shining in the remains of the rain-shower, reflecting the yellow of the streetlight and the illumination cast from the café. No moon shone through the clouds and the darkness reached for Francesca, injecting her with gloom, because she knew violence could erupt at any time. Yet she also knew the violence would be at her instigation and its evolution depended on her. She knew men would die and she hated the thought. Then she thought about Marie, the station and Egger's face. The smugness of his smile and the careless way he shrugged off her tears on that terrible day. The hatred welled up within her and she knew whatever the outcome of this night, she would never look back on it with regret. Francesca felt there was nothing standing in the way of her revenge now, not even her belief in God. Her Catholicism was weak and she knew it, but she knew in equal measure she cared about France. Rationalising her beliefs over her wish for vengeance, she knew she'd never thought she was doing God's work, but she felt certain God would forgive her and it was enough.

The cold anger, thinking of her daughter, readied her for signalling Egger's arrival. She felt less like Judas than Joshua, for she wanted to bring down the walls of her own personal Jericho; she wanted Egger dead.

The rain eased and she saw the black car arrive and stop outside the café. Leaning forward, she realised she felt as tense as a wound-up watch-spring.

'That's the car,' she said.

'No one is getting out; maybe he knows something,' Josephine said.

'He sends his men in first and if it is safe, he follows them. We need to wait.'

Jules drummed his fingers on the steering wheel. Francesca took out another Gauloise. She fumbled her matches and Josephine turned and grabbed them out of her hand.

'Are you mad? You want them to see us?'

Realising her mistake, Francesca, chastened, put her cigarette back into the pack.

Josephine said, 'You are such an amateur. I can't understand what you are doing here with us.'

The two Germans emerged from the black car. Francesca said, 'They will come back any minute.'

To Francesca it was like watching a stage-play or pantomime she had seen before. The scene was like when the soldiers came to the gallery. One stood outside and waited and the other entered. Time passed. The soldier came out and standing by the open car window, he leaned forwards, talking. She watched as Egger emerged and stood by the vehicle. He looked up and down the street. He was a careful man, it seemed to Francesca, but he seemed to see nothing unusual and entered the café.

There was silence in the street. Nothing moved. It was a moment of calm before a lightning strike and she understood it. Presently, she saw Seppo walking with Charles towards the Citroen. They had their hands behind their backs. Seppo stopped at the entrance to the café. Charles walked on until he was past the window. Turning fast, he threw a brick through the shiny glass. It shattered. She watched, holding her breath, her mouth still dry and spittle-free.

The driver of the Mercedes leapt out. Charles, whom she realised, must have held a pistol, fired three shots. At the same instant as the driver fell, she saw Seppo throw something into the café. Both Partisans stood with their backs to the wall either side of the café. Five seconds passed. She could see figures moving close to the shattered window. The glass door of the café opened. Then through it a figure flew. The grenades exploded almost in the same instant. Then it became quiet. Smoke billowed out of the wreck, which had once been a café.

Francesca leaned back in the Citroen and began to breathe again. Jules moved the car closer and the tyres screeched as he drew to a halt. Jolted by the movement, Francesca leaned forward, peering into the smoke-filled shell of the café.

'My God,' she said.

'Your God, indeed, come on,' Josephine said, opening her door.

'What?'

'We have to confirm Egger is dead. No time. Move.'

151

'But I'm not going in there.'

'By the blood of Christ himself, you will. We have maybe five minutes before the street is full of soldiers. Now do it.'

Francesca emerged from the little car and next to Josephine, ran into the café. The smoke was clearing and she could see a scene of horror. This time it was not something she would have wanted to paint. Four bodies lay sprawled on the floor. One, she was sure, had been Bassereau. What remained of his face had the dark beard still attached and she knew it was he. The other bodies were the soldiers, their uniforms smoking as if they were on fire. The other, she presumed, was the proprietor of the place. The blackened and bloodstained apron attested to that but there were no limbs attached to the torso.

She covered her nose and mouth with her scarf and realised Egger's body was not here. Where could he be?

Josephine said, 'Is he here?'

This time it was Francesca's turn to be disdainful.

'Of course, he isn't. Do you see an officer's uniform? The back door. Is he through there?'

She heard the Citroen's engine racing. Josephine, pistol in hand, with Francesca following, kicked the backdoor open. There was no wreckage here. They did the same with the toilet door and Francesca saw an open window. Egger was gone. He may have been in the toilet when the explosion occurred. The two women ran. The Citroen revved again and they were away. The whole exploration took two minutes. Seppo and Charles seemed to have melted away, as far as she could see.

There was no pursuit as they crossed the bridge and headed west.

'He wasn't there,' Francesca said.

'No. He got away,' Josephine said.

'Got away? It's ridiculous. He will come for you all. I don't even know if he suspects me now.'

'Why would he?' Jules said.

'He had me followed, didn't he?'

'They do that to anyone who is new in town. You're not so special.'

'He said he wanted me to look at a painting. He will send his men for me. If he comes himself, maybe you could...'

'Don't be silly,' Josephine said, 'we can't do more now for weeks. Egger will know we tried to kill him. We have to hide and hide well.'

'Where?' Francesca said.

'You don't need to know that. We'll drop you off at Madame Arnaud's house. Carry on as normal. If you don't go to the gallery, it will look suspicious. Everything just like this morning, no break in routine, and don't lose your nerve. You hear me?'

'Yes,' Francesca said, as once more she noticed her heart beating fast and her mouth dry.

When she sneaked into the house, she sat first at the kitchen table. She put her head in her hands and the relief of tension brought tears. Sobs came too. Nothing seemed to be going right and Egger still breathed the same air as she did. It was almost worth a prayer.

2

A gentle hand descended upon her shoulder. Tears blurring her vision, she looked up at Marquite. The old woman, dressed in a pink dressing gown and brown slippers, smiled as if it could offer some reassurance to her guest and friend.

'What has happened my dear?'

'Nothing.'

'Then why the tears?'

'Egger escaped.'

'He escaped?'

'He must have gone through to the toilet and the grenades the Partisans threw never got him.'

'Perhaps he has been spared for some other fate. It is not for us to question. Justice will win through in the end, I am sure of it.'

Marquite opened a bottle of Burgundy. The rusty cork-screw creaked as she drew the cork. Smiling, she took two glasses and set them on the table. She poured the wine, the dark red aromatic wine.

'I don't know if this wine is a great one, but in times of worry surely it does not matter.'

'No. You are right. There will be other times, other opportunities.'

Francesca dried her eyes on her coat-sleeve and smiled. It was a genuine smile of understanding and to some extent, pleasure. She knew she was with a friend and the comfort the thought gave her was worth gold, in her estimation.

'Marquite, you are right. There will be other times and then revenge can have its turn. Tonight was not one of those occasions. I just wanted him dead. When my child lay in my arms on that railway platform, I swore I would have revenge. I will yet.'

'We have a saying here in Bergerac. Wine is good, whether you have to wait years or weeks for it.'

Francesca smiled. 'Yes,' she said. 'I don't seem much good at doing these things but I am good at waiting for the right opportunity. I will do as you say; I will wait for the time. You

154

think it will come?'

'God's justice comes to us all. It is not the sin of commission, which he punishes, rather the sin of omission. You at least are doing something. It is more than many do in these troubled times.'

'You know you have been my saviour, don't you?'

'Saviour is too big a word. A friend is enough. Friendship in these days is worth risking anything for here, now, in Bergerac. You must act as if nothing has happened. They won't suspect you unless you change your routine. Say what you like, these Germans are clever. They spot the smallest change and then they swoop like hawks from the sky. Did I tell you about when they arrested my husband?'

'No.'

'It was four in the morning. We lay close together and for some reason, André was affectionate. He cuddled me in, as if we were young again. Then the door flew open. We had not even heard them break down the front door. Looking back now, I think maybe Annette, the maid who betrayed him, let them in, but I had no idea at the time.'

'They hurt him?

'No. it was much more civilised than that. They saluted and asked if he would accompany them to the Mairie. He asked for privacy to be allowed to dress. I lay in bed, watching as he put on his clothes. He donned his Gendarme uniform, he was a Colonel you know, and then he sat at the desk scribbling for twenty seconds and gave me a note for Inspector Ran. He told me to hide it.'

'They took him then?'

'Yes. They did not touch him. He walked between the two Germans and settled into their car as if it were a simple pickup for a rendezvous with friends. He was foolish, even to the end. I would have fought tooth and nail to be free if it was me. But there you are, I suppose. Maybe he was protecting me, I don't know.'

'Didn't the SD come for you as well?

'Yes, they came next day and ransacked the house. They took me into one of their cars but a man in the front told them to let me go. I don't think it was one of the SD's men. He was an officer but in a green uniform. It means he is Wehrmacht, a regular soldier, not one of these torturers from Berlin. Anyway, they let me go at once and I spent three sleepless nights waiting for news. In the end, it was Eugene who came. He told me what they had done to poor André. Like you, I swore revenge, but what can one old woman do against them?'

'I don't know. My telling you the truth makes you one of us. The thing that hurts most about tonight is Egger getting away. I know it was not his finger on the trigger when they shot my daughter, but he was in charge of the men on the platform. He allowed them to fire. These Germans don't care at all whether French bystanders are killed, you know that?'

'Yes, but this man, I don't know him. I knew Brunner, one of his predecessors. He was an evil man. Someone killed him. Eugene thinks it was a policeman called Inspector Ran but there is no real proof. That dirty fellow Dufy shot one of them. Shot him in the face. I hope he gets a decoration again.'

'Again?'

'Yes, my husband was full of it. He told me repeatedly until the stories were coming out of my ears. Apparently, in the First War, the men lay in trenches, we all know that. But what was different was that Dufy was sent across the trenches, to hide in trees or on hills and target the officers on the other side. André said Dufy killed two generals and several colonels.

156

I don't know if he exaggerated but it explains how he killed that man, Meyer.'

'Meyer? Who was he?'

'He was one of these secret policemen. It was on the very steps of the Mairie. The dirty old man, Dufy, got away and there were reprisals of course. The Germans shot seventeen innocent men for that, but you know, there is a price for everything in life. In this war, it is the Germans who exact the price but we French have to pay it. I still think the resistance is our only hope. Maybe not to kill the enemy, but to shape our minds, our determination to free the country... I'm talking too much, you must be tired.'

'No, not tired. I am frustrated. I have none of these clandestine skills, these weapon skills the Partisans possess. I wonder if my coming here has all been a huge waste of time.'

'No. Each of us has a role to play, however small. Even if your actions do no more than help some of the Maquis, to carry a message, to turn a road sign round or anything, you are helping in the fight. Say what you like, it is all noble. It is for France.'

There was silence then, each of the two women deep in her own thoughts. Francesca felt she knew the truth of it. She had come to Bergerac because of Charles. She loved him. If he had not fled, she would never have left Paris; she would have found some other accommodation and waited her time out until the end of the war, or until the Nazis established their evil supremacy. Now she was here. Now she was fighting. As she ascended the stairs, a little the worse for the wine, she smiled to herself. She knew this life, the one with risk and danger, frightening her so much, was more worthwhile than any other, particularly so, since she was alone, without Marie. Francesca, however she analysed it in her head, knew bitterness was not part of her make-up. Bad things in life made her angry, ready to fight, but not bitter. She knew she was a warrior at heart and as her smile faded, entering her bedroom, her mouth set in grim determination. She knew she would avenge her daughter's death; there was no doubt in her mind any longer.

Chapter 23

1

Francesca looked behind her at every bend in the road. She was sweating despite the cold wind into which she cycled. The early morning sun hid behind a grey canopy of cloud above her, and at times, the half-light created illusions. She almost stopped, thinking a small tree was a soldier. She did stop once on the Dordogne Bridge, imagining a black car swept across towards her, only to find it was a farm-wagon drawn by a donkey.

She turned left after the bridge, then right up a cobbled road past a café towards the church of Notre Dame. Its tall spire threw a dark shadow across the road and she rode on, to the left, to the tall, bare elm trees surrounding the old market square. She saw no one; all was quiet, apart from the autumn wind rushing by. Her unease remained. Egger might have someone concealed, watching, ready to snap her up like the hand of God. She shook her head to clear away the thoughts and, parking her bicycle outside, rummaged in her pocket for the gallery door key.

The bell sounded and she cursed. She was in no mood for its merry jingle and she wished she had asked Bassereau to remove it before she let the Partisans kill him. The thought made her stop still in the middle of the gallery. Had she really done that? Was that man's death her doing? Inside, she knew it was true. If she had not told the Partisans about him, he would still be alive, following her, spying and reporting to Egger. What else could she have done? Was it not self-preservation? Surely, she urged herself, if Bassereau had continued to inform on her, Egger would have become a threat. Egger, he was the one who caused Marie's death. He was the cold, heartless man who had turned his back on her grief and horror.

Egger had escaped. She wanted him dead but when she analysed why, she could not explain it to herself. She entered the kitchen and boiled a pan of water on the ancient gas stove. She wondered whether she wanted revenge on Egger as some kind of symbolic means of challenging the invading Germans. Somehow in her head it was all becoming mixed up: Egger, revenge, the Jews, the German war-machine, and her poor France, raped and plundered by a smug and cruel army.

She poured the chicory into her demitasse and sat at the kitchen table. It was a rickety affair and she almost toppled over as she placed her elbows upon it. Recovering, she lit a Gauloise and watched as the smoke hung in hazy patterns across the room. She wondered if she could recreate those patterns on canvas but realised she had no subject to paint. Her inspiration seemed to be drying up. Internal tension was never good for her inspiration, she thought.

It was then she heard it. A faint sound of footsteps above her. Francesca seldom went upstairs in the old building. There was no need, since she had a place to sleep at the Arnaud house. She used the upstairs for storage, nothing else. It had to be SD or some other security police, maybe even the Milice. Her hand trembled as she held her cup, but the sound of the rattling china irritated her, so she put it down on the gallery counter.

160

What to do?

She was sure they had no reason to arrest her. They could not know she was involved in the café bombing. She wondered if she could brazen it out and pretend she knew nothing. Francesca also knew they had ways to make you talk, unless you were tough, like Arnaud and like Jean Moulin, the resistance leader they had arrested in Lyon the previous year. She felt a tight feeling in her throat as she mounted the stairs.

'Who's there?' she called. 'Who is it?'

Silence greeted her. Still she climbed. On the first floor were five rooms. She stood still and listened. Nothing betrayed anyone's presence.

'Hello?'

Still no answer.

On the top step, she heard a sound beyond one of the doors. She strode down the landing and stood listening outside the room. The speed with which the occupant opened it made her jump. A scream framed itself on her dry lips. In the same moment came relief.

'It's us.'

'Charles? What are you doing here? You got away? You came here? Don't you know how dangerous it is to be here?'

Charles reached for her. She noticed blood on his hands and as she returned his hug, she saw Seppo. He lay on a mattress in the corner of the room. Francesca noticed a pool of blood next to the makeshift bed and a pallid, corpse-like look on the big Finn's face. He did not speak nor even appear to know she was there.

'Seppo?' she said.

'He's hurt. We've been here all night. He's bleeding.'

Francesca could hear the tension in his voice; she could see the tears forming in his eyes. Her disquiet prevented her from comforting him. She had no time now for pleasantries and comfort. Seppo's need was much greater than Charles' was.

Francesca knelt at Seppo's side. She could see a cold sweat on his brow. He breathed fast as if he hungered for the very air rasping through his throat and lungs. Untrained and unschooled in such matters, she had no idea what to do. She felt his pulse. It was thready and it raced.

Turning to look up at Charles she said over her shoulder, 'He needs a doctor.'

'No Nobel prize for you. Any idiot can see that. There are no doctors, no hospitals for us Partisans.'

Charles knelt down and gripped her shoulders.

He said, 'Don't you see? He's dying. I can't bear to see him like this.'

Charles reached forward and stroked Seppo's forehead. The movement so gentle and with the back of his hand, seemed to force tears from his eyes. Francesca heard him sob.

He said, 'Oh, my poor boy. What have they done to you?'

Francesca said, 'Where is he shot?'

'It's his chest. At first he was all right; we ran and got away from them. Then he stumbled and he fell. I had to support him all the way here. He's going to die, I know it.'

Charles wept bitter tears and Francesca, to her own surprise, felt unmoved, as if launched into a different plane of emotion. She came alive, as if this were something she could help with.

'Stop snivelling, Charles, it doesn't help. If he lives or dies, it will depend on what we do today. You must calm yourself, or you are no use to any of us. Hear me?'

Charles wiped his nose and then his eyes on his coat sleeve.

'What?' he said.

'There is a doctor. Eugene Dubois. He is Marquite Arnaud's cousin. He helped François Dufy once. He can do it again.'

'Can he be trusted?'

'I trust Marquite. If she says her cousin is a sympathiser, then I believe her. You have a better idea?'

'What… What do we do?'

Francesca leaned forward and stroked his cheek. His familiar face, the one she had once been accustomed to love.

'Look, I can't leave in case Egger comes for me or sends his men. You have to cycle to Dubois' place and bring him here. He was here, interested in buying a painting. He has reason to return. Please, hurry.'

'But I don't know where he lives.'

'Look, go to Marquite's house; she will direct you. If she consents to come with you, she can persuade him. No one can withstand her.'

'But…'

'Get a grip on yourself. You hear? Go.'

Charles walked, unsteady at first, out of the room. He left Francesca alone with Seppo. The Finn's face seemed a pallid mockery of the once big, strong man, and it frightened her. It was as if she cared for him. It came to her in an instant; she did care for him, more than she had ever admitted to herself before. She realised how, if he died, it would bring back her feelings of grief, like when Marie died. This time, she knew there were things she could do. Death was not immediate this time, not inevitable here. She examined his chest.

2

Snow fell, dense and cold outside, as Francesca and Pierre

made love in their apartment. The place was a small, two-roomed affair and all they could afford, overlooking the Rue Montparnasse around the corner from the park. She held him tight as he thrust into her. She had finished long before and the third time seemed to her to be an excess. She began to feel like a receptacle for his body fluids, as if she were some kind of cup into which the germ of life was being mixed. Pierre had abandoned contraception in the first throes of their lovemaking and she said nothing. He was her man, her husband; he knew what he was doing and at first, she felt content for him to lead her. His love was like hers, a permanent feature of their lives, of their marriage.

He finished and rolled away from her and they lay there, touching, stroking, and whispering.

'Pierre?'

'That was nice.'

'No. I was thinking about the painting.'

'I make love to you three times and you think about a picture? What bloody picture?'

'*Le Mur Rose.*'

'Oh, for the love of Christ. That thing? It is nothing in the scheme of things. No movement. No emotion. It is a flat, boring thing.'

'No. You don't understand. It's a picture from a man who felt what he painted. The emotion is there. They called him a beast but he was France, or part of our country at least. The picture means a lot to me. Can't you see?'

'I'll buy you a copy and you can hang it on the wall. If it makes you emotional, I can fuck you. In fact, if it guarantees that, I'll buy you half-a-dozen.'

'When we first met, you said you would impress everyone with your pictures. I haven't seen more than one. You don't

164

even have a job and yet you risk my becoming pregnant. If my work stops, what do we do?'

'You worry too much Francesca. Something will come up. Who knows? Maybe the Germans will want a French draughtsman for the resurrection of their Aryan state.'

'I mean it. If I cannot work, how do we pay the rent? How would we buy food? You are irresponsible.' She raised herself to her elbow. 'Sometimes I think you don't care.'

Pierre got up in silence. He walked to the bathroom. Francesca could hear him urinating and she thought the tinkling sound seemed appropriate. She felt as if it mimicked the tears trickling down her face.

Chapter 24

1

Time passed in a gradual ebb for Francesca as she sat next to the blood-stained body of the big man. Somehow, she managed to pass strips of dustsheet under Seppo and tie them tight around his chest. She hoped he could breathe, but although he grunted a couple of times, he did not awaken. She stroked his forehead and she whispered to him. She encouraged, she prayed.

Prayer, of course, was a new thing to her. Apart from church at Christmas and Easter, religious words never crossed her lips, but today, she wanted them to stave off death, to save this beautiful man. A picture of his smile came into her mind. She could almost hear his deep, throaty laugh and she pictured him slapping Charles on the back with his pile-driver hand. She felt a restriction in her throat. She wanted him to live. Francesca wondered why she felt so much emotion over someone she did not know well, someone with whom she shared so little. She understood Charles and his emotions. They would both miss Seppo if he died and she wondered if she felt more than friendship for this man. He was in her thoughts often when he was away, but she knew Charles wanted him. She saw no signs of Seppo expressing an attraction to men and since she had become close to Charles, she had evolved into an expert in those little mannerisms or expressions revealing so much about a man. Francesca felt she even understood how Charles thought. Were they not alike in some way?

The back door slamming drew her from her thoughts as if a hand pulled her out of some dreary seascape, half-finished, on canvas. The sound on the stairs and the fast-moving steps approaching the room seemed reassuring, as if help would come at last. The rounded doctor would save Seppo and life would continue as before, with tension and expectations and laughter and with all the other things making up her daily existence, now she was alone, without Marie. Always without Marie. That thought put her life into perspective. She felt it was all meaningless somehow.

'Look, I told you, I'm no surgeon. I have only a little equipment. If he's been shot, I can't help him really. Take your hands off me. You hear?'

Francesca looked up. It was the balding, round pathologist, his circular, gold-rimmed spectacles on his nose and a frown on his face. She stood up, noticing he carried a brown paper bag as if he were shopping and bringing home his purchases. Charles gripped his arm, knuckles white. Marquite stood in the doorway.

'You have to help him. You have to,' Charles said.

'Charles,' Francesca said, 'let go of the good doctor. He can't help if you manhandle him so.'

She turned to Dubois and said, 'Please, doctor. He is badly hurt. It's his chest. I've wrapped some strips of cloth around him and the bleeding seems to have stopped.'

Turning to Charles, Dubois said, 'Leave me with him, would you?'

Francesca made for the door.

'No, not you. You can stay and help. Marquite, make this

fellow a coffee or something.'

Dubois grunted as he knelt by Seppo's side and took out a clean, white towel from his bag.

'Get me hot water and any clean sheets or similar that you have. Hurry now, girl.'

Francesca went downstairs and boiled some water. She brought another clean dustsheet and began tearing it into strips, as if by instinct, knowing it was required. The pathologist had taken down her dressing, cutting away Seppo's shirt with scissors, and was examining the wound. He clucked, then began humming a tune.

'Rib's broken. Lost a lot of blood.'

Dubois leaned forward, placing his ear to Seppo's chest, first on the left, then the right. He percussed the chest, using his fingertips, tapping on his flattened left hand.

'Hm.'

'What is it, doctor?' Francesca said.

'Doctor? Oh yes, you would call me that.' Dubois chuckled, then said, 'Not used to that. Feels odd. This is not my kind of mystery, you know. Most of my patients reveal everything to me. This one doesn't, but there again, he isn't dead. Look, as far as I can judge his problem is just blood-loss and the chance of pneumonia from the fractured rib. Why can't people learn that all bleeding stops if you press on it for long enough? That idiot who fetched me should have known it. It could have saved your friend's life.'

'He's dying?'

'Maybe. I can't tell. He's shocked. If I had a cannula and a bottle of plasma, I could put up a drip, but he needs to be in a hospital for that and moving him now might be too much for him.'

'We can't just watch.'

'No, my girl, we can't. I hope you aren't squeamish.'

'No. I don't feel sick or anything. What are you going to do?'

'Did you know you can absorb fluids from the rectum?'

'What?'

'An old-fashioned technique and much depends on whether there is any bowel circulation to ferry the fluid to his bloodstream. It's all we can do.'

'It's ridiculous.'

'Yes, but I am a pathologist, not a real doctor. Maybe if you got a horse doctor he could give better treatment. None of my patients complains normally, you know.'

'You helped Dufy?'

'Him? That old drunk? Yes. They shot him in the leg, not the same thing at all. He did well enough, though.'

'You think this will work?'

'I have nothing else to offer.'

'What do you need?'

'A couple of litres of water with a table-spoonful of salt dissolved in it. It must be warm. A small funnel would help. You had best be quick.'

Francesca left the room again. She wanted to tell Charles and ask his advice. She did not entirely trust Dr. Dubois. It seemed a strange technique and she noticed his hands shook. She heated water and found a funnel among the kitchen things. Five minutes later she found herself helping Dubois roll Seppo onto his uninjured side. As she lifted his uppermost leg, she wondered whether there was something perverted in the procedure; she had never heard of such a thing.

They used four instillations through a makeshift tube-feed, fifteen minutes apart. Francesca noticed the doctor's stitching as they rolled the prostrate form of her friend onto his back again. It was a neat blanket stitch. She realised then this was no fool. Seppo lay with eyes closed, immobile and absent. Within twenty minutes, a faint rose colour returned to his freckled face.

Dubois, who sat on the floor, continued to feel Seppo's pulse. 'It's slowing a little, I think. Feels stronger, too. He may live. The sooner he absorbs the fluid, the greater the likelihood his kidneys won't get damaged. What time was he shot?'

'Why do you need to know that?'

'So I can warn the SD, of course. What do you think? He had almost no circulation for a time. I need to know how long he was losing blood. Don't worry, I don't want any details.'

'Around midnight, from what Charles said.'

'He has a chance. He needs another litre of saline in an hour's time. He's tough, this one. In the last war I saw many with less blood-loss who died.'

'Thank you for helping. We had no one else we could turn to.'

The Pathologist reached out and squeezed her shoulder as she knelt beside him.

He said, 'You're fond of this man, I can see that.'

'He's a friend.'

'If you say so. Now, if you'll help me up. The only time I sit on the floor is after a bottle of Calvados, you know; today, I'm desolated to say, I'm sober.'

Francesca stood up and, offering her hand, helped Dubois to his feet.

'That reminds me, anything to drink around here? A glass of wine, perhaps?'

'If I had it, I would gladly give it to you. We only have chicory, I'm afraid.'

'Another time, perhaps. I must go. I still need to go to the

170

hospital as if nothing has happened. I will return tonight. Keep a close eye on his urine; measure what he passes and note it down. You may need some kind of bottle placed around his privates, so the urine doesn't cause a pressure sore.'

'I will do as you say, and sit with him.'

She followed the rotund fellow down the stairs. 'One moment, doctor,' she said, disappearing into the gallery. A moment later, she returned with a framed picture.

'It isn't a bright and sunny landscape, but it is a picture of my beautiful daughter before they shot her.'

'I cannot take it. It means a lot to you, I can see that.'

'No. Please, I insist. I have others; it is the only way I can repay you. It contains real feelings of love, precious ones.'

Dubois took the picture, looked into her eyes, then smiled before turning away. He departed through the front door, the painting under his arm, accompanied by the merry chime of the doorbell, as ever. The incongruity of the sound struck her and she almost laughed. Had she been a musician, she might have seen the contrast as tragic under the circumstances, but she was becoming fond of the sound. It was like some bright spark of light in a dark wilderness, foolish but kind.

She turned as the door shut and entered the kitchen. Marquite sat at the table. Charles was nowhere to be seen.

'He's gone?'

'Yes. He became very emotional and stormed out, muttering about his dead friend and how he would get revenge. He's dead?'

'No. On the contrary, he seems a bit better. I have to nurse him and your cousin will return tonight, so he said. He is a strange fellow, your cousin.'

'Eugene? He is one of the few happy men in Bergerac. He has means and he has a family. His wife and daughter are safe in England. He sent them away. As long as Hitler doesn't invade England, they will be safe. He is a good doctor, knowledgeable and resourceful. When he did André's post-mortem, he came to me immediately and told me everything.'

'His hands shake.'

'He likes a drink.'

'I must go. I need to sit with Seppo.'

'Seppo?'

'Yes, my friend. I have an unpleasant treatment to give in half an hour.'

'What did Eugene do to help?'

'Marquite, you don't want to know. He helped, that is all that matters.'

The old lady turned to the back door. As if a sudden thought came to her, she turned and said, 'You know, I am still really glad you came to Bergerac. You have given me a way to fight. Vive La France.'

Francesca smiled as she mounted the stairs, 'Cliché, cliché,' she thought.

It would be a long day.

2

The hours passed and Francesca counted every minute. She ensured not a single drop of urine spilled and she administered the next litre of saline as if it were her calling. A thought prodded her. She wondered whether, now she was alone in the world, she should become a nurse. Like in that story of King Arthur where his wife—what was her name?—went into a nunnery. She realised as soon as the thought arose that nursing was not the same as being a nun. The thought made her smile.

Today's experiences showed her she was neither squeamish, nor frightened to see blood, and it surprised her. She had never before thought of herself as someone who could deal with the bitter gut-realities of life. Francesca had always managed to escape such things as blood and death until they shot Marie. She thought about her daughter's corpse as she wiped the sweat from Seppo's brow and as she checked his urine output. How she wished she could have nursed Marie back to health. If only she could have saved that one life, the one that mattered to her more than any other did. She wished they had shot her and not her daughter. She would have given anything for that exchange. Her little girl.

At midday, Seppo opened his eyes. He mumbled something in a foreign language, then slept. She hoped it was sleep, not coma. She had no way of telling the difference; without training, how could she?

Although the doctor had not told her to, she administered another litre of saline in the afternoon. It seemed the right thing to do, but she worried in case it was wrong. She hoped Dubois would not be angry, though she could not imagine him scolding anyone.

As the hours ticked away, a kind of peaceful stillness descended. She existed only in that room. No one knew she was there; the gallery was shut; no one disturbed her vigil. She held Seppo's hand, she stroked his brow, and it was as if for the first time in many months, she experienced peace, stillness and a kind of satisfaction. She had something to do here, something important, and it mattered to her. Of more significance to Francesca, she felt useful. That seemed to her to be the key. Once she was alone in the world without Marie, she had felt purposeless. What was the point of living? It was the one thought pursuing her day to day, month to month. Today, she knew if she achieved nothing else for the rest of her days, at least this act of vigil, this nursing and care, would prove she still had a purpose in life.

Francesca looked at Seppo's face. For the three-hundredth time, she touched his cheek with the back of her hand and sighed. What was the feeling she experienced when he opened his eyes and saw her? What was the emotion stirring deep inside her when she touched his body, his flesh?

She felt aroused, not sexually, but emotionally, and she knew it; yet when it came, she rejected the notion she might love this man. The thought startled her. It was ridiculous. How could love for an unconscious person rear its head? It was not a love born of mutual respect and sharing. It was a pitiful thing, she decided, to have feelings for someone, simply because of her own act of caring. Ridiculous. Yet she recognised, too, that something was happening to her. Something stirred within her mind. It was not something she understood, nor had she the power to control it or shrug it off. She questioned whether it was because she herself was needy. Francesca wondered whether she was projecting her own need onto what she was doing and gaining some kind of satisfaction from it, even love.

As the daylight waned, her stomach rumbled and she realised she had been sitting there at Seppo's side since morning. Her knees ached, her back complained, yet she felt no inclination to shift. She wanted to be here, nursing him. She realised, too, she needed him as much as he needed her. His need was physical, hers emotional. The strength of those needs were the same and they were equal in their importance. She still fought against the feeling she might love him. It made her angry with herself. She had no right to feel it. Seppo was not a man of such importance in her life and besides, she knew Charles would never forgive her; that fact seemed obvious. Despite those thoughts, scenes came into her mind, of Seppo, his arms around her and the feeling of his lips on hers.

No. It was stupid. Had she been alone for so long that any kind of physical contact, even with an unconscious friend, was enough to arouse her?

Still she sat. She dared not move. The feelings stirring within her were powerful enough to make her stay. It gave an odd contentment, too. Francesca realised then she wanted to be there at Seppo's side. She wanted him and it began to frighten her.

Chapter 25

1

Dusk. The fading sun threw long shadows across the floor and Francesca realised she had no light now in which to assess her patient. She felt like a professional nurse at the end of a shift, tired but certain her day's effort had been worthwhile. Picking up her pack of cigarettes, she lit one and coughed, inhaling the blue smoke, and she watched as it hung in the air. She tilted her head to one side and wondered whether it might be bad for Seppo and so she stubbed it out. Getting to her feet, she noticed how her back ached and her limbs felt stiff. Wondering whether her age was expressing itself, she stretched and crossed to the sash window. It opened with a creak of reluctance, and the cold, biting, fresh air seemed to refresh and awaken her.

The sound of the bell on the gallery door made her jump. Faint and cheery, it rang twice as the door, opened, then closed. She crossed to the door of her sickroom and stood, listening. It could have been anyone, the doctor, Charles, or even one of Egger's henchmen coming for her. Wondering what to do, she checked Seppo's breathing and went to the stairwell. There was no lighting and since she had not been down to light any lamps, any shape climbing the stairs seemed daunting.

'Hello?' a voice said.

Dubois.

Was he alone? He could have brought the Milice or the SD. Francesca had no way of knowing whether she could trust him or not. True, Marquite vouched for him, but how could even Colonel Arnaud's widow know for sure?

'Hello. It's me. I'm coming up.'

Francesca backed away. She wished she had some kind of weapon. Her hands shook and she noticed a cold sweat on her forehead.

'You are alone?'

Her mouth was dry as a burning Gauloise and she struggled to articulate. She could see the rotund figure climbing the stairs. The pathologist breathed hard as if the two flights of stairs were an insurmountable obstacle. He stood on the third step down and tried to recover his breath. Moments passed.

He said, 'Francesca? You are there? Something has happened?'

'You are alone?'

'Naturally. Did you think I would bring Marquite at this time of night?'

'No. Not Marquite.'

'Ah. I understand. You don't trust me. How very wise you are. You are no slip of a girl, I suppose. Don't fear me. I hate them as much as you do. André was my cousin by marriage. You think I could ever forgive what they did to him? They even made me do the post-mortem examination. How is our patient?'

Francesca relaxed as she appreciated his logic. The feeling spread over her and she realised how tired she felt.

'Doctor, I think he is much better, very weak and a bit confused, but he is not dead.'

Dubois padded up the last few steps and crossed to her,

still wheezing.

'Do you have a lamp? There is no electricity in the town tonight.'

'Yes, I think there is an oil lamp in the kitchen.'

'Good. I'm not sure I can manage these stairs more than once. Would you go?'

Francesca found herself rummaging in the kitchen and she located the lamp. She carried it upstairs before lighting it. Dubois was in the room where Seppo lay. He was on his knees and feeling the pulse with his index finger. She lit the lamp, replacing the bulbar shade with trembling fingers, unable to understand why she felt so unsettled.

'Ah,' Dubos said. 'Florence Nightingale. There you are. A woman who saves lives. I wish my work were different. All I get is patients who refuse to move, cannot communicate. After a while, you cease to care and it makes it doubly shocking to have one who talks back to you.'

'Are you drunk? Your speech is…'

'Slurred? No, my dear child. I have had enough to drink, but I am sadly, not drunk. Here, give me the lamp.'

He took it from her hand and held it over the sleeping Finn. Francesca was reminded of a Rembrandt she once saw in the Louvre, depicting an old, grey-bearded man sitting below a wooden staircase, the only source of light pouring from a window above him, all else in gloom.

'How… How is he?'

'Heh, heh. I don't know. I'm not sure whether there was any point in my coming. Perhaps it was curiosity or maybe a wish to demonstrate my concern, I don't know.'

'You don't know?'

'Well, his pulse has settled but his breathing is still a bit too fast for us to relax. Has he spoken?'

'Only in Finnish. I don't know what he said.'

'Finnish is a mystery to the entire globe except to the Finns. He doesn't have a temperature, at least. I will sit with him tonight. You go home and come back as early as you can. You need to rest.'

'But…'

'No buts. I have no one at home, nothing to do but drink my wine and Calvados. Tonight, I shall sleep little, but you know? At my age, sleep is overrated. It only makes me unproductive. I have a book to read and a bottle of our beautiful apple nectar and I will take my turn at this vigil. Did you give him more fluids?'

'Yes. I gave him some more in the afternoon but it only came out of his…'

'Maybe he didn't need it. He is as strong as a horse. Tomorrow he will be a lot better. His bone marrow is very busy just now, manufacturing all those little blood cells. The human body is remarkable, you know—an infinite capacity for repair. You have nothing to give him by mouth?'

'I… I thought the fluids I gave him were enough.'

'It is a good job I have made some broth. If he awakens in the night, I will feed him. I will leave the rest downstairs for you to warm for him in the morning.'

'Should I not stay?'

'Naturally, you will wish to stay, but tomorrow may be a long day, too. You gain nothing by making yourself ill. You won't be able to do anything for him if you don't get some sleep.'

'Very well, I'll go back to the Maison Anglais. I will come as early as I can.'

Francesca cycled back to the Arnaud house. It was dark, chilly and windy; to top it off, it began to rain with that particular cold, unpleasant rain that only October can bring. The moisture penetrated her coat and it ran down her face below her hat. Francesca noticed nothing; her mind remained fixed upon Seppo and focussed upon her bitter fears for his life. Those anxieties were not only for the wound, but also for the SD or Milice who could swoop in at any time. Dr. Dubois' life would be of no value to anyone, either, if they caught him. She knew it and her heart went out to him. It seemed to her, everyone around her displayed courage, and she began to wonder where hers was hiding.

Thoughts of Charles began to permeate. Where had he gone? Considering how he seemed so intent upon trying to form a relationship with Seppo, she wondered why he had run away. It seemed inconceivable. If he cared, would he not have stayed? She did not think he was a coward. Had she not seen him at the café? He threw the brick, he stayed and watched while the grenades flew inside, and he shot the driver as if he had nerves of steel. This dependable, competent man who brought her to Bergerac, now had fled. Francesca puzzled over it. No rational solution came to her and it was a welcome relief from her thoughts when she entered Marquite's kitchen. At least now, she need no longer agonise over Charles and his behaviour. She wanted someone else to focus upon.

2

The autumn wind wrangled with her coat as Francesca arrived at the gallery the next day. The force of the breeze took the door and slammed it behind her. She kept on her coat and climbed the stairs with fingers clumsy from the cold. She felt like a woman visiting a sick relative in hospital: desperate to know, but frightened of what she might find. Although she knew she had left Seppo in the best of hands, guilt feelings grabbed her as she mounted the stairs. She had not kept the vigil. She had gone home and slept. She was faithless, in her own mind. Seppo could be dead, for all she knew, and a feeling of remorse came over her.

It was then she began to wonder what the big Finn meant to her. There was a constant feeling of foolishness when she thought about him, as if she were some teenage girl with sexual and ruminant thoughts about a hero, feelings acquired in her mind yet unfulfilled in reality. She wondered whether her feelings meant a lack of faithfulness to Charles. He had expressed emotional bonds and she wondered now whether the feelings within her were some kind of betrayal of him, her friend, her "father confessor", as she had always referred to him.

But where was Charles now? He had run away and had not shown his face throughout the previous day. It could mean a lack of interest but she knew it could equally mean an inability to cope with the consequences of loss.

Pushing the door open, Francesca took in the scene. Seppo lay propped up against the bolster behind his head. Snoring, leaned up against the Finn's left side, was the good doctor, the pathologist with skills offered now to the living. Dubois slept as soundly as an infant and Seppo seemed awake and alert.

'Seppo?' she said.

'Francesca. What is happening?'

'You are awake?'

'Of course. Who is this man? He has lain like this half the night. I can't move my left arm. I am afraid I couldn't budge him. I feel so damned weak and he wouldn't wake up. He's even been snoring.'

Francesca, unable to resist smiling, reached down and shook Dubois' shoulder. He stirred, then opened his eyes. A fleeting look of confusion came to his face and he sat up.

'Oh. Sorry, must have dozed off. Too much Calvados, perhaps.'

The pathologist turned to Seppo and said, 'So, you are awake.'

Seppo, face pallid, half smiled and said, 'More than you, my friend. You've slept like a baby all night. I don't usually share my bed with men, you know.'

For Francesca, there was an odd reassurance in his words and she knelt down by his side.

'We were very worried about you. Doctor Dubois stayed to keep an eye on you. You lost a lot of blood.'

Dubois checked Seppo's pulse.

'He's on the mend. His pulse is almost normal. It may take weeks to recover your strength, my boy, but I have no doubt you'll make it if you rest and eat well. Move your legs around in bed and take big deep breaths to expand your chest whenever you think of it.'

'I can't stay here, wherever here is. I'm in the gallery?'

'Yes,' Francesca said.

'I need to get away. Did they get Charles?'

'No. He was here but he left yesterday; he was concerned for you.'

'Yes, I suppose he was. I remember we ran a long way and the Germans were shooting at us.'

Dubois stood in the doorway. Shuffling from one foot to the other, he grinned and said, 'I must go. There is some broth downstairs and some bread. Eat as much as you can, my boy. Francesca, you will look after him? He needs to rest. The idea he can go anywhere for about a week is ridiculous. I will look in, in a day or two.'

'Thank you, doctor. I will manage. You have done a wonderful job, considering how your usual patients fare.'

They smiled at each other and when she heard the doorbell chime, she turned back to her patient and sat beside him.

'They shot you in the chest. The doctor said the bullet broke a rib but did nothing more. You bled so much, we thought you were going to die.'

'Damned painful. What did you do?'

'I'll tell you later. Now you rest and then I will feed you.'

She got up to go.

'Francesca?'

Turning in the doorway, as Dubois had earlier, she studied his face. There were lines of strain painted on his pale forehead and she realised how much she cared for him.

'I'm endangering you. I must leave as soon as possible, you know that.'

'No. You stay until you are strong enough to move. If you go now, the bleeding could start again. There is no reason for the Germans to search here. Rest, you heard the doctor.'

The stairs creaked as she descended. An overwhelming feeling of relief flowed over her. There was more than relief, too. She realised she felt happy. It was not a happiness threatening her usual feelings of remorse and grief over Marie; that would have been a betrayal, but it was a feeling that here was something from which she could absorb some kind of joy at last. Seppo was alive, he was safe, and she knew she had been instrumental in that. Busying herself with heating the doctor's broth, she smiled to herself and her imagination painted a scene in which she lay in the Finn's arms, nestled, secure and warm.

Chapter 26

1

Seppo possessed remarkable powers of recovery, according to Doctor Dubois. Francesca, at times during the next two weeks, needed to calm the pathologist's ardour for taking notes preparatory to writing a journal article about him. By two days, the Finn was able to stand and take a few steps; by ten days, he could dress himself and walk around the upper floors of the gallery. He tired within minutes, it was true, but Francesca was always there for him, an arm under his, a warm smile and words of encouragement when he stumbled.

Autumn began to cool and the wind never let up, still blowing the swirling, brown elm leaves into the ground floor whenever Francesca opened the door. There were no customers. No one wanted to buy pictures. The devaluation of the franc meant no one had money, but she kept the gallery open in pretence. It was a show. She wanted to look as if every day was business as usual and as if she wanted to sell. She knew the truth and she revelled in it. Francesca knew she was there for a purpose but that reason sometimes seemed to evade her. She knew she was not there for Seppo's sake. She saw no divine, omnipresent force commanding her to be there, yet she understood this was something she had to do; there was a need to fulfil.

And still she grieved. Marie constantly impinged on her

thoughts, even at those times when she prepared food for Seppo. The thought that this was a dish Marie loved, and another was a favourite dish for them in their weekly routine, hovered in her thoughts like an itch she could never scratch. Seppo, always appreciative, always calm and friendly, seemed to revel in the nostalgic stories she told him of her daughter and how they once lived together, yet apart.

'This is wonderful,' Seppo said.

'What is?'

'This stew. No wonder your daughter loved it so much. She must have been very fat.'

'What?'

Francesca frowned. They were in one of the attic rooms, eating from a spread tablecloth with plates laid out upon it. Dusk threw a faint cold light across their meal and Francesca was breaking a piece of bread in her hands. Seppo lay on the floorboards, propped on his right elbow, running a slice of bread across his plate, mopping up the sauce as if it were his last meal.

Swallowing, he said, 'With a mother who can cook like this, she must have been eating all day. I know I could.'

'Marie was beautiful. She was slim and fit. We ate enough, never too much, and she was never a fat girl.'

'Now I've offended you with my humour. I'm sorry. I didn't mean it that way, you know that.'

Francesca reached across and took his wrist. He dropped the bread. Their eyes met and she felt a warmth in his gaze. Francesca felt goose pimples on her forearms. Seppo grabbed her hand. His fingers, big, bony and strong, clasped hers and he squeezed, a momentary pressure. As he looked up at her, Francesca leaned forward. This was the first time she had experienced that sensation inside, the stirring of inner feelings

185

absent since Pierre left her. Her heart raced and she felt a flush descend upon her cheeks. Seppo, for his part, remained immobile until their lips met. They kissed but he drew away.

'Francesca. I'm still too weak for this.'

'For what?' she said.

'It will be weeks before I can make love to you.'

'I never asked for that.'

'Oh. No… Sorry. I meant only…'

She smiled at him and crossing the wide valley of pink tablecloth, she settled behind him, one arm around his waist, the other propping her up. She leaned her head on his shoulder.

'It is enough to hold you. Enough to feel your body next to mine.'

'I don't think I can kiss you like that without feeling… you know what.'

'What? Is that what you call it in Finland?'

He smiled and said, 'You are a terrible woman. You threaten to make love to me and you know I can't do it. Are you a temptress from Hell? Are you here to goad me into undoing all your work?'

'Hush. Enough humour. Hold me.'

Seppo turned, groaning with pain from his broken rib as he did so. He held her in his arms and their lips met again, this time, no fleeting contact, but deep, emotional and caring.

Francesca drew her head away and looked up at him.

'It will keep. My feelings for you are as solid as the foundations on which this house is built. I am here only for you, Seppo.'

Darkness descended and they lay in each other's arms, not caring how the time passed. Francesca knew at last she had found a man she cared for, perhaps enough even to give

186

herself to; yet the fates were cheating them both. All they could offer each other was warmth, emotion and a feeling of anticipation. As her eyes closed, she wondered whether the platonic nature of their affection was a relief or whether she truly wanted a sexual relationship with Seppo, or with anyone else, for that matter.

2

A further week passed. The big Finn recovered more quickly now, and Francesca found she revelled in his progress. His tolerance for walking around the upper floors of the gallery increased and with the growth of his stamina, his desire for her seemed to her to grow stronger daily. She stayed alternate nights in the gallery. The bed she purchased seemed lonelier with each passing night and it was not until the third week of Seppo's convalescence that her loneliness was assuaged.

Sleep brushed her face that night and as her eyes closed, she thought of her daughter, out of habit perhaps, but with no less feeling than the day on which she had lost her. The wind moaned outside, disconsolate yet urging, and she turned onto her side, pulling the blanketed sheet around her neck. Eyelids drooping, she heard him come. Seppo's footsteps, soft yet audible, approached and she felt his weight as he sat upon the bed. Francesca felt his hand on her shoulder through the blanket and turned, feeling uneasy, as if this were the beginning of something she yearned for, yet was reluctant to start at the same time.

'Francesca.'

His voice was husky, subdued.

She reached for him. The big muscular hand on her shoulder squeezed a gentle pressure and he leaned towards her. He drew away with a suddenness, which surprised her, and she heard him grunt.

'Damn this rib,' he said.

Francesca said, 'Come.'

She shuffled across to make room for him and she heard him grunt again as he lay down next to her. She touched his cheek with a gentle hand and she sensed he was smiling in the dark.

'I wondered if you would come. Hold me.'

'I'm trying. I can't lie on this side though.'

She got out of the bed and walked around it, icy floor-boards pricking her bare feet.

'Here,' she said, and lifted the covers, descending on him as if they were some old married couple, years into their marriage, each reading the other's needs.

He took her in his arms and their lips met. For Francesca it seemed less strange than she imagined it would be. She recognised she wanted him and their bodies seemed so natural together. He touched her hair, stroking with a softer touch than she ever imagined from so big a man.

Francesca could feel the strength of his arousal against her flesh and it made her feel more alive than she had for a long time. He touched her breast and she felt shy, wishing her body could have been what it was when she first met Pierre. Then she cursed herself mentally for thinking of that man who had betrayed her all those years before. Yet Pierre was there some-how. He was the man who shaped her view of men, who deserted her and left her with Marie to care for.

Those thoughts dissipated as soon as they arose. He was touching her. His hands fondled, they stroked, they teased and she felt herself relax, abandoning herself to the pleasure of contact with another whose feelings she still needed to understand, explore and enjoy.

Minutes later, Seppo turned and lay on his back.

'I can't do this. My rib is killing me. Maybe we should wait.'

'Lie still, cherie, lie still.'

Francesca, the blanket still on her shoulders, moved over him, straddling him.

They made love. She felt him thrusting as she moved over him, feeling the mounting pleasure as if she were walking fast up a steep slope and then resting, then racing on, each gentle slope bringing her to a place where light shone and an electric ecstasy transfixed her. She heard him breathing and realised she too was rasping as they both reached the summit of their pleasure and then it came. It came in waves, making her cry out.

'Oh God,' she called but it was not God she wanted; it was this big, handsome man, this Nordic god, and she realised she loved him, knew he was everything to her now. She realised how in this bitter, torn and twisted world, he was the one point of hope and pleasure, hope and reassurance, a hope making her remain human and part of it all. Francesca understood at that moment too, how this love, this unexpected liaison formed by circumstance, meant more to her than anything else.

She could not shed her customary grief and her hatred as she lay in Seppo's arms. The thoughts intruded still as he caressed her, but this time they seemed almost fleeting, hovering on the brink of her consciousness, ready to reappear, yet kept at bay by her feelings of love and endearment.

They slept and it was only dawn's early light, brightening her vision, which awakened her. But there was a sound too, clattering into her conscious mind and making her startle, eyes wide and alert.

A sound of footsteps came and then before any reaction stirred in her, the door opened. In the faint cold light of dawn, she saw a face. The visage stirred emotions in her and she gasped, involuntary and sudden, as she regarded the intruder. Fear took her then, not fear of physical violence, but a trepidation of what was to come and how she could deal with it.

3

He stood there. It was not his expression; it was the eyes. Something about his gaze made her shudder. Seppo snored and half-turned. He did not awaken.

She whispered, 'Charles?'

No reply came and the shadowy figure, dark and forbidding, disappeared.

Naked, Francesca arose and scrabbling for her clothes on the floor, she realised she was stabbed by guilt. Buttoning her skirt, she questioned why she felt like an unfaithful lover. It made no sense. She had taken nothing real or tangible from Charles but she recalled the look in his eyes and sensed how he would react.

Descending the stairs, she began to identify with Pierre. It was surreal. She knew his affairs hurt him at the time and she realised now, it must have been a painful process, this cheating in love. She stopped halfway down the stairs. She thought this was nonsense. Seppo was not a man to be involved with Charles in a romantic sense; had he not proven it to her? No. Charles was wrong. His imagination, his fantasies, were driving him crazy. Seppo had never been his and Francesca knew it. It was never an infidelity, there was no one to betray.

She could hear Charles moving around in the kitchen below and she knew she needed to face him but also understood she needed to be gentle. She loved them both, after all. Had Charles not been her salvation in the dark times after Marie died? Was it not Charles who saved her life that suicidal night in the apartment? How could such a sensitive man be so wrong about Seppo?

Charles sat at the table, a cup of chicory in his hand, his rifle resting propped against his thigh. The light, more powerful now, fought to illuminate the room and she looked at her friend's face, questioning and inquisitive. Rays of sunshine picked out his features like a portrait by Klimt.

'You betrayed me,' he said.

'No.'

'Yes. You took Seppo away with your womanly charms.'

'Womanly charms? Is that what you think, you fool? He is not a man for men. He loves me. He loves women.'

'You spoiled it all.'

'How?'

'All men have a germ of love for other men. I wanted to crystallise and nurture that. You took it away. You stabbed me in the back.'

'Charles. I love you. You were the only one in our lives, when Marie was alive. You helped me through the pain, the grief. You think I would take away a lover of yours? No. It is nonsense. Seppo is not like you.'

'Like me? Am I diseased or something? You don't understand men. All of us have a capacity for loving each other; you women will never understand. You think it is as easy as meet a man, get married, have children? There is a kind of bonding between men that you will never understand. You've robbed me of the chance of sharing that with Seppo. You deny him an ecstasy you will never understand.'

'Charles. This is nonsense. He is not that kind of man. If you confronted him with it, he would either laugh or become angry. I know him.'

Charles stood up, gripping his rifle. His knees pushed the chair back behind him and it fell, clattering to the floor. The sound imposed a momentary silence, then Charles looked into her eyes. His own eyes narrowed.

'I loved you once, but this betrayal, when you knew how I felt, takes all that away. How could you?'

She reached for him and he shrugged off the outstretched hand.

'No,' he said, 'don't touch me, you bitch.'

'Charles, you are the only friend I have.'

'Friend? You think this is friendship? Get away from me. Go back to your filthy bed and suck his cock. I don't care anymore. If I never see you again, it will be a good thing. After all I have done for you.'

'You fool. You think you can treat me this way? You ran away. I didn't. He was dying. Doctor Dubois came and saved Seppo's life, and where were you? You ran away because you believed he was dead. You are the coward. It is you trying now to project your guilt onto me. Stupid man.'

'If I could take back the last few years, I would. The biggest regret I have is ever meeting you.'

Charles crossed to the back door; gripping his rifle, knuckles white, he shouldered it and left.

Francesca stood looking at the battered green door as it banged shut. Her anger dissipated; she felt a bitter grief, a familiar feeling for her, akin to the loss when Pierre left her.

She knew she loved Charles and he too was gone now. He was abandoning her and she knew deep inside it was no more her fault this time than it was when her husband ran away with his lover.

Sitting down at the table, she reached for the now cooling cup of brown liquid, feeling bereft; as she brought it to her lips, she realised her tears were dripping into it. Bitter tears, as bitter as the nasty brown brew of chicory she was drinking.

Chapter 27

1

Francesca knew Seppo was well enough to go; his presence in the gallery as a convalescent was now a pretence between them. They slept together and Francesca spent more and more nights at the gallery. She knew it might look suspicious but her burgeoning love for the Finn chased away all caution; all she wanted was time with Seppo. It had to end, and she knew it. His restlessness came as no surprise to her, either; it brought only regret.

The snow came early and the mornings greeted them with a chill unfamiliar to Francesca. At home, in Paris, there had always been good heating in her apartments; hot water was constant and she took it for granted in those days. Not so now. The only source of heat in the gallery was the gas stove, but she felt she could put up with any inconvenience to preserve this island of peace and love.

They lay in the bed in the attic. Dusk eroded the daylight and the room darkened fast as she looked at his face.

He smiled and said, 'My darling, I will have to leave, you know. We have taken risks already and if I stay any longer, your life will be in danger. I could not bear for anything to happen to you.'

'In a week maybe?'

'No, it must be as I said. I am strong enough now and I

need to find a way to rejoin the Partisans. Charles will have told them I survived.'

'Charles? Yes, perhaps.'

Her face clouded but he could not see it in the advancing darkness. She still could not bring herself to tell Seppo how Charles had fought with her when he left. Although he had not come back, Seppo never questioned Charles' absence.

'I'll go at first light, or maybe a little before, and head south to where I last saw the others. There are a few likely places. Maybe they will find me first.'

'You'll come back?'

'Nothing will stop me.'

'You'll be careful?'

'Always careful. I have a reason now.'

She touched his cheek. Trembling, tentative fingers, stroking.

'Me too. Before this, I didn't care what happened. Now…'

'The war will end and we can be together forever,' he said.

'Perhaps the war will never end; it could be years.'

'No, Hitler made a mistake in opening the Eastern Front. The Wehrmacht are in tatters or so the paper you brought said.'

'There is no one to fight against the Germans here in France except people like Josephine and you.'

'The Rosbifs will come. Even the Americans will come into this now. We must persevere. It is the only hope.'

'I never understood why you did not go back to Finland.'

'They killed my brothers. I want to fight. Anyway, getting home to Finland would bring little pleasure. The Russians seem to think it belongs to them.'

'Hold me.'

Their embrace kept them warm as evening descended.

From the outside, any passerby would never have realised anyone was there in the tall, grey building overlooking the market square. To an observer, it was an empty shell, but to Francesca it was the nearest thing to home she had felt since Marie died, as if it were a means of staving off her grief. Her love for Seppo felt like an island to a shipwreck survivor, a place of hope and shelter within her.

When he left, neither of them spoke. There were no tears, no last-minute entreaties, only acceptance. They were both old enough to understand and bear the darts of inevitability driving him away and making her stay.

Francesca stood in the kitchen, smoking. She stared long and hard at the door through the blue-grey smoke, wishing it would open again and she could see Seppo's smiling face. It seemed to her, all her life had been filled with partings and anyone she loved was destined to leave her. There was a catch in her throat as she turned away and trudged up the stairs.

2

Francesca felt as if Seppo's departure was like a sobering up after a long evening drinking beautiful wine. It had been a wonderful time, closeted in the gallery with him, but there was the real world to consider, too. She began to analyse the issues impacting her life. She had been coddled since childhood, first by her parents, then by student life and later by Pierre, as she thought at the time. Now, without Seppo, she felt she was alone and needed to look after herself. She existed only to serve the resistance but she found their way of life so hard. She hated the long, lonely nights waiting for them to contact her, the time spent with cigarettes and wine, hoping

Seppo would come and take her in his arms.

She took to wandering around the gallery building, smoking Gauloise and drinking cheap Bergerac wines, often staring out of the windows at the bleak winter-bitten square below. When the doorbell rang, she felt almost reluctant to descend to watch customers perusing her paintings and then walk out again. Francesca sold one picture to a plump woman in a grey woollen coat sporting a fox-fur collar. The woman wore a large hat with a feather that bobbed up and down as she spoke. There was a black netting veil hanging from the front of the bright green straw hat and as the woman spoke, it wafted and waved with each word as if, like Francesca, it yearned to fly away and be free.

As the broad backside of the purchaser navigated the doorjamb, Francesca realised it had been two weeks since Seppo left and almost two months since Egger said he would send for her. She felt reassured by the absence of Egger's attentions. Perhaps he would forget. If he did, he might leave her alone. The way he caressed her breast at their last parting had rung alarm bells in her, but she knew there would be little she could do if he had amorous intentions. Who was she to object? There would be no way to defend herself from a big man like him. The thought angered her. She felt like a woman in an abusive marriage, subject to beatings at the whim of a bully and thinking she could do nothing to escape. Her anger served only to make her question what she was doing in Bergerac. Following Charles and hoping he would lead her to some kind of Promised Land of revenge upon the German army, seemed now as absurd as it was unachievable. Yet deep inside, some portion of her being refused to let go of that grain of hope, her wish for justice; her desire to see the invaders dead or gone.

The more she thought about it, the more she realised her

anger was fuelled as much by their violation of her country and culture, as it was by Marie's death. And then the circle became complete. Marie, grief, anger, they mixed in her mind like some vicious tornado, swirling, flying through her thoughts. It made her drink. The thoughts seemed attenuated when she drank, but they never left her, and she knew it was not a solution to her negative musings; it was only a sticking plaster on a broken leg.

But Egger had not forgotten her.

One cold, frosty evening, as she mounted her bicycle, she heard footsteps behind her. She glanced over her shoulder and replaced her ride on the stand. She knew what was coming. Her heart beat fast as she realised the time had come to face the killer of her daughter. Two men in black uniforms approached and Francesca wondered why she had not noticed the black Mercedes from which they alighted. Perhaps they had parked it a while before, sitting inside as it crouched with German malevolence in the shadows, waiting for her to emerge. Did they suspect her? Had they connected her with the café bombing?

'You are Pascal?' one of the men said.

She had no idea what rank he might be but realised he must be an officer from the flashes on his black uniform.

She said, 'Yes, that's me.'

'You will come with us.'

Nothing else, no explanation, no invitation, only the curt order from an occupying military officer. She swallowed.

'Now?'

'Yes, you are expected. You are not under arrest.'

'Under arrest? Why would I be under arrest?'

Francesca spoke and listened to the slowness of her own reply. It seemed as if she were talking at a snail's pace to delay

198

the inevitable.

The German clicked his heels and gestured toward the car with a wide-flung arm.

There was no opportunity to refuse. The simple gesture said everything. Egger had sent for her. Her heart beat a tattoo in her chest and her arid mouth made her swallow hard. Nausea came, too, but she managed to control herself enough to obey the command.

Francesca sat in the back seat, head banging, with a German either side as the vehicle made its way to the Mairie. Why the Mairie? Egger did not live there. The only reason for being there was if they intended to question her. A sense of panic took her. Her eyes darted, as if looking for some way out of the car, but she knew there was none—not all logic had departed as her fear escalated. The car entered the cobbled square where the Germans had taken over the centre for Civil Administration when they occupied the town. The Mercedes stopped by the steps of the building. The German on her left side got out.

Francesca tried to follow but the other man restrained her with a hand on her arm.

'Not you. You stay.'

He smiled, though it gave her no reassurance. She had no trust in these men.

They waited. Five or so minutes later, Egger emerged and seemed to skip down the stairs. He smiled and leaned into the open car.

'Francesca, how nice to see you, and so kind of you to accept my invitation.'

Egger looked at the German in the car. He said, 'Schumacher. You can go.'

The man next to her got out and Egger got in, sitting next

to Francesca. He smiled and said, 'If you move up a little, we will both have room.'

Feeling stupid now, Francesca shuffled to the other side of the car seat and the driver started the engine. It sounded smooth and efficient to Francesca, like all things German, clinical and clever. They set off towards the south of town and she realised another vehicle was following. Egger was a careful man and she realised he had an escort. It took little imagination on her part to understand why. Egger patted her leg and smiled.

They turned into the Rue Bastide and the car pulled up outside a three-storey block. Ushered out of the car, she found herself escorted up stone steps towards the entrance and climbing the stairs to the first floor. Outside an ornate wooden door, Egger fumbled for keys and opening it, he gestured to her to enter. The main feeling in her mind was one of relief Egger was not pushing her into some dank cell in the Mairie. Whatever Egger planned, it could only be better than that.

Chapter 28

1

A long corridor greeted her as Egger guided her through the doorway. Coats and scarves hung from a hat-stand to her right and she noted the pale green wallpaper, with its adornment of darker green flowers, to Francesca's eyes seeming lacklustre and unwelcoming. The shade of green reminded her of hospitals, government departments, and official buildings and she felt no warmer as she entered than she had felt in the car.

Egger guided her with a gentle hand on her lower back and although the restraint of his touch could have seemed benign, she resented it all the same. She hated this man, not because he had killed her daughter, but because Marie's death was his responsibility and he had shown no remorse that day on the platform. Even more insulting to her, had been his lack of recognition when he saw her in the gallery. He did not care at all who she was.

'Please, Liebchen, enter.'

The corridor opened into a large room with high ceilings, painted covings and a chandelier lit up in a splendorous brilliance above her as soon as the German flicked a switch. There was a thick-pile Turkish rug on the floor and antique furniture occupied the room. The furniture looked ornate and old, but she was uncertain whether it was genuine antique or reproduction. Furniture was not her speciality. She noticed a tall olive-green safe in the corner. It seemed out of place in a room full of decorative and opulent items. She paid little attention, however. Advancing a few paces, she paused because the sight greeting her forced her to catch her breath. Propped on an easel in front of the unlit hearth, was a painting. It was one she recognised. The flat blue sea and the almost lilac tint of the sky stung her with recognition.

Paysage Le Mur Rose.

It was the Matisse, with which she had always identified; the one painting she always felt represented what her country meant: a place now defiled by the German presence, her home. An expectant shudder trickled down her back and anger came in its wake. This painting could surely not be here in the possession of a man like Egger. He had not even the right to look at this symbol of her French heritage.

She said nothing; common sense took over, despite the emotions swirling within her. If she could have scooped up the canvas and run away, she would have, but she was no fool. Since Marie's death, emotion no longer drove her every action. She was now neither impetuous nor impulsive. It was as if that part of her had died with her daughter. Francesca knew how she had changed. She understood why she reacted in such a different way to what her previous self would have done. She had felt she had nothing left to live for until Seppo came into her life. Now, here, she became passive. There was nothing she could do; Egger had the painting. Egger was in charge and she must remain silent, burying her true thoughts, because survival was an instinct, even in a world where living day to day seemed meaningless.

She stood rooted to the spot, drinking in the flavours of a great artist, absorbing the aroma of his brushwork and the passion of his creativeness. Matisse, her Matisse, would he not have understood? Would the great man not forgive her for her languor, here in a place where a mistake could cost her life or the lives of her friends?

'You like it?' Egger said. His voice was soft, almost as gentle as the hand with which he had steered her into the room.

It was hard to speak. Francesca swallowed and said, 'It is a very average landscape.'

'Average?'

'Yes, it's probably not genuine. The original was in a private collection; maybe this is just a copy.'

'You can tell at a glance?'

Egger stepped forward. He drew the dagger at his waist. He said, 'Then I will destroy it. No use keeping a copy, is there?'

'No! Don't!'

Egger turned, and smiling, said as if taunting, 'But why? It is just a fake.'

'No,' Francesca said, 'I could be wrong. Let me look at it properly. This light is deceptive.'

'Deceptive?'

'Yes. More light, I'll need to see it closer, too.'

Egger walked towards a doorway and returned with a standard lamp. He plugged it into a socket and stood back.

'Please,' he said, indicating the painting.

Francesca approached and squatting, peered at the picture.

'I think now I was wrong. This signature is genuine. It is a Matisse. His early work. Not his best, of course, and maybe not worth very much money either, but a nice keepsake nonetheless.'

'A Matisse. That is exactly what I thought. We must celebrate. I have some champagne. Krug, I think. Yes, a celebration.'

Egger disappeared into an adjacent room; Francesca imagined it was a kitchen. He emerged with the bottle and two champagne flutes. Popping the cork, he poured the wine and handed her a glass.

'Prost!' he said, sipping the sparkling wine.

Francesca drank. Her nervousness drove her to down half of the glass's contents and Egger refilled it with an indecent eagerness.

'Come,' he said, 'let us sit. Well, that is very good news indeed. My colleague, Hauptsturmfürer Barbie in Lyon, seems convinced all the great paintings in France have been sent to Germany. He is wrong. I have one here. I'm so pleased.'

Francesca said nothing. Her mind worked in fury. Could she kill this man? Could she escape with the Matisse? It was absurd, of course. She possessed no means of subduing the German and even if she had, she could not walk out of here with the picture under her arm and ask Egger's driver to take her home. It angered her. She drank more. Whenever she emptied the glass, Egger refilled it. She lost track of the amount in the end. Egger seemed to sip his own drink and Francesca, whose empty stomach rumbled, began to feel dizzy.

The German leaned across the couch, placing a hand on her knee. Francesca crossed her legs—a reflex. Egger puckered his lips and closed his eyes, trying to kiss her, and she moved away along the couch. He tried again. This time she raised her glass to her lips and he collided with it. The wine spilled on Francesca's skirt. She stood up.

'Here let me wipe it away,' Egger said.

'No. Champagne does not stain. I must go.'

'But you can't leave now. Not all wet. Take off your skirt. I will dry it.'

Francesca stared at the German.

'Come on. Take it off.'

It sounded like an order, though he smiled as he spoke.

'No, I must go.'

Egger placed his hand on her leg. He moved it upwards under the damp skirt. When it reached her buttocks, she could no longer control herself, and she stepped away, leaving the German seated on the couch.

'Want to play games?' he said.

'No. I want to go home.'

Egger stood up. His expression now was one of anger and determination. He towered above her. Looking down, he said, 'I don't think you are going home yet. I am a conqueror and you are the... How do you say? The vanquished. Yes, that's it. Vanquished. You will do as I say. Now take off that skirt.'

Stepping further away, Francesca said, 'No. I want to go home.'

Egger raised his arm and the backhand slap on her cheek, when it came, held enough force to project her to the floor. She lay there, propped on her elbow, looking up. The world rotated around her, though it was not from the champagne this time. Then she laid herself down on her back.

'Do what you like, I don't care anymore.'

She spread her legs wide. She remained like that, passive, immobile, looking up at her tormentor.

A look of fury came over the German's face.

'You French bitch.'

He kicked her leg. The booted foot struck her calf and she felt the pain but lay still.

Egger knelt next to her.

'You fucking whore. You think you can reject me? I wish it were your daughter instead. She would have been worth the effort.'

It felt almost as if he had dowsed her with ice water. A sudden clarity came to Francesca then. He knew who she was. He remembered. All this time Egger had been playing with her. He must have enjoyed the idea of killing the daughter and seducing the grieving mother. The shock of that realisation was so acute, Francesca lay immobile, unthinking, for moments.

Egger stood up. He grabbed her by the arms, dragging her to her feet. Pushing her towards the door, he said, 'Go to hell, you bitch. Old meat. You have nothing to offer me. Go and die somewhere.'

Francesca moved towards the entrance to the corridor. Entering the narrow space, she felt a sudden blow on her buttock and realised Egger had kicked her. The pain made her stumble and she landed against the wall by the front door.

In her mind, she wondered whether some unseen force worked its will upon her. Her right hand rested on the key board. A bunch of keys invited her grasp and grasp she did. It was a large bunch of keys and she knew it was similar to the one Egger fumbled with when they had entered. She grabbed. She held onto those keys as if they were a lifeline. The night was perhaps not wasted after all. With her left hand she fumbled, then opened the door. Another booted foot struck her a glancing blow and she lay on the doorstep, bruised and dishevelled. The guard outside lowered his rifle and turned away. Egger flung her coat at her and she was aware, again as if by divine intervention, it covered the hand holding the keys.

'Filth,' he said.

The door slammed.

Francesca smiled.

2

'You're sure no one followed you?' Josephine said.

Francesca said, 'Yes. I'm certain. I went out of the back and the front door still looks as if the gallery is open.'

They sat at Roland's kitchen table as the late morning light crept through the window. Frost twinkled outside on the ground and formed an ice-pattern on the windowpane like a delicate frosting of adhesive sugar. Roland stood behind Josephine, and Jules, sitting beside her, fiddled with a saltcellar. Egger's bunch of keys lay in the middle of the table, a small but perhaps insurmountable obstacle to Francesca.

He said, 'He'll change the locks. It's pointless. Anyway, there are two permanent guards; they will raise the alarm in no time. We also don't know if he keeps any official documents there; we don't even know if the door-key is on the key ring. I say we do nothing.'

'But don't you see? It is a golden opportunity,' Francesca said. 'He probably doesn't even know they are missing. They are his spare keys. How would he know? I'll bet he doesn't miss them for days.'

'If he finds they are gone, he will know it was you,' Roland said.

Francesca said, 'How? It could be anyone. Even if he suspects me, he can't prove it—not if we replace them on the way out.'

'Men like him don't need proof. He's SD. He can have you shot on suspicion if he wants to,' Josephine said.

She looked at the faces of her companions, then grabbed the saltcellar from Jules, 'Stop fiddling with that thing and pay attention. I think Francesca is right. It is worth the risk as long as it is soon. It will have to be today. While he is at the Mairie.

There will only be two guards if Francesca is right. If she's wrong, it will be a trap and we are all dead.'

Jules looked into her eyes; he said, 'But I don't understand what you expect to get out of it? Money? Jewellery? It's crazy.'

'You're sure you saw a safe when you were there?' Josephine said.

Francesca said, 'Yes. In the corner of the room. A big green thing.'

Roland reached across the table and picked up the German's bunch of keys. He separated one of them, a big heavy one.

He said, 'This is a safe key. We have such things at the Prefecture. The woman could be right. The trouble is, if any documents are missing, they will know we have them and we will achieve nothing.'

Francesca said, 'Can't we photograph them?'

'You have a camera?' Jules said. 'Then don't say stupid things. I vote against this foolish plan.'

Josephine looked up at Roland. 'And you?'

Roland stroked his bearded chin. He was silent for a moment then said, 'It is maybe worth the risk. We can take whatever documents seem useful to London; they will know what intelligence we have taken, and how the Germans will react to the theft. It may work both ways and might prevent them from doing something important. Better still, we may have a list of collaborators or spies. I say we do it.'

Francesca said, 'I think it will work.'

Jules looked up at Francesca, 'It doesn't matter what you think. You aren't one of us.'

Josephine said, 'She is as much one of us a Dufy or Dreyfus. I trust her, remember that.'

She stood up. 'I will get back to the camp. You two stay

here. Francesca, we will pick you up behind the gallery, assuming we can get a vehicle. Midday, understand?'

Francesca nodded and stood to leave. Josephine reached across and squeezed her arm. 'You did well, Francesca. As long as you can remember the way there and which building it was, we may get something out of this. If Egger is unwise enough to come home early, he's a dead man.'

Cycling back to the gallery, Francesca began to feel she had achieved something at last. She hoped Josephine and Roland were right. Any intelligence was useful, even if the Germans knew it was open knowledge. Losing information would be disruptive, whatever happened in the aftermath. Icy rain fell as she rounded the corner of the cobbled street at the market square. She looked around to ensure no one was about and sneaked to the alleyway behind the gallery. Stepping fast, she drew the collar of her coat around her neck and searched for her keys. A picture of Egger came into her mind; his leering grin as he groped beneath her skirt the previous evening, seemed embedded in her memory. She hoped her actions now would damage him in some way. He knew all along she was the mother whose child his men had shot at Saint Lazare. Hatred burned in her again but it failed to keep her warm, and she shivered as she entered the kitchen.

Chapter 29

1

Francesca sat in the stolen red Renault between Seppo and Jules. Seppo squeezed her hand with his. She looked up at him and smiled. His presence seemed to chase away the anxiety she felt inside and she wished she could be alone with him again and feel the touch of his body against hers, but this first reunion was miles away from how she had imagined it.

They parked the car around a corner from the German's apartment and they all saw a green-clad soldier standing to attention outside, next to the doorway, as they drove past. Francesca knew there would be at least one other inside and she wondered whether they would be wiser to abandon the plan. Jules might be right, after all; perhaps there was nothing worthwhile inside the apartment. To Francesca, the risk of discovery and someone raising the alarm seemed insurmountable. She felt as if something had forced her to this; this whole escapade made her feel as if she were a speck of dust, flown here by some powerful wind in an involuntary and inescapable role.

Francesca thought about Charles. No one had seen him since the day they had argued over Seppo. She wondered where he could have gone and how he was. It was as if she experienced some kind of grief at the separation. Charles had once been her lifeline and losing his friendship hurt. He was also part of that past-life when Marie was alive, even part of Francesca's relationship with her daughter. She bit her dry lips and felt a deep sadness. All for Seppo. Yet she was not in control of her emotions any longer. There was a passivity to her life now, as if events moved her rather than the converse, and she realised she had not the strength to fight the inevitability of her present, let alone her future. Still, she missed Charles.

Sitting between the two Partisans, she watched as a little sleet began to smear the windscreen and she shivered, then leaned towards Seppo, nestling into his big frame. The overcast afternoon sky darkened the shadow-less street, but they would need complete darkness to attack the guard on the front steps, as far as she could see. It seemed to be too open, too risky, to Francesca. Seppo smiled, however. He betrayed no sign of fear as he checked his Luger semi-automatic pistol. He got out, followed by Jules and then Josephine, who had been sitting in the front.

The Partisan leaned into the car. 'Coming?' she said.

'Me?'

'Francesca, you have to identify the apartment. We could be there for hours, trying keys in the wrong door. Come now,' she said.

'Yes, of course.'

She walked next to Josephine behind the men. She knew Josephine would never let her off the hook, wriggle as she might. As they rounded the corner, she wondered whether *Le Mur Rose* would still be in the apartment and whether...

Seppo strode along on the inner side of the pavement. He would come level with the guard first. They walked as if they were out for a stroll and Francesca prayed no one would look too closely. She was perspiring and her heart beat a tattoo inside her chest, a now-familiar accompaniment to her every-day life; she was becoming used to it.

They were level with the steps leading up to where the guard stood. Still, they walked. Josephine seemed to stumble and trip. She sprawled headlong across the lower step. That split second distracted the guard. He raised his rifle and stepped forward. With a speed belying his size, Seppo leapt up the steps. He landed a punch with the force of an express train. The left hook lifted the German off his feet. He lay crumpled against the doorway. He did not get up.

Jules hammered on the door and Seppo flattened himself against the other wooden portal.

'Help, he's ill. You friend is ill, he fell over.'

The second guard opened the door. He did not even raise his weapon. He looked around the door at his colleague. Seppo struck again. This time, his fist came from below. The guard's head flew back as the pile-driver blow connected with his chin. Jules caught the now-prostrate man under the arm-pits and sidled inside, dragging the unconscious guard. Seppo pulled the other up the steps and Francesca and Josephine followed.

'Tie them up,' Josephine said. 'Which apartment?'

Leading the way, Francesca ran up the grey stone steps and stood outside Egger's apartment. The pressure of Egger's hand on her back came to mind, then the feeling dissipated as Seppo arrived with the keys. He began trying them in the lock.

Jules said, 'Hurry, damn it. We have only minutes.'

'Calm down, my love,' Josephine said, placing a flat hand on his arm, 'we have plenty of time. Egger never leaves the Mairie until late afternoon.'

'All the same.'

Seppo said, 'Yes. Success. Francesca, you go first, you know the way.'

She strode ahead as he asked. The others followed and Jules shut the door behind them. She heard the loud click of the closing door and began to calm down. Entering the sitting room, she pointed to the tall, green safe standing in the corner like a watchdog. Looking around, she saw no sign of *Le Mur Rose* and wondered, while her friends tried keys in the safe, whether the Matisse was still there. She crossed to the bedroom.

'Where are you going?' Josephine said.

'Nothing, just looking.'

'Stay here, in case we need you. This is no time for pilfering.'

The insult stung her but she ignored the suggestion she would steal, even from a German. She heard a click and the safe opened. Jules began to scrabble inside. Francesca did not wait. She began her own search. She almost missed it but as she left the bedroom, it caught her eye. She had not expected the painting to be on display. Egger had moved the Matisse to his bedroom. It hung from a hook on the picture rail opposite his bed. She reached up and took it down. Struggling with the weight of the ornate frame, she came back to the sitting room, where her companions were poring over some files and papers.

Jules looked up and said, 'What are you doing, you silly woman? This is no time for stealing things. We can't carry that thing back to the car.'

'It's a Matisse. It must be saved for posterity. For France.'

'Don't be silly. Josephine, tell her.'

Josephine looked up from the file on her lap, as she sat on the sofa where Egger had felt under Francesca's skirt. The fresh memory of the ordeal made Francesca angry and she turned it onto her companions.

She said, 'You fools. Saving this picture is as important for France as any silly paperwork you might find here. Don't you understand what it means?'

'Keep your voice down. You can't carry that out of here,' Jules said.

'Seppo, have you a knife?'

Seppo reached into his pocket and withdrew a Laguiole knife, its olivewood handle shiny from long use. She snatched it from him and struggled to open it, her fingers clumsy with haste. The blade seemed stuck.

'Here, I'll do it,' Seppo said and took the knife from her grasp. He opened it without any obvious effort. He said, 'What are you going to do? You're not going to destroy it are you?'

'We've got what we wanted, let's go,' Josephine said.

'No, wait,' Francesca said. There was a plaintive note in her voice.

'No time,' Jules said. 'We're going with you or without you.'

'Shut up, Jules,' Seppo said, 'You go without me, then. Hurry, Francesca. We have no time; he's right.'

Josephine checked her wristwatch, Jules stood by the doorway, shuffling from foot to foot.

'Let her take it.' Seppo said, 'it means a lot to her. She led us here, after all.'

Francesca said nothing; she turned the frame over and loosened the wooden stretcher and bent the retaining nails back, then began levering out the painting. It was not a large canvas and it fitted under her arm as if that were its proper place. She crossed to the bedroom and took a pillowcase from the bed. As she slipped the painting into it, she emerged into

214

the sitting room, almost tripping on the empty picture frame. To Francesca, the empty frame seemed almost sad as it lay abandoned on the rug. As they left through the apartment door, Seppo replaced the keys on the keyboard. Francesca hoped it would look like an art theft but suspected Egger was not that stupid and he was sure to know why the raid had taken place.

They ran down the steps and out into the cold, wet, November day. Francesca felt sure no one saw them as they passed like shadows in the dusky sleet. The Renault coughed and spluttered. Minutes passed.

'You could have stolen a newer car,' Seppo said at Jules, leaning across Francesca.

'It was all I could get. Let me try.'

The little car seemed to have heard him for it burst into life and they were away. Francesca, with the painting on her knee, knew this time the Matisse would be safe. She knew how to hide it and she knew she stood a chance of preserving it for her country. It seemed to be her first stroke of luck since coming to Bergerac.

She felt more than lucky. Now she had a real chance to contribute to the struggle. *Le Mur Rose* was her way of resisting. For too long, she felt, she had stood on the sidelines, passive and expectant, wanting to fight, yet being powerless to do so. At last, she possessed a key, her weapon, her way of struggling against the oppression of the invaders of her country.

2

The antique, fish-scale American kitchen-clock struck four, its deep boom announcing her arrival, as Francesca pushed past Marquite at the back door of La Maison Anglais. The smile on her face forced raised eyebrows from the old lady and Francesca, shivering in her thick woollen coat, realised she was, for once, full of hope. This was a memorable day, not least, she thought, because for the first time since they had shot her daughter, she had something to celebrate, something tangible to make her smile. For those few moments, while she stood on the doorstep waiting for Marquite to open the door, she had thought of Marie, wishing she could tell her, wishing somehow she could communicate her elation over what she had done.

'You're smiling, young lady.'

'Yes,' Francesca said. 'The smile is real enough, though I'm hardly a young lady.'

'You grin as if you just had your first kiss,' Marquite said. 'What's that under your arm?'

'It is part of our heritage and I've saved it from Egger's filthy hands.'

'Heritage?'

'Here, let me show you. We have to hide it somewhere safe.'

Francesca removed the pillowcase. She held up the painting so it caught the lamplight.

'Ah,' Marquite said, 'a landscape.'

'No. Not a landscape, but *the* landscape. Matisse painted it when he was a young man. My friend, whom the Nazis took away, owned it. She understood its importance and they stole it. I have stolen it back but if they get it back again, it will be lost to France forever.'

'Not so fast. I need time to understand, my child. You stole this from Egger?'

'With a little help from my friends, yes.'

'By the Holy Virgin, they will come here looking for it then.'

'No. Why should they?'

'They are beasts but they are not stupid beasts. Anyone could connect you with me, with this house. It is dangerous to keep it here, however well we hide it.'

'Are you too fond of your pictures here to lose one?'

'Eh?'

'I will nail another canvas over it and refit the frame. It will look as if it belongs and we can re-hang it. The dust-marks on the wall will make it look as if it has always been there. They will never know it has a secret face behind the old picture.'

'Yes, it could work. I suppose you know your business. André had some tools in the cellar. I'll get them. Don't tell me which picture you use. They could make me talk perhaps. Are they looking for you?'

'No. We were in and out very quickly and although Seppo, you know, the one who was shot? Well he laid out the two guards. I don't think they saw my face under my scarf. It all happened so quickly.'

'But they could have?'

'I think not.'

'They could have. You take too many chances, dear girl. Open a good bottle and we'll celebrate.'

The old woman descended the cellar stairs leading down

from the kitchen. Francesca looked through the remaining wines. There were only six bottles left. She chose a bottle of Vosne-Romanée, her favourite Burgundy, and she pulled the cork with care. She stood it on the kitchen table to let it breathe and waited for Marquite to reappear.

Presently, the old woman emerged, clutching a small hammer, a pair of pliers and a handful of anodised nails.

'Will these do? They were the only ones I could find.'

'Perfect. Now you need to go upstairs and I'll call you when I've done. You can inspect the hall and stairs to see if you can spot my handiwork.'

Francesca looked around the hallway. There were family portraits and copies of some famous paintings, among them, Van Gogh's *Field with Poppies*. She searched for one almost the same size as the Matisse. She found a small oil painting of a cornfield with a young woman in the foreground. Taking down the picture, she stepped into the kitchen and began her work.

First, she removed the cornfield painting from its frame. With fingers deft and gentle, she took the canvas off its wooden support. Careful not to damage it, she laid it face-up on the table. Next, she removed the Matisse from its base-frame, nail by nail, inch by inch. She was one of the few people in France who knew with precision how to do this without causing damage. When she nailed the two canvases together onto the first one's frame, she made certain there was no overlap and she used the exact same holes for the nails. Inspecting the rear of the pictures, she felt satisfied there were no clear signs of tampering.

She lit the candle on the kitchen table and then extinguished it. Using a little lamp-black, she disguised the age of the new nails. Then she replaced the original on its hook

218

above the stairs. It broke her heart, but she burned the wooden original canvas supporting frame in the stove. She knew that wood had held the Matisse for all those years and it was as much a part of the picture as if it was part of the canvas itself. Matisse had handled the wood himself a hundred years before and it made her feel as an atheist might, destroying a religious relic.

Calling up the stairs to Marquite, she said, 'You can come down now.'

As the old woman descended the staircase, Francesca smiled.

'You can look and guess, but I won't tell.'

Marquite did as Francesca said, but she could not identify which picture now held the Matisse.

'Remarkable, Francesca. I cannot spot which one. I shall be guessing every time I come down now. What fun.'

They settled down at the kitchen table then and raised their glasses to France, to art and to Matisse. When the bottle stood empty and sad before them, Marquite said, 'You know, with all that fuss about the painting and the wine, I forgot to put on the stew, but we should eat something. Another bottle would go well with bread and cheese, would it not?'

The two women busied themselves laying out bread, local cheese and some pork liver paté. For Francesca, it felt like one of the finest meals she had eaten since coming to Bergerac. It was not the taste of it, nor the beautiful wine; it was the company and the knowledge she had achieved something at last. She felt elated to be useful again.

3

Although it seemed impossible to Francesca, a week went by without a word from the Partisans and without enquiry of any kind from the SD. She found it surprising, but it fed her sense of relief. If Egger did not pursue her, then she could not be under suspicion. She became convinced the guards outside the German's apartment could not have seen or identified her and so, with each passing day, she felt more secure. It was true, without her Partisan friends, she was in the dark, but she felt content with that. The thought of *Le Mur Rose* lit her path for her. She had saved it. She thought sometimes of the story of the Holy Grail. The long quest and the saving of humanity through its salvage. The feelings she experienced were akin to that tale. She had saved the painting, rescued it from a barbarian horde, and she felt proud. If only Marie were here to see what her mother had done for France and for posterity.

These thoughts were interspersed with thoughts of Seppo. She missed him and his face seemed to haunt her wanderings around the gallery. In the end, she found relief in her oils and canvas. The first day saw only a charcoal sketch of the grid into which his face would steal. On the second, she began to add features. His blond hair, the eyebrows, and his chin seemed to spring from her brush, the shades, and the shapes coalescing on the canvas, distilled from her memory; but it was too concrete a memory. It was then she needed to feel his touch, hear his laugh, and see his naked body. How could she finish the picture without his presence? She wanted him. Francesca realised she loved the big Finn and her portrait of him needed not only that emotion, but physical contact too, for the picture to complete itself. She never saw her work as a conscious expression of her thoughts, but each brushstroke seemed to evoke the next and when the right mood consumed her, the paintings painted themselves.

A week after the break-in, she stood in the afternoon light emanating from the ground floor window of the kitchen and stared hard at the work in progress. Winter seemed both cold and dark but she preferred to paint with natural light since shades and colours seemed more alive to her then. Francesca felt she was stalling in her efforts and as she thought about the big man who had lain there in the attic close to death, she heard a sound outside. Startled from her thoughts, she peered through the net curtain and her heart leapt. He had come.

4

Standing at the kitchen door, enveloped in the strong arms of the big man, Francesca experienced a warmth and solace she had never imagined she could feel. There was a feeling of security, as if his muscular arms were enough to protect and deliver her from the cold, hard world in which she had found herself in the last few years.

They climbed the stairs and, entering the attic room where her bed stood, she realised how anticipation heightened reality. Her imagination, feeding her thoughts of Seppo, made his touch electric as they collapsed on the bed, and as they made love, her thoughts propelled her to a place she never dared to imagine before. When they finished, she lay in his arms, warm between the sheets and blankets, and it came to her they had spoken little since he returned. Guilt came then.

221

She wondered whether all they had was a physical relationship, but deep inside she knew the truth. It was not only her sexual self, nor was it her need to feel secure; she loved this man with her whole being and she knew she would never recover from that.

'Seppo, where have you been? It is a whole week since the break-in. I have been alone here, wondering what has been happening.'

He stroked her face and said, 'I could not come earlier. Josephine ordered us all to stay in camp. She was worried the SD would be on the alert now. Egger has done nothing?'

'No, nothing. Maybe he does not connect me with the theft.'

'Theft?'

'The painting.'

'Is that all you think about? We took lists of names, collaborators, and German spies. There was even a map of the defences and munitions factories on the German border. We have sent all we have to London. An English flyer whom we smuggled out took copies of the documents. London radioed and they will check the information with care. They trust no one and seem to think it was all subterfuge by the Germans. They think we were set up.'

'How do you mean?'

'Well, if the Germans knew we had the keys, they might have left false information in the safe. It is what I would have done in their place.'

'There was no time for them to do that, surely?'

'You said yourself he recognised you.'

'Yes, but he does not know I am in love with a huge Finnish Partisan, does he?'

'Love?

Francesca fell silent.

'You love me?' he said.

She raised herself onto her elbow and looked at his face.

'You think,' she said, 'I would lie here with you if I did not love you?'

'No. I know I have loved you from the moment I first laid eyes on you. In that forest, your face, your skin…'

His verbal clumsiness made her place her index finger on his lips and he fell silent. They remained regarding each other, and in that moment, they both understood what they felt.

The afternoon came and went and they punctuated the time with eating bread and cheese, drinking a rough Bergerac wine and making love. When evening came, they slept in each other's arms and the day seemed to Francesca to be a perfect one. She felt, however, it was a stolen moment, one that might so easily never come again.

And she thought about Marie.

Where was her daughter now in the scheme of things? Francesca wondered, as this new love grew, whether it made Marie into a fading emotion, a diminishing spirit, dissipated by her mother's distraction with her newfound affection. Yet Francesca knew it was not so. Her love for another could never mean betrayal of her love for her dead daughter. Inside she knew one can love many people and loving anyone need not ebb the love for another. They could live side by side, those loves, neither reducing the other.

She was sure of it.

Chapter 30

1

Dawn brought no relief from the cold investing everything around her, and Francesca shivered as she and Seppo descended the stairs. They embraced on the back door-step. Francesca wished it could be like the time when he was recovering from his wounds. As he kissed her lips, she realised she had not even asked how his wound had healed and whether he had pain. She had felt the scar as they caressed in bed but never asked. She began to think she had become selfish and self-obsessed.

It was all on the tip of her tongue, when he said, 'Here, we need you to deliver this.'

Seppo drew a letter from his coat and handed it to her.

'What's this?'

'It's a note to Roland. He hasn't been home when we've called and it needs to be put into his hands. None of us can hang around on the off-chance he will turn up.'

'Have they caught him?'

'Unlikely. They have no reason to suspect a member of the police.'

'But maybe he was seen with one of you?'

'No. Not possible. He is a very careful man.'

'How do I get it to him?'

'The message is in cipher. It's addressed to "Didier". That's his codename. He should be at work after six. Go to the

Prefecture and ask for him. The more discreet you are in handing it to him, the better.'

'What's in it?'

'You don't need to know. I don't know myself. Josephine arranged it all. You'll do it?'

'Naturally.'

'I told them we could count on you. Tell the man at the desk when you enter, you are a friend of Roland's and it is personal.'

'His second name?'

'Aubrac.'

'Dangerous?'

'No. I don't think so. No one suspects you.'

'When do I do this?'

'Later today, this morning.'

Then, he said, 'I love you.'

'Yes. I love you too.'

'When this war ends, we will be together for always.'

He kissed her lips and cuddled her in.

'Seppo?'

'What?'

'What happens to hatred when it is spent? Does it colour your soul forever?'

'Hatred? Who is it you hate?'

'I want the Germans to die, in pain, in misery.'

'You know about my brothers?'

'You said…'

'I want the Germans to suffer like they made me suffer. Can you imagine the grief when you see your little brothers shot? Boys who came to France to earn money as carpenters and bricklayers? They never hurt anyone. They we innocent but their papers were not in order and the SD colonel felt they might be spies. They were shot in public, as if everyone afterwards could go home and enjoy a feast—you know—roast goose and the like. I hated them for that. They cheapened and scorned my brothers' lives as if they had no meaning. I'm going to show them that meaning.'

'I understand. It was like when they shot Marie. They didn't care, and that was what mattered to me most. I loved her and she was everything to me. Egger was there. He ordered them to shoot, and when I cried over her dead body he shrugged it off as if it were of no consequence. You think I don't understand? I do.'

Francesca leaned back, looking up at him. Neither of them said any more. It was as if they both understood how protracted goodbyes were not needed, indeed were dangerous.

She watched as he shut the back door but she stood for long moments, wishing the door would open again, revealing his indomitable smile. Still, she remained a realist and so she turned back, shutting the door. Loneliness filled her. Charles had gone, Seppo too; all she had of him now was the lingering warmth of his lips still on hers. Lighting a cigarette, she stood in the kitchen.

Francesca took the sheet from her canvas. She looked at the rudimentary face staring back at her, and in anger and frustration, she tore at the half-finished painting in front of her, until, fingertips red-raw, the canvas glared back at her in tatters. Pure emotion flowed through her and she realised her fury was indeed almost spent. In all this death and decimation that men called war, there was only one man she wanted to see dead. It was Egger.

2

Snow. It began as small, occasional flakes, and by the time Francesca plucked up the courage to leave her gallery, it descended in wind-swept flurries. Closing the door to the accompaniment of the merry chimes of the bell, she looked down at the pavement. White, spreading like a thin blanket, adorned the cobbles and she thought about happier times. She recalled five-year-old Marie's sled and the fun they had shared on the hill in the nearby park at home. The word "home" seemed to echo in her brain. She had no home, all was gone now, and only memories remained to her. Biting her lip, she locked the door and stuffed the key into her pocket with fingers slow and numbing already in the cold. The morning was dark, as if it heralded some ill fortune, but Francesca shrugged off the feeling of gloom. It was not her nature to feel depressed, even now. She wondered why Egger, having recognised her, had kept silent. Was he watching her still? The letter sat uncomfortably stuffed into her waistband and she felt it crumpling as she walked the twenty yards to the Prefecture.

A sudden tension took her as she approached the stone steps leading to the tall, iron-studded door. What if Roland was not there? Suppose the Germans had already arrested him. What would she do?

She shrugged off these concerns. Seppo would never ask her to risk her life for a forlorn hope. Francesca heard a car pull up behind her. The door of the vehicle opening rang in her ears as if magnified. Her heart leapt at the sound and sweat broke out on her forehead as if she had exerted herself climbing the stairs. She kept walking.

'Madame Pascal?'

The voice behind her carried only a trace of accent but it was German. A chill descended upon her. She shuddered as she turned.

'Yes?'

'You will come with us.'

A short man in a black uniform confronted her when she turned. He smiled as if this were a source of amusement to him. His right hand rested on the holster at his waist and before he could reach her, another man in a black uniform emerged from the car. It was one of Egger's men, Schumacher.

'Where to?'

'We want to ask some questions. Nothing serious. Only some questions.'

'Can I come later? I have business here.'

'No. I think you need to come now. It won't take long. Half-an-hour perhaps.'

'What's it about?'

'Oh, nothing to concern you. Come.'

The man gestured the black car. Francesca noted the flags bearing the swastika mounted on the front wings of the vehicle, the bright colours belying the evil they represented to her, and she shuddered.

'Really, I'm very busy. Can't it wait?'

He sounded almost kind. Like a man admonishing a wayward child, reassuring but firm. It was the look in his eyes frightening Francesca. There was an icy coolness expressed in them and she realised he did not care what happened next. She considered running but standing on the steps with the car below her, and two armed soldiers each with hands on their weapons, forced her to realise flight was not an option. She relented then. Francesca Pascal, artist and conservator once employed by the Louvre, understood who she was in the scheme of things. Now she was a Partisan. Now she was a captured rebel and the consequences of that would follow. Now there was no avenue of escape.

Marie was dead. She reassured herself it no longer mattered what they might do to her. Her only regret as she entered the car was that she had never killed any of these evil people.

Chapter 31

1

The two soldiers, one on either side of her, said nothing. It was like the last time when Egger wanted her to come to his apartment. Perhaps this time he would emerge from the Mairie and get in with her? No. She knew it would not happen this time. She tried to steel herself for what was coming and she was realistic.

They would find the letter to Roland. They would question her, then kill her. The thought of them shooting her seemed almost attractive. There was no purpose to life without her daughter. She had not passed anything of herself to the world for future generations. She would be shot, she would die and although Seppo might mourn her for a while, that would be the end of her miserable life.

Deep inside her, though, there was a spark. It was like a tiny glow at the very beginning of a great blaze. The feeling grew. She would not give in. Whatever they did to her, she would say nothing about Roland until twenty-four hours passed to allow him to escape. That was her duty. Seppo had told her that. All the Partisans knew that when one of their number was caught, they would have to hold out for a day to allow the others to escape. Francesca bit her lip. She had never seen herself as strong. How could she hold out? What could they do her to make her talk? Yes, they might beat her. Yes, they might try to persuade her with lies to tell what she knew. But what did she know? She knew a few names. There was nothing strategic she could tell. Josephine had kept her in the dark and perhaps Seppo too, had never told her anything useful to the sauerkrauts.

The car stopped with a jolt in front of the Mairie. The man to her left got out. He gestured to her to follow. He extended his arm and his fingers flexed twice. Francesca looked at him. There was no smile this time. They had her. There was no longer any need for pretence and she knew it from his face. Her bladder reacted. She was desperate to pass water. It would have been a foolish thing to ask if she could. Francesca Pascal, the artist, knew then she had to face the consequences of her ridiculous presence in Bergerac. As they took her arms and pulled her up the Mairie steps, she glanced behind over her shoulder. A feeling this would be the last time she saw daylight reflected on snow, came into her head. Dizziness came then. It was as if the certain knowledge the SD had arrested her made her head swim. She heard the doors slam behind her and then there were more steps. A grand marble staircase flew by as they took her up to an office.

They pushed her through the door and the high-ceilinged room seemed almost civilised. A desk, a chair, paintings adorning the walls. It appeared to Francesca as if she were about to have a job-interview. The room was silent. The men shoved her towards the chair in front of the desk, her feet stumbling. She sat. The men left. Nothing happened. She was alone in a big room in the Mairie.

'What was there to be frightened of?' she thought. Perhaps this was only the brief, friendly interview the soldier promised.

Then Egger came and fear came with him.

2

He entered through the door by which the two SD men had left moments before. His face seemed calm. She was struck by the fact he carried a tabby cat under his left arm. It would have seemed comic to Francesca to see this big man cradling a cat but in his right hand, he carried a horsewhip. He stood looking at Francesca, tapping his boot with the whip. His mouth was smiling but it looked like a knife cut; it was the look of his eyes, too, she found frightening . They were pale and moved with rapid shifts of his gaze. They reminded her of a caged creature, a wild beast looking for a means of escape or even attack. There was a feral quality to those eyes, yet they held a cod-cold quality too, and Francesca realised there was no humanity in the glance, once his eyes rested upon her.

A shudder ran down her spine. She said nothing. Watching him as he regarded her, she knew there was nothing to say. He knew who she was and worse still, she still carried the letter for Roland.

Minutes passed. He approached and crossing to the other side of the ornate desk, sat down, still clutching the cat. With movements quick and precise, he placed the whip on the desk and reached down, pulling out a drawer. Egger extracted a bottle of some pale liquor and two tiny tumblers. He filled them both, re-corked the bottle, and pushed one of the glasses across to Francesca.

This seemed to be a game to Egger. Francesca refused to play. If they were going to hurt her, she wished they would get on with it. She began to wonder how much they knew about her and the Partisans, about Seppo and most of all about Roland.

He said, 'Drink. It will be, I'm afraid, the last drink you have in a long time, Frau Pascal.'

The emphasis on the last words was an insult and she knew it.

'It seems you have something of mine. I was foolish. I hung it and should have taken it away instead, out of temptation, from your grasping Partisan fingers. It never occurred to me you would be there, let alone steal my painting.'

'I... I don't know what you mean.'

'Drink. Please. I'm not trying to poison you.'

He took his own glass and downed it. He grimaced at the sting of it, then smiled again.'

'You seem to think we are fools. Yes?'

She was silent.

'There are no fools in the SS or the SD for that matter. Do you know what it means to be in the SS?

Francesca refused to speak. There was nothing to say. She was here, and he was here, and soon he would beat her. It seemed as plain as the thin coldness of his smile.

Egger stood up and said, 'Each one of us is chosen by the Fürer himself. They check our background for four generations and if our families are strong, German and clean of Jewish blood, we are tested. They test our intellect; they test our bodies and our fortitude. Only the cream rises to the top. So you see, when a small intellect like yours is matched against the SS, you can stand no chance.'

Egger's pale eyes narrowed and he began their darting dance; he frowned. Taking the whip, he thumped the desktop. He leaned forward across the desk. Their eyes met again.

'I want the painting you stole. If you take me to it, I will let you go. It is a simple choice. Believe me, you will not like our kitchens down below, but you will see them soon enough if you resist.'

It was the word "resist" which triggered it. The anger she felt grew and as it did, she realised there was nothing she had to say to this mockery of a human being. He caused Marie's death. He wanted to take the only thing in this filthy war Francesca could protect. She had failed to protect Marie and she felt pain whenever she thought about it. At least she could protect the painting from Egger. She would never let him have *Le Mur Rose*.

Her voice, slow and measured, Francesca looked up at the German and said, 'You killed my daughter. I have nothing to say to you. You can hurt me. You may kill me but I have nothing to say to you. Now get on with it, I'm ready.'

Laughter.

Egger laughed at her.

There was no humour in the sound and she knew it. It seemed to be some kind of pantomime. In defiance, she took the glass in front of her and she drank. She emptied the glass and realised it was some kind of vodka. It burned her throat but the feeling came as a sweet relief from the tension racking her.

'Francesca. Please. Be reasonable. I would spare you what is to come. If you give me the painting, I will free you. I don't care about you. You are such small fry, no one will ever know whether you live or die. They all talk in the end anyway, no matter how brave they are. Listen to reason.'

He reached across the desk and still smiling that razor-sharp smile, he squeezed her hand. The warmth of his fingers served only to impress upon her how alone she was. Here in this high-ceilinged room, with the man responsible for her daughter's death, there would be no escape, no reprieve. What would happen would happen.

She drew her hand away, her movements slow and deliberate.

'I have nothing to say to you.'

Egger sighed in pretended resignation and rang the bell in front of him. Two soldiers came through the doorway. Neither carried rifles but there were pistols at their waists. They said nothing. They pulled her from the chair and dragged her towards the stairs. Regaining her feet, she allowed them to manhandle her down to the ground floor, then down another smaller staircase. She was going to Egger's "kitchens" and she knew they prepared no meals there, only a diet of pain.

3

Francesca had never imagined how it would be if she were arrested. She had always refused to acknowledge the possibility, as if it did not exist. The reality of the fact caught her almost unawares. She experienced an overwhelming feeling of loneliness. It was an isolation so deep, it penetrated every corner of her being and she realised this was her greatest vulnerability. The two soldiers took her down to a small room. There was a rough-hewn wooden table with two chairs on one side of it and none on the other. It was not a place where the interviewee was expected to sit. At the other end of the room were two objects and Francesca was unsure of their purpose, though she could guess, and that mental picture forced a shudder from her. There was a stout metal frame, six or seven feet tall, with two rings at either end of a cross-bar. The other was a large, white, enamel bath. Brackish-looking yellow water filled it. There was a faint smell of urine emanating from it.

The smaller of the two guards, his face impassive, shoved her into the centre of the room.

'Remove clothes,' he said. The tone was flat; his eyes cold.

'Now?' Francesca said. She could conjure no other meaningful response.

'Clothes off, or we take them off.'

The accent was a guttural German and she wondered whether he spoke much of her language. It occurred to her they might rape her.

With no other choices at hand, Francesca began removing her coat and then her blouse. Each button seemed be a step nearer to an abyss from which she would be unable to return. Something Seppo had said to her once about the intimidation of arrest came to mind and she bolstered herself by trying not to give in to her feeling of fear. Her fingers gained in strength and dexterity and she resolved not to show these men the naked terror deep inside her.

Almost with an air of disdain, she threw her clothes onto the empty table, careful to keep the letter to Roland out of view. She knew it was a forlorn hope but she wondered whether she might be lucky and it would remain hidden when they destroyed her clothing, if indeed that was what they were going to do.

Naked, she stood there before them. She folded he arms in front of her. In her mind now was only determination. She would not show them fear, only French disdain, whatever happened. If they raped her, she would go limp. She would not give them the satisfaction of even a token resistance. She wanted to show them how a true Frenchwoman could behave.

The soldiers did not even glance at her body. The taller of

236

the two began rummaging through the pockets of her clothing. He found the letter. He cast a quick glance at her and said
something in German to his companion, then walked from
the room. Francesca still stood there naked. It was as if she did
not exist to the remaining man. He showed no more interest
in her than if she had been fully clothed and wearing a hat.

Minutes passed. She shuffled from one foot to the other.
Still scared, she realised the letter would change how they
treated her. She would now be a Partisan in their eyes, not a
simple thief. If only she had managed to discard it. They had
proof now, though she did not know the contents of the note.
Perhaps if it was enciphered, they would be unable to implicate her. She knew nothing of such things and it would be
useless of them to ask, though she was certain they would.

Presently, Egger entered. He still held the cat and the
whip. His bemused smile seemed out of place.

'Put on your clothes,' he said, 'you look ridiculous.'

As Francesca dressed, he said, 'Who is Didier?'

'What?' she said.

'The note was addressed to Didier.'

'I don't know what you are talking about.'

'Are you Didier?'

'No. I don't know who Didier is.'

'Then how could you deliver the note? Or maybe you are
Didier. Either way, you are implicated.'

'I was asked to leave the note in the square and walk away.
I never saw the man who brought the note, only a written
instruction which I destroyed.'

Egger stood up. He moved around the table and said,
'Who is Didier?'

'I don't know.'

The speed with which the whip struck her face was like a

237

snake striking. It caught her across the forehead. It stung like a knife-cut. It took a moment for the pain to register. It was as if the shock of the blow delayed its message. Francesca's head whipped back and she raised her hands. She wanted to cry.

The words came in a slow forceful sentence once more.

'Who is Didier?'

Francesca said nothing. She sobbed, then was silent. She knew she would say nothing. It was as if she wanted pain. It was nothing compared to losing Marie. It would cease in the end and she knew it. Maybe it would continue for a few days, but in the end, they would shoot her. A few days are nothing in a lifespan. If they were going to shoot her anyway, she thought, maybe it would be as well for them to do so learning nothing.

'You are Didier, aren't you?'

Silence.

She heard Egger say to the two soldiers, 'Wait outside'

The door clicked as they left.

'Francesca, I'm sorry I was so... so brutal. It is simple. All I want is that painting. I don't care about who your Partisan contacts are. We will catch them and eliminate them anyway. You can save yourself a lot of pain by just telling me where you have hidden it. I will let you go. You will be free to go wherever you want. You will tell me in the end. You will beg me to listen.'

Francesca knew there was nothing to say. She would not give this brute the Matisse. It meant too much to her. Handing over the picture, for her, was like a religious man denying Christ. It would be like becoming German. She knew she had suffered the mental pain of loss and now she was ready to face up to physical pain as well. She would not talk.

Egger said, 'I will give you time to think about my offer. I have plenty of time. You are alone; no one will come to your rescue. Tell me what I want to know.'

She looked up at Egger. She knew he was right, but in one sense, she thought she was not alone. She still held on to her indelible mental picture of Marie. It was the only defensive wall she could erect and she knew it was powerful. It would last. Her life, her pain, was as nothing compared to the bond between her and Marie. The sooner she joined her daughter, the better. It became a source of strength to her and she knew she would keep silent.

Chapter 32

1

The cell was clean, bare concrete flooring, no furniture or even a mattress, only stanchions in the walls, projecting from them like an acrobat's rings, but at floor level. The manacles she wore chaffed but it was neither their tightness nor the weight, it was the restriction of movement that hurt. Francesca had three feet of movement only and although she could turn and change her position, she could not stand upright. Hunger gnawed her as evening fell and the boredom of isolation came, too. There was room for six others, she counted, but the other stanchions remained empty. She wondered what was going to happen. The heavy door was made of iron bars and she could hear occasional groans from other cells but from her position in the corner, she could not see out. There was a faint smell of disinfectant and faeces. A bucket stood next to her and she used it, though she found the act hard with the restrictions of the manacles.

The plain, smooth, whitewashed walls were in themselves a kind of deprivation. She viewed them with an artist's eyes and the absence of texture or any kind of view made her isolation harder, since she had nothing to focus upon. She found herself longing not for company, but for something to look at. When she closed her eyes, she could see images, but when she opened them, there was nothing. The blankness of her surroundings became as hard as the manacles on her wrists.

Francesca still wore her coat but shivered with cold all the same. There was no source of heating and so she curled up, shivering against the wall, grateful they had not taken her coat. She bent her head on her knees and despite the dark, despite the cold and hunger, sleep came.

She thought she must have slept for minutes only when the door of the cell opened. It was dark so she understood she must have slept for some hours, though she possessed no knowledge of the time. Two guards in brown uniforms entered. Looking up, she could see an officer also in brown behind them. Unlocking the manacles, her captors pulled her to her feet. The officer spoke to them in German, his voice calm and unhurried, though she did not understand what he said. He looked tense.

They took her to the same interrogation room in which Egger questioned her before. They stripped her of her coat, blouse and brassiere, leaving her skirt and shoes. This time there was a third chair in front of the table and she sat down, legs and arms crossed as if it would protect her.

On the table, a variety of objects lay on an outspread blanket. With a strange curiosity, she looked them over, as if she were a diner in a restaurant, examining the cutlery before her meal arrived. The thought made her smile. She knew something was happening inside her because she felt untouched by emotion now, resigned but determined.

Egger entered. He still held his riding crop but there was no cat this time. The guards looked relaxed with half-smiles on their faces. Egger said nothing. He picked up a set of handcuffs from the desk and handed them to one of the guards, who took them almost eagerly, Francesca thought. She felt as if she were not there, but witnessing all this from somewhere else, as if this were some play or pantomime in which an actor called Francesca Pascal played the part of the Partisan prisoner and Egger was the co-star. Francesca wondered whether the casting was appropriate and wished the end credits would roll.

Grabbing her wrists, the man held her arms out in front of her and snapped on the cuffs. There was pain then and Francesca realised there were blunt spikes inside them, biting and pressing her flesh. She must have yelped then, for she heard the guard say, 'Shut the mouth.'

The two guards dragged her to the frame by the wall and hoisted her up with a chain strung between the rings. Standing on tiptoes, she felt pain radiating down her arms as the spikes dug in and Francesca thought she would faint, but no such kindness was forthcoming. Looking up, she could see Egger picking up a rubber truncheon; he weighed it in his hand and turned towards her.

In silence, he approached and he smiled a humourless smile. Francesca remained uncertain whether he smiled from pleasure or if it was some kind of pretended gesture, a way of relieving his own tension. What happened next, left her in no doubt; it was pleasure.

His eyes darted over her face, her chest and he still said nothing. He poked her left breast with the truncheon. Still smiling, he raised his arm and with deliberate whipping force, he struck her. The pain shot through her. It was unbearable. Francesca had experienced labour pains and she knew there was no pain as bad as that, but this made her sweat and whimper.

Another blow. This time she cried out as the truncheon struck her in almost the same place. She knew he was making that area his special target. Tears ran down her cheeks and

Egger smiled again, as if he experienced as much pleasure as she felt pain.

The German walked away and sat in the chair Francesca had occupied only minutes before. He took a cigarette from a gold case and lit it with a match from a gold matchbox-holder. The grey-blue smoke hung in the still, cold air and he placed the cigarettes on the table beside his assorted instruments. It signalled to Francesca through the watery view she had that they would be here for some time. Apart from her screams, the whole pantomime proceeded in silence.

Egger stood up, truncheon in hand. She wondered with a strange curiosity whether he was waiting for the bruising to reach its maximum. He began again. He poked; she winced. Then he hit her again. The pain seemed to make her head swim and she screamed again. No words. An animal noise this time. Sweat ran down her face, despite the cold, and she felt faint.

The scene repeated itself several times. In her agony, she lost count. No words. Screams and silence; silence, then screams. Waves of pain and nausea washed over her. Her wrists became numb but the pain in her chest seemed worse than anything she had ever imagined. Her head fell forwards and still conscious, she felt as if it were impossible to endure this horror.

Egger was smoking again. She wished he would choke. She wanted to be anywhere but here in this silent mortuary of a place where she knew she must die or live in pain. Then it was as if a voice somewhere in her head said, plain and clear, 'Maman, let me help you. You should not be doing this by yourself.'

It was a strange thing and she knew it was an illusion, but it helped her. Egger had not asked any questions; he only gave pain. Each time he stood smoking, weighing some kind of instrument from the table, there was an uncertainty whether he would use it or not. He approached. This time he did speak.

'Francesca, are you Didier?'

She raised her head, eyes wild.

'I don't know who Didier is. If I did know, I would not say.'

He struck her again but with a flat hand across her face and she felt warm, red blood trickle down her chin.

'Maman, let me help you.'

The voice came again and this time she smiled. She wondered if she were becoming just a little mad. Perhaps even insane enough to stay mute in the face of this German whom she hated.

Egger turned to the guards at the door and told them to leave. The door shut with a metallic clang.

'You know, you have two breasts. I have only started on the left one. The right will be the same. Then the left will be sensitive enough to begin again. We can keep that up for a few days, then there are other more interesting persuasive measures.'

He raised the rubber truncheon and struck her on the stomach this time. The pain shot into her back and she would have doubled up, had she not been suspended by her now-benumbed wrists.

'The painting, where is it?'

Silence.

He raised the almost-finished cigarette and extinguished it on her left nipple. The swelling must have numbed it, for the pain was not as bad as she thought it should have been or perhaps the mental picture of Marie was helping her. Their

244

eyes met. His, cold, pale and mobile; hers, steady and burning with the bitter fires of hatred.

'You are stubborn to the point of stupidity. From the moment you arrived in Bergerac, I have known who you were. Yes, even when my men stopped you and that old bat on the bridge, we knew who you were. I knew you took the keys; I knew you and your friends, perhaps even this Didier, tried to kill me in the café. You have been my toy, my experiment, if you like. You have underestimated me. Now, where is the Matisse?'

Another backhanded blow to the face. She yelped this time and felt her lips swelling.

'You don't understand,' the words spoken through her swelling and bleeding lips seemed mumbled and faint.

Egger leaned forward, 'What?'

Clearer and with difficulty she said, 'You don't understand what *Le Mur Rose* means to a Frenchwoman. It is part of me, part of my country's heritage. It symbolises France and the beauty of my home. I can no more tell you where it is than I can stop breathing.'

'You will stop breathing in a few days, don't worry. What state you will be in then is up to you.'

Egger stepped towards the door. Opening it, he called his men back.

Francesca heard him say, as if from a great distance, 'Get her out of here and bring the man.'

With her head swimming, and her legs unstable beneath her, they took her back to the cell and her manacles. She tried to feel her chest with her hands, but the numbness in her fingers made them clumsy and weak. This time her blouse lay by her side but her coat was gone. She began shivering but whether it was from shock or cold, she did not know.

Francesca wondered whether she could face another session like that. The numbing ache in her breast, the swollen lips and the feeling of faintness all seemed overwhelming and unendurable.

2

It was a long night. This time, try as she might, she could not sleep. Only pain sat upon her shoulders, weighing her down, robbing her of any certainties, if indeed she had ever possessed them. She wished she knew where Seppo was and whether he was still safe. Would he know what was happening to her? Would he try to save her? She knew she could resist better if such foolish hopes did not come into her mind. It was a matter of remaining hopeless and accepting what was to come. How long she could do that, she did not know, but as the pain increased in the cold cell, she became more determined to remain silent. The only thing she knew was she had nothing to say to Egger.

Francesca understood how he coveted the picture and as she sat hugging her knees, back against the cold stone of the wall, despite everything he said, he had been stupid. Egger did not understand she would be there when the Partisans broke into the apartment. If he had anticipated her being there, he would have hidden the picture. It gave her hope. The painting was the only thing in all this sorry mess of her life, which made her cling to her silence. That, and her feelings of Marie watching over her, strengthening her when she was tempted to weaken.

Time passed until she saw a sprinkling of morning light coming through the bars of the tiny window high up on the wall of her cell. It was as if the dawn light brought with it a sense of hope. She could not understand why she felt like that. She knew there was no hope of release, no chance of capitulation on her part, either. There would be pain, then death, and no one would know whether she had suffered or not. The SD would shoot her when they finished with her and escape, rescue and deliverance were impossible, ridiculous goals.

Francesca's thinking changed then. It did not matter how much pain she suffered, or how long they tortured her. It was finite. It would end. The rescue and release she sought depended upon her silence, not her giving way. If death was inevitable, though she could not speed its arrival, it made her even more determined to tolerate. If she talked about the painting or even about the Partisans, her death would have no meaning; Marie's death, too, would be useless. No. She would not talk. Egger would never get the painting.

The morning wore on. She could move only with difficulty and her breast must have swollen for she could feel the weight when she shifted. Every movement brought pain. Then the cell door opened and a brown-uniformed man approached. He held a cup of water and a lump of bread. Placing them by her feet, he said nothing and left.

Reaching forward to the bread, she began to eat. Her swollen, cracked lips smarted as she did so and the meal became slow and laborious. The water had a metallic taste but was clean enough. Finished, she replaced the empty cup on the floor.

The door opened again and it made her jump. The two guards from the previous day appeared. They unlocked the manacles and Francesca now knew there would be more pain. The knowledge allowed her to prepare herself for it in anticipation. She would show courage this time.

The room had not changed. The chairs remained but there were no truncheons or whips. Instead, a bottle stood on the table. It held no label but there were two small tumblers. It looked like the vicious brew Egger had offered her the previous day, or was that, she wondered, several days ago? No, she was sure it had been only two days before.

She sat down and waited. She still felt faint, as if the pain and the hunger combined to weaken her. Staring at the bottle, she rehearsed in her mind how she would sketch it, charcoal, smudged at the edges against the backdrop of the rough wooden table. An hour passed. The two guards stood in silence at the door.

Francesca looked at their faces. She wondered what kind of people they were. Could any man watch human suffering and not be touched by it in some way? Were these two men so isolated from the human race, they could stand and watch as Egger tried to beat information from her or anyone else for that matter?

Neither of the men looked at her. It was as if she were an object, tangible but inhuman. A crying, screaming machine and because she did neither of those things at that moment, she did not exist for them. It angered her. She stood up. The pain in her cramped legs began to ease. Both guards crossed the bare concrete floor and pressed her down into the chair. Shrugging off their rough hands, she remained sitting this time.

Presently, Egger arrived. He still held the cat under his left arm but carried his horsewhip too. He stood on the opposite side of the table, tapping his black boot with the whip. When he sat down, he poured two glasses of the clear liquor. As before, he pushed a tumbler across to Francesca. Her head swimming already and with painful movements, she took the drink, gagging as she swallowed; it burned her broken lips. The alcohol and the pain seemed to bring clarity. She put down the glass and noticed the bloodstains where her lips had caressed it moments before. She needed no mirror to know what she must have looked like and what they had done to her face.

He said, 'I am sorry I was so rough yesterday. You must think me most inhospitable. Your poor chest must be painful. All so unnecessary too, don't you think?'

She was silent, looking at his face, wishing she could sink her nails into the sallow flesh.

'Nothing to say? I understand. I was unforgivably rude yesterday. I will make it up to you. Are you hungry?'

Francesca said nothing.

'When you go back to your room, I will have some food sent down to you. You must be starving.'

Francesca still said nothing. The word "room" seemed ironic. It was as if Egger was an hotelier describing his best accommodation. Perhaps he would offer her a shower or a room with a bathroom and toilet. Perhaps... She knew, however, he would either feed her or not; it was, after all, beyond her control and therefore something to accept or not; it made no real difference to the ultimate outcome. She knew she was going to die here.

'My dear Francesca, you won't realise how much I hate these methods, but they are necessary. You have something I want. I need you to tell me. If you behave, there is no need for punishment. Come, Francesca, who is Didier?'

'I don't know.'

Her reply seemed almost to be as he expected. He laughed, though the sound was mirthless. His eyes narrowed.

'Francesca, Francesca. I mean you no harm. This is not

249

personal. In other times, you and I might have been friends, lovers even. Now I will ask you again. Can you identify Didier to us? Point him out, indicate where he is? It will end all this cruelty. I don't enjoy it at all.'

'I don't know who Didier is. I told you. If I did, wouldn't I have told you already?'

Egger looked up at the guards by the door. He said, 'Leave us.'

The door shut and she knew what he was about to say.

'Look,' he said, 'I need the painting back. It is mine. If you tell me, I will ensure you have a smooth ride. This Didier business is nothing but a sideshow, as far as I'm concerned. The painting, however, is worth a fortune to me. An original Matisse would fetch enough for me to retire after the war. Along with the other smaller trinkets I have, I will be very comfortable. You see, you stand in my way. Now, where is the painting?'

'Even if I knew, I wouldn't let you have it. I would rather see it burnt.'

'Look, that attitude will give you nothing but pain. Where is it hidden? We have already searched your gallery and the old woman's house. Where is it hidden?'

Francesca realised now the painting was safe. If they had indeed searched the English House and not found the Matisse, they would never find it.

She tried to smile through her bloody and swollen lips. She said, 'I hope you suffer in the eternal fires of Hell.'

Egger thumped the desk with his fist. He became flushed; his ears radiated redness and heat. A scowl appeared on his face, then he calmed. He leaned back in his chair and called his men. They returned her to her cell.

Francesca found she was not alone. Another woman

looked up from the ground as the guards chained her again to the floor-level stanchion. The newcomer's face showed bruises and she shifted with pain like Francesca, as the guards stepped back and left.

The two women regarded each other in silence, as if there was little to say which was not obvious to both of them. The new woman was of middle age and her name was Juliette Duprée. Neither of them trusted the other. They spoke little but shared the food when it came. Francesca wondered why her treatment at Egger's hands seemed to have changed. She expected a beating, not conversation and food. They ate chicken and bread, and shared their physical pain. When night fell, the cold made them huddle together and the warmth of each other's bodies was enough to allow sleep.

Before sleep came, she thought about Seppo. She wondered whether he understood he had lost her now. She would never feel his strong arms about her, the contradiction of his large hands caressing with the gentleness of a child, nor feel his lips upon hers. Francesca hoped he would recover but most of all, she hoped he would be safe.

Chapter 33

1

Egger worked hard in the next few days to cause confusion for Francesca. One day he would send for her and make conversation across the interrogation room table, the next, they strung her up and beat her without mercy. Even the beatings were unpredictable. Egger used a horsewhip one day and his hands the next. Slaps and punches bruised her face and flesh. The days merged with the nights until she had no understanding of how long this cycle of beatings and verbal persuasion went on. As the days wore on, she became unable to stand and dizzy came from exhaustion and hunger, mental weariness too, began taking its toll.

Still, she said nothing. Each blow, each slap, made her more determined to remain silent. Somewhere in her jumbled mind, she reasoned that each punch added to the last. If she weakened and talked, all the other pain would have been wasted and meant she should have told Egger everything at the beginning. In the end, nothing could make her talk; giving way would have wasted her determination and her hatred for this monster, who now, even pervaded her dreams. They were nightmares; visual episodes in a fitful sleep until she could no longer recognise whether she were in a nightmare or in reality. She became confused and sometimes laughed when they hurt her.

She found after ten days of this treatment that Egger was showing increasing signs of frustration at her silence. He ranted and raved in the torture sessions. He hit her harder and more often with his fists. Then he changed tactics. They dragged her to the interrogation room and when she was unable to sit, they deposited her on the floor in front of the clean, shiny, black boots of her torturer. Through swollen, almost closed eyes, she recognised him. The tap-tap of the whip on the polished, black leather was unmistakable.

'My dear Francesca, you need a bath. Let us assist you to get undressed.'

Rough hands pulled at her clothes, tearing them, ripping buttons away. They hauled her to her feet. She felt handcuffs on her wrists, behind her back. The men dragged her to the enamel bath. The water stank, even to her swollen nostrils. Seating Francesca on the edge of the tub, Egger placed a chain around her wrists and threaded it under a bar placed across the bath.

'Now, Francesca, we will see if you can swim.'

They pushed her in, face up.

She thought he must have pulled the chain because her whole body arched back and she felt the surface close above her head. There was no distress in her mind. At last she could die. If she breathed in this urine-stained, filthy water, she thought she could die and it would all end. She could see Marie again, join her forever. Peace was coming.

With a suddenness that shocked her, they drew her head from the icy water. Francesca gasped, choking and coughing. Had they submerged her for seconds or longer? She had no idea, but if the chance came again, she would inhale, breathing deep, departing at last.

She heard Egger say, 'Francesca, next time it will be a little longer, and the next time too, even longer. Tell me what I want to know.'

Shivering, Francesca tried to focus her eyes. She wanted to say what a fool Egger was; she wanted to laugh at him. He had lost. She could kill herself now; all she needed was a little time to breathe in when they pulled her under again.

'Marie, wait for me,' she thought.

Then they did it again.

Now, a chance.

Now, death can come.

She tried her best to open her mouth. She wanted to breathe it all into herself, end this charade of life and the pain it brought. As soon as she tried, she coughed. She spluttered and nothing happened. Her throat refused to cooperate. She tried again but the same happened.

The room reappeared. The water in her ears made it hard to decipher Egger's next questions. It made no difference. There was nothing to say. *Le Mur Rose* was locked away and hidden in some deep recess of her mind and she would never give it up, never betray her country or her friends. She felt the suffering made her stronger now.

Francesca, through her pain and anger, heard Marie again, her voice soft, gentle and unlike everything around her. Through the brutality of the moment, her daughter said, 'Maman, here, let me help you. Maman, I'm here.'

In the murky water, Francesca opened her eyes and thought that somehow she could see. She could see her little angel, arms outstretched, a smile on her lovely face and a glow around her. Marie reached for her, touching, enveloping her, soothing it all away.

Then reality bit again. She found herself on the concrete. Her body shook, her remaining teeth chattered. Hard under her, the handcuffs poked her back, bruising, biting. She hardly felt it. Her whole body felt like one great bruise and the bucket of icy water drenching her did nothing, either. She thought perhaps if they put her back into the bath, she would succeed in drowning herself. Hoping Egger would not guess, she looked up through the swollen slits of her eyes and murmured.

'I will never talk.'

Egger leaned close, 'I have seen many like you. No one can take this for as long as I intend to keep it up.'

Looking towards his men he said, 'Take her away, oh, and leave her clothes.

Darkness came then into her mind. The journey to the cell was a blur. The manacles clasping her wrists seemed lighter somehow that night, and sleep or some other kind of absence of consciousness came.

Uncertain what time it was, she felt the manacles released. A blanket covered her shoulders. She looked up. It was a man, a guard. She recognised him as the officer who had come to her cell on the first day.

He pulled her up with gentle hands, then as her legs gave way, her swept her up and carried her from the cell. He placed her in another where there was a cot and more blankets.

'I'm sorry but I will have to take you back there before morning, but at least until then…'

Francesca looked at his face. It was the first time she had seen any emotion expressed by any of her guards.

Whispering through cracked and broken lips, she said, 'Why…?'

'Say it again, I didn't hear.'

'Why did you do this?'

'I am a soldier. This is not why I joined the Wehrmacht. I

joined to fight for my country, not torture women. Hush now. I will come back in time. Egger is out of town, but if they know I have done this, there will be trouble. Sleep if you can.'

She heard the door shut and she curled up to try to warm herself. Some kind of sleep came and in that blackness the next thing she heard was the door opening and she realised it was time to be cold, to be in pain; if only death would come, too.

2

Hunger, terrifying dreams and pain were all she experienced. It had to finish and she knew it. She would never tell Egger what he wanted to know. She knew this now and clinging to that knowledge brought her some kind of satisfaction. Francesca longed for it to end. Perhaps, she thought, the next time they put her into that filthy water, she could succeed in drowning herself. Her failure the previous day annoyed her, through the curtains of pain and confusion.

The day faded and night came. For Francesca, it was just the passing of another day of suffering to be waved away in the hope the next would be her last. She sat propped up against the wall, naked and alone. She thought of Seppo again. The thoughts made her wonder where he was. Remembering their last moments in bed, she tried to smile, but the effort induced pain in her cracked and swollen lips, leaving her with only a flicker of movement.

And Charles? She wondered to what place he had disappeared. Had he gone back to Paris? Was he hiding in the woods with the other Partisans? No, she thought not; he would want to avoid Seppo; seeing the big Finn again would in all likelihood cause Charles pain.

A memory of her father came then and how he would dry her hair in front of the fire when she was a child. His rough farmer's hands would become gentle, with soft movements. He used to sing to her then, songs of France and songs of childish heroes. Her voice cracked and faint, she began to sing. She reflected the sound would seem terrible to a passerby, but she continued trying somehow to dispel the isolation, the lonliness accentuating her pain.

It must have been very late when she saw the lights come on in the corridor outside. Her cell door opened and the two guards she recognised from her torture sessions, appeared. Unshackling her, they dragged her to her feet and away. She thought she knew what was coming. Anticipating the icy waters, she looked forward to ending the Hell into which circumstance had plunged her.

The interrogation room was the same, the blanket with the instruments to her right and the enamel bath to her left. She felt almost eager. She had held out for many days, how long, she could not tell, but now at last, she had both the will and the determination to inhale the grubby bath-water.

The room seemed more crowded than before as she peered through the swollen slits her eyes had become. With Egger, were two other officers. One of them was the man who had covered her with the blanket. He looked away when she caught his eye. The other, a small squat fellow, was drinking from a bottle. She recognised it for brandy. Egger took it from him and drank, too. Francesca realised they were all very drunk.

Egger picked up a whip-handle from the table. On the end was a spiked ball, fastened by a chain. He held it up in front of

Francesca.

'This, my dear Francesca, is a new toy. Klaus here made it especially for you. I have told him about your intransigence. I will ask you one more time. Where is the picture?'

There was no pretence today. He did not even intend to hide what he wanted from her in front of the others and she thought this was strange. She said nothing. Anger overcame her. Why not the water torture? Was she to be robbed even of that?

'Here,' Egger said, gesturing the chair. Her guards pulled her across to the chair and laid her face down across it, her knees resting on the hard, frigid concrete floor.

'Now,' Egger said, his speech slurred, 'now I give you one last chance, then we will try my new mace.'

Silence. She waited. What was he going to do?'

She felt the pain and heard the crack as the spiked ball descended square on her back. Pain like electric, red-hot needles shot down her legs. It was more pain than she had ever experienced in childbirth. It was beyond anything she had ever imagined. Then a dull ache, but still the electrical feeling in her legs, burning, biting.

Blackness came then. The voices faded, the pain too. Nothingness descended and all she was aware of was deep black.

3

Francesca became aware of a bright light. Her eyes opened with difficulty but the sight greeting them made her confused. It was a view of a civilised room, a grand piano to her right and elegant pictures hanging on the walls. A carpet of thick-piled, red and green wool adorned the floor and a French window stood closed in front of her. She sat in a chair facing the view from the doors and she could see snow, stretching forwards to a tree line of tall pines.

She would have thought it was all a bad dream, had it not been for the excruciating pain in her back. She lay face up, slumped across a pillow, and her legs felt weak but still moveable. She flexed her toes and realised she had not lost function there.

Leaning in towards her, she saw a face. It was Egger. He spoke with a soft inflexion, calm and almost pleasant. It did not fool her.

'Now Francesca, I hope the clothes I selected are adequate. I admire you. Few people could have held out as long as you have. Your friends will all be dead soon, anyway, so Didier can wait until we have another suspect. At least we know the name. I want the picture. Where have you hidden it?'

Francesca had nothing to say to him and she thought he knew that, too. Glaring up at him, she tried to spit, but her mouth was too dry, her bruised and bloody lips disobedient to her defiance.

Egger's face contorted. The rage expressed in it showed her who he was. He was a devil, a beast. He poked her chest with his finger, seeking the bruises his handiwork had created. He slapped her face hard.

His voice high-pitched and screaming, he cried, 'Where is it?'

He seemed to recover his composure then and turned to someone else in the room, 'Get rid of her. I never want to lay eyes on this stupid woman again. There must be a train for garbage like this.'

The pain of her return to the Mairie forced tears from her

swollen eyes and whimpers from her mouth. Soldiers pushed her into the back of a truck and the driver seemed in a hurry. The swaying and cornering jolted her and her back felt as if a hundred spiked balls were being driven into it. She noticed for the first time since her last interview with Egger, how she was dressed in a bright yellow, flowery dress, a summery frock useless to keep out the cold.

Unable to walk, they dragged her to her cell in the "kitch-ens" and chained her as before. This time there were four others, none of them in a better state than she was. None of them spoke. Each of them knew what was to come, either a firing squad outside, or a train-ride to a death camp.

Surprised, she saw the guard-officer who had helped her in the night. She heard a conversation in quiet German but the only words she could decipher were "Birkenau" and "mor-gen". The words made no particular sense to her, but the officer directed his men to her and they took off her manacles. Their hands were not gentle but they took her away into another cell, the one with the bed and the blankets.

Time passed and she seemed to sleep or faint; she remained uncertain which it was, once she awakened. The door rattled. Soldiers came.

Again, this endless dragging by German soldiers. She won-dered now if they would shoot her. She welcomed it. Her back was a continuous source of pain, worse with each passing hour, and the radiation of the pain into the front of each thigh seemed to rob her of any ability to stand.

Up the stairs, along the corridor and finally fresh, cold air on her face. She opened her eyes and saw the square outside the Mairie in the early morning light. Surely, they would not shoot her here? Perhaps she was here to wait for a transport to the station? It seemed confusing and puzzling.

The soldiers took her down the stone steps and released her in front of the building. Her legs buckled beneath her and she lay there as her captors turned away. They could have been dumping a sack of potatoes from the way they turned away, uncaring and unseeing.

Francesca tried to stand, but unable to get up, she crawled. Her fingers were numb, her limbs stiff, but crawl, she did, to anywhere but this place of agony. One of the guards came back and aimed a kick at her leg, but to her amazement, a voice rose in the snow-bound little square.

'Stop that at once.'

It was a woman's voice. One Francesca recognised. The person stood at her side and racked by pain as she was, she turned to see who it could be; who would defy the might of the German army?

It was Marquite. In her hand, she held an umbrella. She poked the soldier in the chest with it.

'Do you want to visit the Mairie?' he said. 'This is a prisoner, a Partisan. If you don't put that down, I may shoot you, you old bag.'

'My brother is the Judge Dubois. If you so much as touch me, there will be chaos in this town and I will make certain your superiors know it is your fault. Now get out of my way.'

On one knee, she knelt at Francesca's side. She looked up at the soldier.

She said, 'So this is how you brave Germans treat women? You should be ashamed. You have no honour.'

The man appeared less self-assured than before. The fierceness in Marquite's voice seemed to intimidate him, and he turned, shrugging his shoulders.

'Leave them, just stupid French whores anyway,' he said to his colleague.

261

The second soldier said something in German and they both laughed as they ascended the stairs and disappeared into the Mairie.

Francesca wondered whether she was dreaming. Angels did not ride bicycles; they did not threaten armed soldiers with umbrellas and verbal abuse. But of one thing she was sure; here was an angel, sent for her deliverance, for her salvation.

She had to lean on the bicycle to stand and with one hand on the saddle and leaning across, her friend supported her somehow and they made it out of the square.

'My poor child, my poor child,' was all Marquite could say. Francesca heard the grief in her voice and saw the tears streaming down the old woman's furrowed face. She wanted somehow to assuage her sadness, to say it was all right, but no audible words came from her cracked and swollen lips.

Turning right, they entered the top of the market square, a short, wide lane with elm trees marching down its sides, where the space in between was the designated area for stalls on Saturday.

They passed the Prefecture and the café and then Francesca glimpsed the gallery. The door hung from its hinges and as they entered, she saw the destruction. Every painting lay shredded and torn in the centre of the front room. The Germans had ripped the place apart and both women knew why. Francesca also knew they had not found what they sought and it made the pain in her back seem almost worthwhile.

Chapter 34

1

Their entry into the wrecked gallery was a staggering lurch and Francesca could not stand after they crossed the threshold.

Looking up from the icy floor, she said, 'I can't walk any longer. My legs …'

'I will get help. Here.' Marquite said. The old woman removed her coat and scarf. She draped the coat over Francesca and pillowed her head with the scarf, muttering all the time. She tucked the coat around her injured friend as best she could and left. Francesca thought she must have swooned then, for the next thing of which she was aware was hands lifting her onto a hard surface and a painful, bumpy ride in a cart or some similar vehicle.

She next awakened in the English House, lying on a mattress in one of the front rooms. There were two unfamiliar faces staring down at her from her bed on the floor. One was elderly like Marquite and the other a little older than Francesca. Both were well dressed and looked to Francesca more as if they were attending a function at the Town Hall, than muttering over her battered face.

Marquite appeared.

Francesca, her voice no more than a cracked whisper, said, 'Marquite. Where am I?'

'Why, in my home.'

'How…'

'When I could not move you, I asked for help. Michelle and Madeleine are members of the Women's Guild, like me. We have been friends for years. Madeleine's husband is the chairman of the bank and Michelle's husband is a farmer. He brought you here in his cart.'

'Drink…' she muttered.

Marquite held a spoon to her lips. It tasted like some kind of broth but Francesca could only manage a few mouthfuls.

'Slow and gentle. We will not leave your side. Eugene is coming. He said he would look to see how badly hurt you are but you know what these men are like. He insists he does not have the skills to help, though I suppose he will know who has.'

'Egger beat me, broke my back.'

'Yes, those German pigs will pay one day. But they let you go. We have been taking it in turns to watch the Mairie, hoping for news of you, for twelve days. I was going to give up, but there you were. They spat you out like a lemon pip, and here you are.'

'Are they still watching?'

'We have seen no one. When they let someone out, they don't usually bother with them again. Perhaps it is because they have what they needed from them.'

'I told them nothing.'

'I know,' Marquite said. 'I thought they had shot you because they did not find the picture. You must be strong, like my husband was.'

'Nothing. You hear?'

Francesca tried to raise herself up but the pain in her back made it impossible to move.

'Now, then, my little one. Hush now. Rest here and we

will tend you.'

There was the sound of a doorbell and Marquite said, 'Ah, that must be Eugene.'

Doctor Dubois entered and to Francesca he looked cherubic. She thought how all he needed now was a set of wings and he would ascend to heaven. His round face and encouraging demeanour reassured her he could help.

He removed his round gold-rimmed spectacles and making soft tut-tutting noises, he replaced his spectacles and examined her from top to toe, shaking his head and then muttering.

'They have beaten you very badly, my little assistant,' he said, his voice soft.

'My back?'

'I don't know. You say the pain goes into your legs?'

'Not now, but there is a numbness.'

'Yes. I know. This needs an x-ray. We need to get you to the hospital, I'm afraid.'

Marquite said, 'The Germans might come for her again if they know where she is.'

'Why would they do that?' he said.

'She told them nothing. They may come back for her.'

'You think they won't search here then? You are mad.'

'Eugene, she must have help and peace and quiet.'

'What are you, Doctor Arnaud all of a sudden? I'm the doctor, not you.'

Their banter continued for more minutes and Francesca followed less and less of it. Her thoughts took her far away. She was thinking about Seppo. She was wondering where he could be and whether he was alive and well. Charles came into her mind, too. She realised she missed them both more now than even when she was in the Mairie. At least then, she had no hope of seeing either of them. Now she needed them and that need grew from day to day.

In the end, Doctor Dubois consented to obtain the opinion of an orthopaedic surgeon of his acquaintance in Lyon before moving Francesca.

The consultation resulted in an x-ray at the hospital and a plaster of Paris jacket.

Francesca remained with Marquite. Her three months' sentence in a rigid plaster jacket frustrated and angered her. She began to think of Egger as the sole reason for all her ills. She began to top up her hatred. That hatred kept her determined. It fed her will power and despite the cumbersome shell making her every waking hour inconvenient and difficult, she struggled on. Through it all, almost like a forgotten word on the tip of her tongue, she thought about Seppo and wondered where he was and if he were safe.

Doctor Dubois' sense of humour failed to amuse her, either. His references to "turtles" and "tortoises" on his visits stimulated no laughter, although she knew he was only trying to elevate her mood.

It was March before the flashbacks eased. Marquite might be washing her hair and her mind would fill with a vivid scene of the enamel bath with its yellow water, or see Egger's face with its knife-cut smile. The worst of these unbidden visions, these pictures of the past, was the rubber truncheon, striking, beating her flesh. Some objects triggered the visions; sometimes it was the sound of distant laughter, bringing back not memories, but a reliving of the moment. When this happened to her, her mouth would dry up, her pulse would race, and she could feel both her heart thumping beneath her ribs and a cold sweat breaking out on her forehead and hands.

At times like that, she thought of Seppo and calmed. Her mental pictures of the man she loved were strong, visual, and

266

sufficient to drive the living memories from her mind. Although she had not heard anything about Josephine's group, she felt certain he was alive and he would find her in the end. She missed his strong hands on her body, she missed his deep masculine laugh, but most of all she missed his mental support.

The nightmares, too, were a source of terror. They always involved Egger and she often awoke in a sweat as the torturer's face appeared in some other, alien setting. The recurrent nightmare was of holding her daughter in the night, cuddling her, reassuring her and as she looked at the face of her child, it changed with brutal suddenness into that of the evil SD officer.

Both the waking and sleeping terrors faded with time. Doctor Dubois said he thought it was a testament to her resilience, but Francesca knew the truth. It was an overwhelming hatred and her certainty that she would achieve vengeance on the man who had made her life into a living hell. She plotted and planned. Each scheme seemed so real and so plausible, but when she re-examined them in the cold, clear light of reflexion, she realised they all depended on her being someone else. She found, in the end, she was no Mata Hari and killing her adversary herself would not be within her grasp. She recognised she needed to bide her time and wait for the war to finish because then people would hear or read her story. She nurtured her hatred as if she clutched a growing child to her breast, waiting for the violent infant, like some kind of succubus, to grow enough for her to release it from her nurturing.

Two months later, there was the sound of celebration in the streets; liberation had come.

2

Although standing or sitting remained agonising, Francesca could walk without pain. She formed the habit of walking for an hour every day. It seemed to her the exercise strengthened her back, although climbing stairs was only possible on a good day and there were few of those. On a warm spring day, with the sun shining above her, she and Marquite went to town. Crossing the bridge over the Dordogne, she saw that its brown waters seemed to swirl beneath her as if welcoming the new day, a French day, and a day without German oppression. The countryside was green and yellow to Francesca's eyes and she knew there was something to celebrate at last, something perhaps to dispel the gruesome visions in her head.

Hundreds lined the streets and the jostling crowd made hard going for the two women. At the market square, they encountered a yelling crowd bustling like a wind-tossed cornfield. Curious, they managed to edge their way forward, though Francesca found it hard, since each shove and jostle jarred her back. No one obstructed them, but like all crowds, the people moved as one large monster, calling and gesturing. The two women became separated in the mob, but Francesca became filled with curiosity about what was could be causing all the commotion. It took huge efforts on Francesca's part to push herself through to the front of the gathering.

A six-foot platform stood beside the monument to the Great War dead. It looked rickety, as if someone had erected it in haste. Upon the platform stood two Communists with rifles. In front of them and facing where Francesca stood were two women and a man. She realised two things at once. First, she understood this was a trial of sorts. Secondly, she recognised the face of one of the prisoners.

268

It was Charles.

She shouted. She waved her arms. No one took any notice. It was as if she were invisible to all those who stood around her. She heard one of the Communists read the charges.

'Natalie Dulong; collaborator, sleeping with German soldiers—head shave. Bernadette de Valois; collaboration and sleeping with enemy soldiers—head shave. Charles Duprey; treachery and passing information to the SD—death by firing squad, sentence to be carried out tomorrow morning.'

Francesca became confused then. Charles, a traitor? No. it was impossible. He was a patriot. She knew him to be a Partisan, a fighter.

Before she could force anyone to hear her objections, a familiar voice came to her from the left. Turning her head, she recognised the speaker. It was Josephine, her face drawn and pale, and her eyes alight with a fire Francesca had never seen before. If she were here... Francesca heard her words as if they came from a long way away as she searched the faces around the young Partisan.

Seeing no one she recognised, she concentrated on what Josephine was saying.

'This man led us into an ambush. He was once one of us. He betrayed us and the sauerkrauts massacred us. He is a traitor and deserves to die.'

The crowd roared.

As soon as the hubbub died down, Francesca, with weak legs tripping and stumbling, made her way to the front of the gathering. She turned to face the crowd.

'No. You're wrong. It cannot be true. He was an editor of an underground newspaper in Paris.'

'Shut up. He's a traitor,' a voice called from the back of the crowd.

'No he isn't. He saved me from the SD. He fought with the Partisans here.'

The crowd made catcalls. Others gesticulated.

'I saw him try to kill an SD officer. He shot a German soldier. He would never betray France. This cannot be true.'

She looked up at Charles but his expression showed no welcome, not even recognition. Tears of hopelessness began to form in Francesca's eyes. This was a nightmare. Charles was her friend and the war had ended. There was no place for this wickedness in the world. She saw the faces in the crowd, angry faces projecting themselves into her field of vision. She realised much of the rancour was directed now towards her.

Francesca heard a female voice to her left again. It was Josephine. Hope stirred within her and she turned towards the Partisan while scouring the crowd for Seppo's smiling face. He was nowhere to be seen. She faced her former fellow Partisan.

'Josephine, how can you denounce Charles in this way? He was always one of us.'

Josephine walked towards her with clenched fists. Above the background cacophony, she said, 'That man is responsible for Jules' death and almost everyone in my group. Seppo knows, too. Now do you understand? Charles is a traitor. He led us into an ambush and when all was done, Seppo and I saw him talking to the German officer who led the attack. I barely escaped with my own life. Jules died covering our escape. You hear me? My man died in front of me because of this man's treachery. Now, tell me what a patriot this man is.'

'There must be an explanation. I have known him for ten years. He would no more betray his country than I would.'

Josephine turned to the crowd behind her. 'I say he is guilty. I saw his treachery myself. If this woman says he isn't, then maybe she is in league with him.'

Many turned towards Francesca. There was only anger expressed in those faces. Francesca shrank back. She said, 'I was tortured by the SD. I told them nothing. You think I'm scared of you? There is nothing you can do to me I haven't suffered already. I tell you, I know this man to be loyal.'

Hands reached out for her. They pulled her towards the platform. Unable to ascend the steps, she felt her legs fold beneath her and she lay in the mud, looking up at her attackers. For the first time, she felt scared. These were her people. The world was insane. They had all gone mad. Surely, they knew who she was. They must know. Yet they declaimed her for complicity in treachery.

A man wearing a long grey raincoat and a black beret grabbed her arm and pulled her up and towards the steps.

'Get up there where you belong, you German-lover.'

The faces around her were ugly. They showed the beast she had once seen in Egger's eyes, baying for blood, anyone's blood.

'Shave her head,' she heard someone say.

'Yes, shave her.'

Others took up the call.

'I've done nothing. Nothing.'

Hands reached towards her. They pulled her and as she staggered forward, others dragged her to a bench next to the two women collaborators, under one of the old elm trees.

Where was Josephine? Why did she not intervene? Surely, she knew Francesca was no traitor?

A short, plump man approached; he held a cutthroat razor in his hand. Although most of the crowd concentrated on the platform, about twenty or thirty men and women stood looking at Francesca. The man stood poised, razor in hand, and pulled at her hair.

Chapter 35

1

Francesca looked at the faces around her. She wanted to fight. She wanted now to defend herself but knew resistance was futile. She felt as helpless as she had in the Mairie. There seemed to be nothing she could do but be as passive with her own people as she had been with the Germans. Somewhere inside her, she found the similarity ironic. She did not hate any of these people who leered at her here. They were not German but they were using the same kind of wickedness to expunge their own hurt, the damage done to them all by the occupying forces so recently gone from their midst.

As the razor touched the skin of her forehead, a figure appeared in front of her. It was a tall, blond hulk of a man and his voice held a tone of outrage.

'What the hell do you think you are doing?'

It was Seppo.

Francesca wanted to shout with relief and pleasure. He was alive. He was here.

She saw her man grab the barber's hand in one of his big fists and her heart skipped. The razor fell to the cobbles at Seppo's feet. Francesca stood up and encircled her arms about his neck. He held her to him and she yelped with pain.

'What?' he said.

'My back, it was damaged.'

'Your back?'

A broad, stocky man approached. He grabbed Seppo's arm. Another followed close behind, holding a sten-gun.

'This woman is a …'

In the space of time it took the man to speak those four words, Seppo released Francesca and his right fist flew forwards as he turned. Catching Seppo's blow on the side of the jaw, the man slumped to the cobbles as if he were a sack of potatoes. The second man tried to level the gun at the Finn. Seppo was on him with frightening speed, surprising for such a big man. He wrenched the gun from the hapless man as if he were taking a toy from a child. He struck him with the butt. The sten-gun-carrier fell to the ground. He did not get up.

Seppo looked at the crowd. The mass of people were becoming aware of the disturbance. Seppo fired several shots into the air.

At the top of his deep voice he shouted, 'Anyone here wish to argue with me?'

Silence spread through the mob. Francesca saw angry faces; men and women were muttering. One of the Communist Partisans called across.

'I know you. You're the Finn. Stay out of this.'

Seppo said, 'This is Francesca Pascal. She is a great woman. A great patriot. She suffered torture at the hands of the SD when no one here lifted a finger to help her. She is my woman. I'll kill anyone who touches her.'

A voice from the crowd shouted, 'She's a friend of the traitor.'

'I was friend of his too once. You know I'm no traitor. This man needs trial by a court, not by a mob. You hear? You will all be murderers. He must be handed over to the authorities.'

Josephine approached. She reached up and hugged the big man, then stepped away, but threw an angry glance towards Francesca. She spoke to Seppo in rapid, low tones and Francesca could not hear what they said. The crowd watched, silent, threatening.

Josephine turned to the assembled people.

'That woman is innocent. The traitor on the platform is not. Carry out the sentence.'

Francesca called out, 'No.'

Seppo backed towards her, holding the gun in front of him.

He said, 'We must go. You don't know the whole story. We must go.'

'But… not Charles.'

'We must go. This is a mad place, a place of revenge and death. Come with me. I love you.'

They faced the crowd and retreated, backing up as far as the trees and Seppo turned, grabbing her hand. As Francesca turned, she saw the mob turn away from them and face the platform again. She could do nothing more and she knew it. The big man's hand held hers and the warmth of that grip felt to her as if another angel had descended and was leading her away from Hell itself. She could not run but she walked as fast as she could and Seppo placed his arm around her.

A black Renault stood by the kerb near the road leading to the Mairie. Seppo unlocked it and they climbed in. He leaned across and kissed her lips. Then he held her at arm's length and looked into her eyes.

'I knew you were alive,' she said.

'I escaped north after Jules was killed. Josephine went in a different direction. I joined the Communist group in the north and later we fought in the mountains. I never stopped

274

thinking of you. You have had a terrible time.'

'Yes. Egger. He must pay.'

'Not your old ideas of revenge, surely?'

'I can't be with you or anyone else until he is dead. He broke my back. He tortured me for twelve days. Will you help me?'

'I would do anything to be with you. You know that. Where to now?'

'The Maison Anglais. I'm living here. Marquite has looked after me as if I were her daughter. She has been my saviour.'

He squeezed her hand and pressed the starter. Driving across the bridge, Seppo was smiling.

'What will happen to Charles?'

'You heard them. There is no civil administration here, only the British army. The judges worked for the Germans, even that Dubois fellow. The Communists seem to have taken over for now. They may well shoot Charles in the morning and I for one will not be sorry. He did betray us, but I can't understand why. Josephine and I saw him talking to a German officer over Jules' body. They embraced.'

'Will they let me see him?'

'Why would you want to do that?

'He was my closest friend for many years; he helped me raise my daughter. If there is anything I can do to help him, I would.'

'That traitor? You're mad.'

'Look, I must see Egger dead, but even so. I must speak to Charles. Maybe it is only that I want to know why he did it, if he did it.'

'Believe me, he betrayed us.'

There was silence then, the car bumping on cobbles and swaying on the corners. They reached the Arnaud house and remained in the car. At first, they said nothing, as if they were adolescents confronted by their closeness and neither daring to begin. Then slowly, as if the re-living of it was the most difficult thing in the world, Francesca told him her story. She described Egger's abuses of her in detail, as if leaving nothing out would assuage her of the pain and chase away the nightmares. It was as if she hoped Seppo could dissipate it all with some simple words of endearment and she need no longer suffer the mental canvases painted by memories.

When they emerged from the car, there were tears in the big man's eyes.

2

Like everything else the Communist Partisans created, the "prison" where they confined Charles only approximated what it should have been. They had no access to the Prefecture, and its cells, which someone had locked and boarded up. They chose the baker's shop next door to the café and put their prisoner in an upstairs room with guards posted outside. Seppo drove the Renault to the doorstep and helped Francesca out. She smiled as his strong hands grasped hers and felt as if his strength made everything in her life easier. She knew, also, her love for him would see her through the torments threading her mind. Despite her own pain and the time without Seppo, she still thought of Charles.

Francesca's internal visions of Charles always pictured him in his role of friend. She recalled how he had always shown patience and kindness towards Marie and how when either of them needed him, he was there. How could she contemplate neglecting to visit him now?

The baker's shop was similar in construction to the gallery. There was a shop front and a back room, and a curtain separated the two. The baker had extended the back room into the kitchen and this formed the work area where they kneaded, proved and baked the bread. The place still smelled of yeast. The guard in the shop guided them upstairs and in one room, there was a makeshift cell. Another Partisan armed with a shotgun sat on a chair outside and Francesca saw yet another inside the room with Charles, where he sat in a corner, wrists behind his back.

The guard inside the room refused to leave until Seppo persuaded him. She was alone now with her condemned friend as the dim light of an oil-lamp shed a flickering light from the centre of the floor. He did not look up when she entered, nor when the guard left.

'Charles?' she said.

Silence.

'Charles, I'm here to see you.'

The slow movement of his head as he looked up made her wonder if he was drunk or drugged, but when she saw his eyes she realised they were closed by swelling. They must have beaten him, and Francesca empathised. It was only months since she had seen the world through the same red slits.

It seemed to her the world was becoming a confused and twisted portrait, like a painting by some surrealist, where reality overlapped with nightmare, and the evildoers left behind them a legacy of their cruel actions to be taken up by those who remained. Like a disease, the wickedness spread, and even the ordinary people of France were now infected.

She crossed the room and kneeling, placed a gentle hand on his face.

'Charles, it is Francesca. Don't you know me?'

'Yes, I know you.'

'What has happened? They say you betrayed everyone. Jules and Josephine and the others. Tell me the truth.'

'I have nothing to say to you. It's all your fault.'

She took her hand away as if an electric shock had passed between them.

'My fault? How can it be my fault?'

'You took Seppo away from me. I loved him.'

'How can you love someone if they never showed you any kind of affection apart from being friendly?'

'You stole him away before I could tell him. In the end, there was nothing left for me but pain. I wanted him, but if I couldn't have him, I wanted to be certain you never could either. I failed and so I'm here. Never forget it's your fault, you bitch.'

'Charles, I loved you. I loved your friendship and I owed my very life to you. I am not responsible for Seppo's feelings for me. You must know that.'

'You knew my feelings before you tempted him away.'

'I knew you were infatuated but you had no reason to embark on these fantasies. He isn't like you.'

'You've certainly proved that, haven't you? All my life I have sought a companion, a true lover. Every time I thought I had found him, he turned out to be wrong in some way. All my fucking life. The loneliness burns you in the end. It sets you on fire. You will never understand the strength of it. You took from me the only man I knew would be right for me. You destroyed my life. You, with your tits and your fanny. You stole Seppo from me. And now? Here to gloat; to rub my nose in my failure. I hate you even more now than before and God knows that was intense.'

'This is ridiculous. I came here to see if there was anything

I could do to help you.'

'Yes. Yes, there is.'

'What? I'll do anything you ask of me.'

'Go away and let me die in peace. That's all I want from you.'

'Please Charles. Did you really do what they said?'

'Yes. I knew if I couldn't get them to kill you, at least I could save Seppo from you. Egger wouldn't allow you to be harmed. He found you interesting, he said.'

'You talked about me to Egger?'

Charles smiled this time.

'You stupid cow. Egger knew about you from the moment you set foot in the town. He knew who I was and he traced us to Bergerac. He even knew what pictures you took. The Rodin sketch. He wanted that as well. You won't find it in the remains of your pictures; he's got it.'

'What else did you tell him?'

'I told him you were in with the Partisans and you could lead him to them. I told him where you were and what you carried that night they arrested you. It was only your silence that made me lead them into the ambush.'

'How could you know? You weren't with them then?'

'I kept in touch with Roland. He said he was expecting a message that day. He wasn't sure whether they were on to him and whether he should try to escape.'

'You told them about him, too?'

'They arrested him before they took you. I hope Egger made you as comfortable as you deserve.'

'Charles, despite anything anyone says, even you, I forgive you. I know about love. I understand you better than you think. I'm sorry for it all. If I could turn back the clock, I would. What makes it worse is that Marie loved you.'

'Marie? Why bring her into this?'

'Because she loved you. Had you no feelings for her when she died? And you betrayed her mother? I don't understand you anymore. It's as if you have become someone else overnight.'

'I loved Marie. She was the nearest thing I ever had in my life approximating to a daughter. True, she was not my flesh and blood but it doesn't matter. One can love many children, even if they are the bastard daughter of some prick who never made the grade. I loved her anyway. You never asked me what I felt when you were wrapped in your own selfish grief. You never asked what I felt, did you?'

'I didn't understand. Please, Charles, say you forgive me.'

'Forgive you? You have cost me everything, even my beliefs. In one way, Marie's death made me face reality. I still blame you. If you had been a real mother to her, you would never have allowed her to cross that platform. I hate you for that as well. She was our little girl. What do you think? You say, "forgive me," and all is forgotten? No. I will go to my grave, cursing you. Now, get out and leave me alone.'

She stood up. Looking down at her old friend, she almost began again, but she realised it was meaningless. As she walked to the door, the realisation that Egger had played a game with her and the other Partisans, fed her anger as much as the torture, almost as much as her hatred over Marie's death. Egger had to pay.

Chapter 36

1

Liberation had come, yet for Francesca it seemed to be nothing but an anti-climax. When she looked around, there were still deprivations, fighting still continued in Germany and nothing had righted itself, in her opinion. The dissatisfaction she felt seemed to her to be a reverse mirror image reflected in Seppo's gentle care of her. He fussed, he discussed, and he listened. It was like a de-briefing. He questioned everything until she told him every detail.

They lived in Marquite's house, they drank her wine, and they ate with the old woman. Yet, Marquite never expressed dissent; she seemed almost invigorated by the presence of the "love birds", as she called them. It could have been a happy time, had it not been for the brooding sense of hatred and anger still stirring in Francesca's heart.

The ruminant thoughts of what she had been through gnawed at her and her mind harped back to the torture in the Mairie inflicted by Egger. She began to realise how even describing her worst nightmares to her man could not assuage her need to see justice; she no longer called it revenge.

Egger. The fact of his breathing the same air as she did was an insult to everything in the beliefs the war had left her. Egger. If there were a God in heaven, He must surely make the torturer pay. Seppo and she made love and the short moments when she held him in her arms took it all away, but in the cold blackness of a long night, as he lay by her side snoring, she ruminated. She needed to see Egger dead. It was all she could think of as she went to sleep and it was there in her mind when she awoke, too.

One quiet autumn morning over breakfast, as Seppo munched a brioche at Marquite's table, she knew she had to talk to him about her need. Birdsong outside, audible through the open window, did nothing to chase away the darkness in her mind, her very soul.

'I want him dead.'

'What?'

'Egger.'

'What about him?'

'I cannot rest until he is dead.'

Seppo spread some honey on his brioche. He said, 'He will be shot, I guess.'

'Do you know if he was captured?'

'No, but I can find out, I suppose.'

'Will you do that for me? I need somehow to know he is not safely hiding in Switzerland or some other safe place, with my Rodin sketch and a pile of things stolen from dead Jews. If he escaped, it would drive me mad.'

'Madder, you mean. I sometimes think it has become an obsession of yours, my love.'

'No. Not an obsession, simply a desire for justice. Can't you see how, if he escapes, my life will have been ruined for nothing? Marie will have died for nothing, too. If Egger is only imprisoned and he lives on, my life will ebb as his grows.'

'No. We will build our own future together. Can we not let the past take care of itself? We should look ahead, not back.'

She stood up. There was a look of utter fury on her face.

'Don't you care? Charles cared. He at least knew what Marie meant to me. The Germans took her from me and Egger was responsible. He has to pay. It isn't the pain he inflicted on my body, it is the pain he burned into my mind. He knew who I was. He wanted to shove his dick into me because he had killed my daughter. It amused him to think he could abuse us both, don't you see?'

'Calm yourself, Francesca. There is nothing we can do. He will be arrested by the English or the Americans. They will hang him or shoot him, as he deserves. Maybe your statement will be enough to hang him. We can track what has happened to him if we approach the authorities. I will go into town and find out, if you like.'

'I don't know. Maybe he got away. Maybe he escaped to Switzerland.'

'If he did, I'll find out. I have friends in the British army. I'll ask them.'

'You promise?'

'Yes, I promise. Now sit. Enjoy the real coffee and don't think about it for the moment. Trust me.'

'I will go with you.'

'Sure?'

'Yes. I have to know if he escaped or if they've got him.'

'All right, this afternoon.'

Francesca looked at his face. She felt her mind was in greater turmoil now than even when Marquite salvaged her in front of the Mairie. All she had heard so far was that Egger was not in Bergerac when the American troops came through. The military authorities took statements from anyone who cared to tell them about war crimes and Francesca was one of the first to tell her story. They told her nothing in return, however, and as the days passed by, she felt she was drifting. At least during the war, she felt as if she had a purpose. Now, she felt like a woman in a boat cut adrift in a calm sea, safe but aimless, floating further and further away from her anchorage, achieving nothing.

2

When they set off, Seppo drove the little Renault as if it were his pride and joy. It was polished and clean and the engine, which Seppo had serviced himself, purred like a cat. Crossing the bridge brought back memories for Francesca. She recalled the first time she met Marquite and the old woman's courage in defying the Germans who stopped them. She shook her head, wondering once more what it was about the old woman that inspired such respect, even from enemy soldiers. She wondered whether it was a maternal, or even matriarchal, aura she carried within her, recognisable to almost any man.

They drew up outside the Mairie. Seppo parked the car next to a black Mercedes and she wondered whether it belonged to a Frenchman, now that the German military were no longer here. They climbed the steps and even that made her shudder. She still recalled how the soldiers had dragged her towards Egger's office when they captured her. In the event, they went upstairs, trudging up the red carpet and onto the wide stone landing. She noted how there were no pictures on the walls of the corridor as they walked to the end office, where the temporary British Commissioner was supposed to be stationed.

They knocked and entered the outer office. A young British lieutenant stood up and looked at them, curious but not unfriendly.

'Can I help you?'

'Yes,' Francesca said, 'we're looking for the commissioner.'

'Well, he's not really a commissioner, he's a colonel. Who should I say is calling?'

'I am Francesca Pascal and this is Seppo Letinen. We were with the resistance and we want to enquire about a German officer who might have been arrested.'

Seppo nodded when Francesca mentioned his name. His English was borderline when it came to communicating with the British.

'Wait there,' said the lieutenant.

He disappeared behind the frosted glass of the door and became a faint ghost gliding beyond it as Francesca watched. She wondered whether the colonel would be prepared to see her.

Presently, the lieutenant came back. He smiled at Francesca and said, 'Colonel Bond will see you now.'

Entering the office, Francesca noted the man who stood behind the desk. He was short and broad, more stocky than plump, and his face sported a handlebar moustache, curled and waxed, the sharp tips pointing heavenward as if they might rotate at any moment and allow him to fly away. Francesca smiled at the thought, and it was her smile, which seemed to break the ice.

Colonel Bond smiled back and extended a hand.

'Cyril Bond, Colonel of Royal Engineers. I've been posted to intelligence here. Tracing the Gerry Sicherheitspolizei, you know, the SD. Can I help you?'

His hand was hard as a hammer and as she shook it, he gestured them to chairs in front of the desk. She noticed how he limped and seemed to be in pain.

'You are injured,' she said.

'Oh it's nothing. Shrapnel. Nasty stuff. Almost healed, though.'

'I am Francesca Pascal and this is Seppo Letinen, my fiancé. We hoped you could give us news about one of the SD officers who was here in Bergerac.'

'What's your interest?'

'We need to know if you catch him,' Seppo said.

'Yes,' Bond said, 'but why?'

'This man, Hauptsturmfürer Egger, is guilty of war-crimes. He tortured me, among others. I need to know if you've caught him yet.'

'Egger, you say? Yes, I know him. I'll have a look for the file. Excuse me a moment.'

Bond stood up and limped to the door. A sound of hushed, incomprehensible conversation came through the door. Presently, the colonel returned, bearing a file. It was a thick one.

'We have this fellow on file,' he said, depositing the documents on his desk and sitting down. He began to thumb through the file, grunting to himself now and again.

Bond said, 'Nasty fellow, that. As bad as Barbie in Lyon. We have plenty of witness testimony about him. Pascal was it?'

Seppo said, 'Yes. Francesca Pascal. She gave evidence a few weeks ago.'

Bond was silent for long minutes as Francesca watched him read the documents, his lips moving as he read.

'Hm. Yes, I remember now, nasty fellow. It must have been terrible for you. I'm so sorry.'

'I am recovering well,' Francesca said. 'You have news of him?'

286

'I'll have a look through.'

The colonel's face changed. His frown disappeared and he looked up at Francesca, his eyes narrowing.

'Yes, they caught him. British troops picked him up on his way to Switzerland. I interrogated him soon after.'

'You have him?' Francesca said. She realised she was sitting on the edge of her seat and leaning forward. She straightened and sat back; she had the feeling she should not show so much obvious concern.

'Yes, let me have a look at the outcome.'

Bond looked up then, his face now expressionless.

'I'm afraid I can't tell you anymore. I'm really sorry.'

'What? Where are they holding him? Here?'

'I'm not at liberty to tell you any more about it, I'm afraid. Classified.'

'Please, I beg you. He tortured me. He beat me. He broke my back. I must know where he is and what punishment he will face.'

Tears began to well up in her eyes and the colonel's eyes seemed to soften.

'Look, all I can tell you is he is in the hands of the Americans. They... I can't say more.'

'Please tell us where they hold him at least,' Seppo said.

'I can't do that, I'm afraid.'

Francesca stood up. 'After what he did to us, he deserves to die. Have you no heart? Can you not understand God's justice? I have to know what happens to him; he is a vile murderer.'

'I can't tell you, I keep saying. I would be court-martialled. You will have to find out by yourself. I can't help you. Wait here, would you, I'll fetch some tea. You'd like a cup of tea, wouldn't you?'

Bond limped his way to the door. Francesca noticed he did not take the file with him. He did not look back. She looked at Seppo. Returning her gaze, he said, 'Perhaps he won't mind if we look, eh?'

Francesca glanced at the door. Bond had shut it as he left and she understood. She crossed to the other side of the desk and examined the file. She began at the back and the first document she encountered was a memo.

```
Memo BER 3414
Transfer of prisoner AZ4279 Egger.
To be sent under full guard to the American
Rangers base at Lyon and then escorted to the
safe house at 3, Rue Andre Philip.
On hand over, no further interest in the
prisoner will be expressed.
Form A36 must be signed on release of the
prisoner to the American authorities.
Colonel John Hill
```

Further documents showed how the British troops had arrested Egger at the German border and how they had brought him back to France. Included in the file was one letter from British Intelligence in Lyon. It was addressed to a General Marks of SOE.

My dear James,

A while since we spoke, but despite the long time between drinks, I suppose the reunion will be all the sweeter, as they say. This fellow Egger seems to be a conundrum. He has probably been guilty of a lot of crimes during his brief time in Bergerac, but the Yanks want him or at least that is what I have been told by General Staff.

They (the Yanks) seem to think he would be useful to them in hunting down Communists and I'm experiencing a great deal of pressure to release him to their custody. I wondered whether you might be able to help. The damned fellow is typical of these bloody Krauts. Arrogant, and full of Third Reich dogma.

My orders are to hand him over to the Yanks in Lyon, but to be honest I would rather court martial the bastard here and now.

Anything you can do to help?

Love and kisses,

'Champagne' Cyril Bond.

Francesca shut the file again.

'We have to go to Lyon,' she said, her voice level and hard.

'Lyon? Why?'

'I know where Egger is and I even know the address. Come, we have no time to lose.'

Seppo stood up with a questioning look on his face. He said nothing more. Francesca reflected it could have been because of the determined look she knew must be plastered all over her face. As they reached the office door, they almost bumped into Colonel Bond. He was carrying a tray.

'I say, aren't you staying for a cuppa?'

Francesca said, 'Cuppa?'

'Tea, old girl. The real thing. Darjeeling; great stuff for the nerves, especially before a long drive, eh?'

'Long drive?'

'Well, you never know where the fates might take you, Madame Pascal, do you?'

'We cannot stay. I am however, delighted to have met "Champagne" Cyril Bond.'

She smiled then. The colonel smiled back and their eyes met. His clear blue eyes told Francesca everything and as they shook hands, he wished her luck.

'It is more a matter of fate than luck, Colonel,' she said.

'I am enchanted to meet you,' he said.

'That is not a good expression. The last man to say that to me was shot by the Germans on a train platform.'

'All the same, the pleasure has been all mine. Can I just say...?'

'Yes?'

'We British, despite anything you French might say about our eating habits, do believe in fairness and the honest pursuit of justice, whatever form it may take. I'm sorry I was unable to help you.'

They both knew what the colonel meant and they smiled, though Seppo seemed not to understand the thrust of their conversation. As they walked hand in hand down the long stone staircase and out of the Mairie, Francesca could feel a sense of relief, as if all her trials and tribulations would soon be over; as if revenge was at last within her grasp.

It was then she thought of her dead daughter, Marie's bleeding corpse on her knee, as she knelt on the platform in Paris. She looked up at Seppo and said, 'It will be God's justice. Nothing will stop me now.'

Chapter 37

1

Heading north through the city, Francesca wondered why she felt at home. Lyon possessed a reputation for its history, and its panache was second only to Paris. She found herself picturing the open-air cafes and the riverboats full of party-makers as the Renault chugged along the bank of the Saone. They headed north and with every mile, Francesca found her spirits elevating; hope had come, hope and a glimpse of resolution. It was as if a heavy weight had left her shoulders, as if her hope of revenge could release her from the confines of her anger. Marie could now be at rest. Francesca could now evaporate or at least diffuse the pain she had suffered in the Bergerac Mairie.

And Seppo? She knew he understood. He spent hours showing Francesca how to hold the gun and how to load it, aim it and fire it. Francesca felt like a woman who after long months of patience now would give birth and the resulting parenthood would last her for the rest of her existence.

They drove to the address in the file. Then they drove past.

'Preparation is everything,' Seppo indicated.

'Yes,' she said. 'Nothing can be allowed to go wrong.'

'We need to watch the place for a while first to make sure he is there.'

'So you say, endlessly. Surely the files would not lie?'

'Not the point. The Americans could have moved him already. Have you heard of the expression "ratline"?'

'No.'

'It's when the Americans send German monsters away by secret routes to safe countries.'

'Why would they do that? The SD are enemies, aren't they?'

'I don't understand, myself, to be honest. Some of them are experts in countering terrorists and spies. Maybe they want to use them against the Communists.'

'Who told you that?'

'I told you. I have friends in the British camp.'

'You hardly speak English; how do you communicate with them?'

'Vodka seems to loosen my tongue as well as my ears. We need to look for a pension where we can stay.'

'No. I want this over tonight.'

'Tonight? Impossible. We don't know what sort of guard there is, and we don't even know whether Egger is there. I know how you feel, God knows I understand, but we must not be hasty. Trust me.'

'Seppo, after all I have been through, do you really think I can wait? We came here to do a job. We must get on with it.'

'Then you will do it alone. I managed to stay alive when the Germans attacked and killed my brothers in Marseille. I stayed alive when a troop of the bastards almost caught François and the others when we blew up a train, and I lived through an ambush at one of our camps when they caught that little Jewish girl. You think it was because I was hasty? No. It was because I was careful. I love you too much to risk losing you now. Listen to me for once.'

Sulking, Francesca stared at the dashboard. She felt Seppo's hand on her knee squeezing, soft, and gentle. She had no reply to give. In her heart she knew he was right, but her instincts rejected his caution. Wanting Egger dead had become her obsession. She thought that as long as he lived, no peace would come to her. She saw his death as her only source of reclamation from a tormented past, and now she was looking back with pain. The agonies she suffered when her daughter died, the pain of the torture, all of it seemed soluble to her now. The answer was Egger's death and nothing anyone could say to her, not even Seppo, would make her wait with patience. Yet she knew he was right. She understood every word he spoke, but the desire for revenge ate away at her and so she remained silent and morose.

They drove around the corner of the street and on in a westerly direction. Where the Saone curved south there was a small hotel, and reluctant still, Francesca followed her man to a small and grubby room on the first floor. Seppo left almost as soon as they arrived and he would not allow her to follow. He told her it would be too risky for them both to go, but she wondered if this was some expression of the nobility in the man. She thought he was once more trying to protect her.

The hotel room seemed cold to her so she wrapped her coat tightly around and sat in a chair by the window. She examined the view as if she intended to paint it, every detail and every street corner. Francesca even looked at the faces of the people passing by below. They were not happy faces, she reflected. The war had taken so much from them all. The thought she was not alone in her grief began to dawn somewhere in her head.

A woman pulling an unwilling child along by the hand, a man lighting a cigarette, standing on a street corner; all normal things to see, but she read beyond the obvious, as any good artist would. She saw a widow, desperate and alone, wondering how her fatherless child would survive, now her man lay dead on some battlefield. She saw an angry man, lighting his last cigarette, embittered by the death of his family in the bombings.

Francesca looked up at the sky and wondered whether God could see it all, too. She wished she could summon the cowardice of religious belief in which anyone could shelter, but she shrugged off the idea. She knew what really mattered and it was the one, singular thought allowing her to hang onto sanity. Without the hope of revenge, she knew she would never survive the ending of this war. She had to have justice as she saw it.

As if the sun were rising, another picture came into her mind. It was an effigy of hope. A picture of a walled house, a departing road, and a seascape entered her mind's eye.

Le Mur Rose.

In her haste to obtain revenge, she had almost forgotten the painting. A feeling of pride came to her then. She recognised how, despite the pain and horror of her incarceration, she had protected the painting. She analysed how it was her one true contribution to her country's struggles that no one else could have made, and she felt pride stirring within her. That was it, she thought. Her purpose in resisting Egger was her way of resisting the German war machine, and she knew she had done it well. Francesca thought how, although she had not saved France, she had saved a symbol of what it was to be French, to be free.

The sun was setting and Seppo had not returned. Still she sat. Still she stared out of the window until her eyelids began to droop. Her back ached. She rubbed her eyes but the soporific effects of a long journey and the rise and fall of the feelings within her, drew her away from the conscious world and she slept, seated in the hotel chair, no longer staring down at the wide street next to the river, here in Lyon. Francesca knew, as sleep took her, Lyon would become her battleground, where all her hopes of peace would be laid bare, but not yet; a moment's pause beckoned.

2

Seppo parked the car twenty yards up the road where they could see the entrance to the building. It was an apartment block much like any other, but they both knew it was special. The mark of that singularity was a man in a dark coat shuffling from one foot to another, collar turned up to touch the brim of his hat, covering the nape of his neck. At intervals he walked up, then down, the street, always looking around, always vigilant. The bulge in his coat over his left chest told Seppo and Francesca much, even if they hadn't registered the way in which the man examined every detail of the empty street.

He glanced towards their car several times and walked past twice. The man showed no sign of interest, however, until the third time of passing. He approached the driver's side of the vehicle. Leaning forwards, he indicated for Seppo to roll down the window. Seppo raised his hands and gesticulated to indicate he could not, then made to get out of the car. The man stepped back. His right hand slipped inside his coat. The movement was fast, almost imperceptible. Francesca looked up and down the street. Not even a cat. It was the small hours after all, and the emptiness of the boulevard reassured her. She got out on her side. She stood facing the man in the hat.

Across the roof of the car, she said, 'My friend's window is stuck. Lucky it is stuck closed or we would have frozen on the journey.'

'You better move on.' He had an American accent.

'You are American?'

'Move on, lady. This place has diplomatic immunity. I'm part of the security. Now move on before we call the police.'

The speed with which Seppo opened the door made it all seem a blur to Francesca. It hit the American square on the chest. The violence of the blow threw him to the ground. He drew his gun. He had no time to level it or get off a shot. Seppo was on him in a second. A flying clenched fist under his chin threw his head back. It struck the pavement hard. The security-man lay still. Moving fast, Francesca crossed to the unconscious man, and between them they dragged him to a basement stairwell. Seppo took a rope and a handkerchief from his pocket, then tied and gagged him.

'He's not dead, is he?'

'No. We must be quick; he may wake any time.'

'Now?'

'Like we rehearsed. The actress in you must perform, cherie.'

Francesca, her heart pounding in her chest and her mouth dry as an American martini, climbed the apartment steps and stood in front of the door. Seppo followed and stood flush with the other door.

She knocked. Her small hands made only a faint tapping sound, but it was enough. The door opened by a few inches. Another American answered. He was no fool, however.

'Yeah?' he said with a New York twang.

'Your friend said to knock,' Francesca said, smiling.

'I ain't got no friends. Now beat it.'

'Please, I have an important message for the prisoner from SOE.'

'Who?'

'British Intelligence. I'm Shirley Doone. You've heard of me?'

'No. Take a hoik, sister.'

'A hoik? Look, there will be serious political problems if I don't deliver the message. At least let me in and I'll explain to your commanding officer.'

There was a long pause. Presently, the door opened a fraction more.

'Gimme da note.'

'It's not a note. It's in my head.'

'So who broke ya nose then, honey?'

'Please, let me in. I need only a few moments with Egger. Then I'll go. I could make it interesting for you afterwards, if you like.'

Francesca tried to look enticing but the feelings stirring inside made her simulated sexuality seem absurd. She changed tack.

'You have a choice. You can turn me away and face the consequences, or you can let me in. I have to deliver my message before tomorrow. You know where he's going, don't you? I can't reach him once he's gone.'

'Look, I've orders to let no one in or out. Until I get official awders to the contrairyness, no one gets in on my watch.'

'OK, I'll tell you the message but I'll have to whisper it.'

The man leaned forwards. It was to be the last thing he would recall on that day. Seppo's fist landed like a falling landslide and it threw him backwards. Francesca tried to open the door but a chain held it ajar. Seppo burst the chain with a shoulder applied to the door and they were in.

3

Seppo checked each door on the ground floor but they were locked. There was nothing to indicate to whom the apartments belonged. Confused, they started up the stairs to the first floor.

Stopping mid-way up, Francesca said, 'This is hopeless.'

She tapped her hand on the railing.

'Let's check each door and then we open every one until we find him.'

'All of them?'

'Three doors to each floor. Three floors. We'll start on the ground floor and work our way up. My shoulder may get a little...'

A sound from above made him stop in mid-sentence. Francesca heard a familiar voice. Egger.

She felt a shudder of revulsion at the sound. That voice was ingrained in her consciousness. She wondered whether it was like those dogs of Pavlov's, she'd once read about, who salivated every time the meal-bell sounded. She felt conditioned to shudder at Egger's voice.

Seppo put a finger to his lips. She said nothing.

'Keep the damned noise down will you? I am trying to sleep.'

The sound came from above and they could see a light from one of the doors on the landing. The door shut with a bang. They climbed the stairs. Both of them knew which door Egger was behind and they waited a moment. For Francesca, it was with as much anticipation as she would have experienced in waiting for a lover.

Seppo stood sideways on to the door, a Parabellum in hand, as Francesca drew her gun. The big Finn had provided her with a British Webley .38 revolver, in the hope she could manage the recoil. Days of practise had made him dubious of her aim, even with the smaller gun, but he told her it was her party and he would not do the job for her.

The big man shouldered the door. It did not give way on the first impact and Seppo tried again. The second time, the door burst open and they entered a darkened room. Francesca felt confused. She searched for the light but Seppo grabbed her hand.

'No,' he said.

With surprising stealth for such a big man, he crossed to an open doorway and stood with his back against the adjacent wall, facing Francesca. Hands shaking and holding her weapon with both hands she advanced towards the doorway.

'Who's there?' she heard Egger call.

'I have a message,' she said.

'Who are you?'

'Elise Van Meuren. British Intelligence. I have a message.'

'You broke down the door. You think I'm stupid? Where are my guards?'

'They're waiting downstairs.'

'I've got a gun. Come in with your hands up.'

In the half-light, she looked at Seppo. She had no idea what to do now. She had found Egger, but how could she reach him?

'I'll put down my weapon on this table here.'

Francesca switched on a small table lamp in the corner of the room. She placed her gun on a low table in front of a settee and she sat down.

'I'm ready,' she called.

A faint shadow seemed to move in the adjacent room. She folded her arms. Sweat began to moisten her brow but she took no notice. Her heart raced and emotions stirred in her. This was the man whose very voice reminded her of pain. The sound evoked a response of hatred and fear at the same time, deep within her. The gun was three feet away. Seppo stood his ground, invisible in the darkened room. A feeling of reassurance came then.

A gun barrel appeared first. Egger emerged, grasping a Luger. He pointed it at Francesca. Shade hid her face and her hat protected her eyes from view. The German took one step into the room. He stopped. She looked up and the lamplight caught her features, revealing her face to her enemy. A look of surprise overcame him.

Seppo's gun prodded the back of Egger's head.

'Don't move,' the Finn said.

Egger turned his head, his gun swinging around as he did so. It was foolish. Seppo struck him with the barrel of his gun, grabbing the Luger from his hand in an almost instantaneous movement.

Egger fell to one knee and Francesca picked up her Webley. Holding it with both hands, she pointed it at her tormentor.

'Recognise me?'

'You,' Egger said.

'Sit,' Seppo said behind the German. As Egger stepped forward, he indicated a chair.

Egger stood, unsteady from Seppo's blow to his head.

'Move.' Seppo shoved the man forward.

'Look, Francesca,' Egger said, 'it was never personal. It was my job.'

'You only wanted *Le Mur Rose*. You said so. That's personal. Anyway, it's no excuse. You animal, you broke my back.'

'It's a bad job but someone has to do it. Believe me, I like you. I didn't want to hurt you. You were just so stubborn.'

Seppo stepped back behind Francesca. He still held his gun but he lowered it.

'We have no time for this,' he said.

Francesca hesitated; the barrel of her gun descended a fraction. Egger must have seen it. He launched himself at her with the desperate speed of a cornered rat. The gun in her hand exploded. The shot hit Egger point-blank in the chest. The recoil pushed her back but she stood looking as Egger slumped back into the chair. Her back ached. It was done. Revenge. Francesca could not move. She felt like a woman who had waited for the end of a pregnancy but no delivery had come, only pain. Egger's death seemed unreal, unbelievable. It was as if she had clutched at something in a fog and it yet evaded her grasp. She was shaking. She felt faint. Most of all, she felt sadness and waves of bitter regret, for everything.

Chapter 38

1

Francesca stood before the blood-stained corpse. She stared at the lifeless limbs, the gore dripping at her feet. She wondered why no satisfaction came. Why had this final act of vengeance done nothing to assuage her feeling of anger? The over-arching sensation of bitterness remained. Marie would never come home; she knew it. The pain she had suffered at her maternal loss and during the torture seemed still to be there, like some spectre hovering before her. And yet, Egger was dead. He would never torture or kill again. She had needed an end to it. All through the hunt and the kill, she had imagined this one act of revenge would bring her some kind of relief. But it did not.

All she felt was sadness, a kind of soulless emptiness.

Francesca felt her knees buckle. She knelt before the corpse of her anti-Christ and her head seemed heavy and unsupportable. With her forehead resting on the corpse's knee, she let it all come out. Tears of pain and bitterness flooded, soaked into the grey flannel trousers, leaving a dark, wet stain she knew even Dr. Dubois would have difficulty explaining.

'Francesca, we must go,' Seppo said, placing his hand on her shoulder with characteristic gentleness.

She looked up at him. Her moist eyes were red and wild.

'No better. No better,' she said.

'Now. We must go.'

Francesca stood up as if in a dream.

Her blood-soaked knees began to function again and Seppo took her arm, guiding her out through the brown mahogany door and down the stone steps. They crossed the street and Seppo opened the car door. A young couple passed by, hand in hand, oblivious to the two in the car. The girl laughed and the boy lowered his hand and grasped at her buttocks. She jumped and passed by in their playful, happy state as Francesca stared after them.

Then she slumped forwards in the front seat, and as she buried her face in her hands, sobs racked her once again, her lungs feeling empty, her narrow frame shaking. Francesca remained so as Seppo started the car and drove away.

They drove until it seemed safe. Stopping the car by the roadside, he leaned towards her shaking body and enveloped her in his strong arms.

'It's over now. We can have a life now.'

'Seppo,' she said, 'I thought when it was over, when that bastard was dead, it would help. It gave me nothing. It is as if the act of killing him meant I was no different from him. It wasn't enough.'

'Hush now,' he said, stroking her back. 'It's over. The war; the pain. They can't hurt you anymore. You have a blank, white canvas before you; we will paint it together but I want bright colours for our future, not dark, sad ones.'

Francesca closed her eyes. A picture came into her mind. *Le Mur Rose.*

It remained hidden in the English House. Was that what all this was about? Had she suffered all that for a picture? No, she decided. It was for France. The picture was France to her. She felt like her country, abused, beaten by that German. It was as if like France, her very soul had remained hidden throughout, but still there, still strong, and still resilient.

She knew then what she must do.

2

Afternoon sunlight sprinkled the room. The curator had positioned the picture so those rays would never reach it. A single picture light shone just above it and the gilt frame reflected the light without it affecting the glass covering the painting. Beneath the picture was a plaque.

It read:

```
Paysage: Le Mur Rose.
  By
Henri Matisse
On loan from a private collection.
With grateful thanks to Mme. Francesca Pascal.
```

A warm feeling overcame the old woman as she stood in front of the picture. Feelings stirred within her. They were emotions she understood. Her empathy with this painting felt so strong, so vibrant, she felt overwhelmed by it. It was as if she were part of it, part of Matisse's story, and she had scored a victory at last.

Then she thought about Marie. She imagined what her daughter would have said about this great and glorious thing her mother had achieved. True, there was pain. She felt her grief as keenly now, as when her dead daughter lay in her arms on the platform of Saint Lazare all those years before. Those feelings had never departed. Francesca Pascal had learned how grief never lessens, it just comes less often with the passage of time.

A scene came to mind. She recalled how once she had stood in the same place as now, holding her husband's hand and looking at the same picture. Pierre thought the painting was just a landscape. How could a man like him ever understand what it meant to her or what that affinity would do to her life? She held up her chin with pride. Her silence before Egger and her retrieval of the picture had been her contribution to that long-gone war, when her country suffered and its culture was attacked. Francesca knew she had become so enmeshed with this one picture, it had meant more to her than anything in those dark days of suffering in Bergerac's Mairie. It was part of her life, her love, her being.

At last, she understood, too, how revenge gave nothing back. Egger's death was a momentary event, bringing her neither satisfaction nor relief. All those hours and days of her life, thinking how much she hated Egger, seemed wasted now when she looked back. She recognised how returning the Matisse was a better source of repair and reclamation than any bullet-driven and bloody vengeance. She understood it all now. That vengeful part of her life was gone, not through Egger's death, but through *Le Mur Rose* and the act of returning it to the Louvre.

Francesca turned and walked towards the doorway. As she descended the steps, she heard a guide introduce her picture to a group of tourists. She smiled to herself. She knew the guide would not say what mattered to her. No guidebook could tell of the pain which had kept the picture hidden here in France, nor the torment and the agony one woman had endured to keep a tiny piece of France from the clutches of a monster.

Outside in the sunshine, she looked around, and then she

saw him. He hobbled towards her. Leaning on the stick in his hand, Seppo stopped short, waiting. She ran to his arms and on tiptoe, she placed her arms around the old man's neck.

'I love you,' she whispered.

'I know, but sometimes I become jealous of that old picture. It's as if the Matisse means more to you than life itself,' he said

Francesca laughed.

'You could be right, but the painting cannot hold me in strong arms and cannot love me back, so you will have to do instead.'

They smiled at each other as they walked arm in arm along the boulevard, and Francesca could feel the sun, warm and comfortable, on her neck. It was, after all that time, still good to be alive.

A Note From the Author

Like any historical novel, the reader will understand that the characters and their environment are fictional. The story arc is made of the history and the characters are as they appear—fictitious. There are some aspects that are real. Claus Barbie the 'Butcher of Lyon' did exist. He was spirited away to South America in a ratline by the Americans because they wanted his 'expertise' to hunt down communists in the days when there was more 'Reds under the beds' paranoia. Some quotes from Barbie's own mouth are used in this book. I felt it added a bit of authenticity.

The Matisse *Paysage: Le Mur Rose* is a real picture appropriated by the Nazis during the war and later returned to Israel and exhibited to the public. It isn't his best. It lacks the bright colours and perspective for which Matisse was known.

What happens to Francesca when she is captured is based upon what really happened to Lise Lesevre, an incredibly brave woman who worked for the Resistance. She held out for twelve days, on nine of which they tortured her, without her ever breathing a word to her captors. What they did to her is pretty accurately described. Barbie did break her back, and at his trial she appeared in a wheelchair to give her evidence. She described Barbie as having 'a mouth like a knife-cut and his eyes were light in colour and darted like the eyes of a wolf'.

So, this book pays tribute to a very, very brave woman. Sadly, I've lived with women all my life and I fear I still don't entirely understand them. Writing from a woman's perspective is the hardest bit of authorship I've ever done. I hope it works for you. If it doesn't, then I'm sure you'll let me know.

The premise? Revenge is not as sweet as it seems. There are better ways to obtain closure.

--

Find more articles by Fred, plus a blog, free chapter downloads and details of upcoming public appearances, at:

www.frednath.com

ALSO BY FREDRIK NATH FROM FINGERPRESS:

THE CYCLIST

A World War II Drama
by Fredrik Nath

"The story is brilliantly executed... Nath's biggest success is
the sustained atmospheric tension that he creates somewhat
effortlessly."
-LittleInterpretations.com

"A haunting and bittersweet novel that stays with you long
after the final chapter—always the sign of a really well-
written and praiseworthy story. It would also make an
excellent screenplay."
-Historical Novels Review—Editor's Choice, Feb 2011

http://novels.fingerpress.co.uk/the-cyclist.html

FAREWELL BERGERAC

A Wartime Tale of Love, Loss and Redemption
by Fredrik Nath

François Dufy, alcoholic and alone, is dragged into the war effort when he rescues a young Jewish girl from the Nazi Security Police.

Then the British drop supplies and a beautiful SOE agent whom Dufy falls in love with. But as the invaders hunt down the partisans in the deep, crisp woodland, nothing works out as Dufy had hoped.

http://novels.fingerpress.co.uk/farewell-bergerac.html

GALDIR: A SLAVE'S TALE

Barbarian Warlord Saga, Volume I
by Fredrik Nath

"Highly commended"
-Yeovil Literary Prize

A tale of love, brutal battles and conflict, in which a mystical prophecy winds its way through an epic saga of struggle against Rome.

http://novels.fingerpress.co.uk/galdir-a-slaves-tale.html

MAGIC AND GRACE

A Novel of Florida, Love, Zen, and the Ghost of John Keats

by Chad Hautmann

"Quirky and funny and heartfelt and rich"
-Ft. Myers News-Press

"A compulsively readable mixture of fast-paced plot, likable protagonist, and subtly deep theme"
-Magdalena Ball, CompulsiveReader.com

"Highly entertaining, often thoughtful, and strategically humorous"
-Ft. Myers & Southwest Florida Magazine

http://novels.fingerpress.co.uk/magic-and-grace.html

Lightning Source UK Ltd.
Milton Keynes UK
UKOW040154290912

199828UK00002B/6/P